From

The W...
124 Shoredit...

Sandi Hall *Photo by Marti Friedlander*

Sandi Hall has been a feminist activist for just over ten years and came to a conscious recognition of her lesbianism halfway through that decade. She is a collective member of *Broadsheet*, a New Zealand feminist magazine, and also of Mediawomen, which is dedicated to changing the image of women on the media and the position of women in it.

She believes that feminists, globally, will have to be prepared, in the very near future, to stop the increasing warfare on this planet.

SANDI HALL

The Godmothers

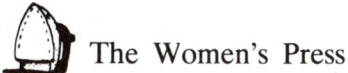 The Women's Press

First published in Great Britain by
The Women's Press Limited 1982
A member of the Namara Group
124 Shoreditch High Street, London E1 6JE

First published in the United States by
The Women's Press Limited 1982
Suite 1300
360 Park Avenue South
New York NY 10010

Copyright © Sandi Hall 1982

All rights reserved. This is a work of fiction and any resemblance to actual persons living or dead is purely coincidental.

British Library Cataloguing in Publication Data

Hall, Sandi
  The Godmothers.
  I. Title
  823[F]   PR 9639.3H/

  ISBN 0-7043-3888-2

Library of Congress Cataloging in Publication Data

Hall, Sandi.
  The godmothers.

  I. title.
PR9639.3.H26G6   1982   823   82-4913
ISBN 0-7043-3888-2   AACR2

Typeset by M C Typeset, Rochester, Kent
Printed in Great Britain by
King's English Bookprinters Limited, Leeds

To all past, present and future women on this and every other world

I wish to thank my supportive and understanding friends
Sarni, Gossi, Melanie, Rosemary and Hilary
whose political discussion with me at the eleventh hour
resolved a major flaw in this story.

Sandi Hall

Time Past

The courtroom was nearly empty. The trials are having their effect, mused Saul Crabtree. Folk are getting scared. Thus is the way of the Lord, he thought with satisfaction. The laws are exactly that, laws, not to be broken. He straightened the papers in front of him, aligning their top edges with the table's edge. A whispered commotion made him turn to see Selina Cross talking to the officer at the door. As he watched, the man reluctantly let her pass. Selina glanced round the courtroom and selected a seat near the front. Tobias Brunt, the judge, came in by the side door. He nodded to the prosecutor, picked up the other paper and began.

The girl under guard was fifteen, dark hair pouring in a tangle down her back, the skin around her eyes smudged with fear. Her breath came in gulps. Slowly, she became aware of Selina Cross' steady gaze.

Selina kept her eyes on Cassie, sending as much strength as she could. She had birthed the girl, easing her from her mother's womb with practised hands. When Bessie Riley had died twelve years later, Selina had gone to Cassie, asked her to come and live with her, seeing the child still in the eyes of the girl poverty had made older than her years. But Cassie wouldn't come, preferring to stay in her mother's hut, where the walls were hung with herbs.

'. . . and having passed by the place where she lived, he greeted her as is the custom, and was reviled and sworn at for his greeting. A se'enight later, he was took to his bed, and pustules came from his body; and under his left breast, a black mark appeared. He was heard by many witnesses to cry out her name, the last time some ten minutes before death came upon him.

'And in the face of this evidence, I declare her a living witch, unholy partner of the Devil, doing his will here on earth. I beseech this court to find her guilty and to burn her to purify her of the Evil Spirit.'

She remembered the hot breath on her face, smelling of cheese and ale. His hands were thick and sweaty and pulled at her jerkin. She struggled, but his strength was much greater than hers, and her struggling seemed to make him stronger. He ripped her skirts awry, thrust a harsh leg between hers as his hand held her two hands pinned above her head. He fumbled with his britches. She felt the thick pulsing flesh thud against her thigh, then pain and pain and pain as he raped her virgin womb.

The moon was beginning to rise as Selina hurried across the wet grass to the jail. Her whole being cried and screamed, but no sound came from her lips. Powerless she was, but at least she could give Cassie a touch of love before – but her mind shied away from the scene it held behind the barriers of control.

'No one can go in,' said the guard abruptly, standing in front of the rough hewn door. Selina drew her energy into one strong beam.

'Don't you tell me that, Elias Broome,' she whispered, 'not when I've just birthed your wife of a fine son, same as I birthed that poor child in there. Where is the mother or the father she can turn to? Even the pastor stays away, but that child has as much right to the solace of the Blessed Virgin Mother as any other folk in this country. You let me pass.'

For a long moment he looked at her, stony and cold, with uneasiness growing in his eyes.

'Let me pass, in the name of the Mother of God,' insisted Selina. And held him with intense blue gaze until he shifted his feet and eventually moved away from the door.

Cassie huddled on the pile of straw. In the far corner, pools of vomit stenched the room. Selina knelt before her, pulled Cassie into her arms. A wordless croon filled the space around them. Cassie began to shake. Huge tremors juddered through her and her breath came in ragged gasps. Selina crooned and rocked her. Presently, Cassie's gasps slowed; her body sagged limp and heavy against the older woman.

'Help me, please help me,' Cassie begged.

'Child, there is no way out that I can see. So you listen and listen hard, hear my words in your heart. They will come at midnight –' Cassie jerked in Selina's arms, and Selina tightened them around her. 'Yes, at midnight they will come. And they will lead you out and tie you to the stake. The wood will be piled around you. They will set fire to it. Soon it will send out much smoke. You must breathe hard of that smoke, with all your lungs. Do not struggle against it, for your body will want to cough and fight. But the smoke is your friend. It will lead you to unconsciousness before the pain of the flame. Do you hear me, Cassie?'

The whimpering girl nodded once, and burrowed more deeply into Selina's body.

'Now I have a potion here, which I want you to swallow when I'm gone, and bury the vial in the corner. 'Twill calm you and make you indifferent to them, so that you can go proud and like a woman to the place of your dying. And when it is done, I swear to you that I will take what there is of your body and bring it home, to bury in mother earth, surrounded by love and prayers. And one other thing there is to remember, Cassie,' said Selina, her voice deepening, 'when you get to the other side, beseech a day of reckoning, for yourself and all the others.'

Cassie raised her head to look at Selina. In the moonlight, only the child Cassie could be seen, the rounded cheeks, the huge wondering eyes.

'Beseech whom, mother?'

Selina kissed the girl's cheeks and hugged her fiercely. 'You'll find them, girl-child. Over the far banks of the river of death, you'll find them. And when you get there, remember, remember.' For long minutes, Selina cradled Cassie. Then she drew a small vial from her bodice.

'It wants a few minutes to eight, and they will not come until midnight. Wait until the moon moves across the space of your window, then drink this. Bury the vial and smooth the earth down. And think of me Cassie, for I will be with you. Feel me with you.'

The girl sobbed and clung closer. Selina held her a little longer, until her small cries had ceased. Then she tore off one long ribbon from her bonnet strings.

'Tie this under your shift, around your waist. I am with you.'

She stood up, kissed the girl twice more, then called the guard.

1: Time-stream Two

I rise up in the morning and am behind myself, wearing the face that shows the mirror surprise. So that's who I am today. I would know simply by thinking, but it's become a habit with me to check the mirror. I am still pleased by that alignment of human features into the state that is called beautiful, which I'm positive is one of the reasons that I also am the dark one with four heirs who has an allotment of days at the food sorting plant. I'm usually weak after I've been her for a while, and have very little to take back Home. What I do bring seems to be satisfactory though.

Today I am one of my favourites, for I love beauty and there are the clothes, the pearl silk shirt and the raw silk trousers, moonstone ring. Piled neatly beside the scriber is the work. I skip through it and become totally myself. I am Lydya Brown, Senior Executive of Holovision International. This morning I am on my way to present my ideas on the kind of programme mixes that are desirable in certain countries. Because I want to do the work, I've brought my latest programme mix.

I am pleased with the results. The mixes for Santiago South, particularly, have blended beautifully; there is an excellent balance among my choice of other cultures, science, politics, a first in medicine, seaming with sculpture as a spatial need and early twentieth-century love songs. The sweetness of the latter is balanced by the non-emotive elements of the former, with the sculpture providing a pivot point between. All are packaged within their own frames of reference and the mixing along these frames is, I thought, the best I'd ever done. When the music is added, its effectiveness will be doubled.

On the high-speed image level, the mix is potent, touching the fear/reassurance emotions in a visual pattern that will also be underscored musically. If you sit and watch any of the programmes in the mix, you will also get an impression of the world's history, chaos down the centuries, the rise of new thinking, the rightness of the present system of order and government. It is very effective.

Cheva, my driving companion, brings the flick round to the front of the house. I am delighted to find that the day is mild and sunny, for spring has been extremely coy. We greet one another with a hug and settle into the wide curved space. She punches the directions through, checks the straps and releases the Block. I've known Cheva for years: our ages are compatible and we went through training together. We have given pleasure to one another many times in the past, but now her liaison with Meriol, which has lasted several months, seems to be developing into something stronger than loving friendship. Cheva is also one of the few women outside Comnet with whom I have mindbonds; though, of course, we don't use the technique much because of the energy loss. The flick takes us swiftly to Comnet, its domed pillar rising out of the huddle of buildings to catch the full sweep of the sun's arm. Cheva brings us gently to the downpoint. I get out of the flick and tell her to check with me later to find out what time I'll be ready to leave. The soft sucking whoosh of the flick's departure pulls my hair straight up; I drop my case to smooth it down and see Cheva's wicked grin. Then, after one last smooth of my hair, I pick up my case and run up the steps into the Comnet building.

The fifth floor, where my offices are, has a view, but not one to make you gasp at the marvels of nature. Apart from the buildings of the city, all around, as far as you can see, is flat, ruler flat, until the land stretches out to a thin line which is faintly stained according to the season. You feel suspended between land and cloud in a changing cloudscape or skyscape. After three years in that office, I know the sky almost as well as I know my own home, and can tell what the day is going to be like from the sky's colour and texture.

Today, it was clear and mild as a baby's smile, light gentle blue, with tiny clouds cuddled next to the land and the sun around somewhere, but invisible from my window. When the location of the Comnet Building was first mooted, I was against Regina, a city of no appeal that I could see. I was pushing for Atlanta, which I loved. But I could see that, as far as the continent went, Regina was ideally situated. You could as easily catch a flick to Reykjavik as Acapulco. In communications, to be central to everywhere was priority number one.

'Lydya, good morning!'

Across my office floor came Marla, another Senior Executive. There were four of us in all; Marla was acknowledged as being the most skilled at speaking, and so she often as not issued messages for us, which made some people think she was our leader, but there are some people you can never change. Berenice and Michou were the others, and Michou was often accompanied by Stella, whom she was training.

'You're looking rather wonderful this morning,' said Marla, looking me up and down appreciatively. I knew Marla felt warmly towards me, and I liked her, but her angular body did nothing for me. 'Good journey down?'

'Mmm, pleasant,' I said, 'I've finished the mixes – want a side?'

'Yes, please!' she returned, and sat down as I got the mixes and plugged them in. 'When is the meeting?'

'Three, I think, in the Solarium,' I said. The picture was fading and opaquing at the edges, so I stopped the machine and adjusted the laser control setting. Another little test run, then I sat back to watch my creation once again.

A holovid mix is a curious concept, a bit like one of those paper shapes you make for children to tell fortunes with. Each 'side' seams with that of the next mix, and though each side is complete in itself, together they form a wholly separate mix, usually on two levels. At first, the top level fusion happened by itself, but as we learned more about it, we could manipulate our base mixes to achieve the top level mix. In every holovid mix, each integral part must be able to be extracted and still leave behind a perfectly sensible programme, so that the EXTRACT button can be pressed at any point, to lift out a whole mixed programme, while leaving another whole mixed programme there to view.

Our viewings were held in the Solarium because it was the most comfortable room in the building, and a viewing always took several hours because everyone wanted to see all sides.

'Oh well done, Lydya,' said Marla, her eyes fixed on the screen. You could feel the cold, smell the reindeer as they fled under the night sky. She had pushed the EXTRACT button then, and the scene had moved without hesitation into a star map of that night sky. The transition was excellent and the stories individual. The extractor was actually a channeler, allowing separation of individual structures during transmission. Normally, the mix went out as a total package, put together with the viewers' needs in mind. The joy of a good mix was the precision of linking, so that each programme had to be related to the other on all sides. Mind-jumping rather than viewing was what it really was.

Holovision allowed a single transmitter to send out up to six programmes simultaneously, and the choice of what to use was completely in the hands of the person controlling the extractor. We programmed for schools, of course, a 'total education' transmission. Commercial transmissions were our money spinners, and Berenice seemed to have an instinct for choosing what would appeal to the public of Western Samoa as easily as what would appeal to the public of western France. Marla really excelled at the classic arts material, and my own grasp of education mixes seemed to come from somewhere inside myself that I couldn't call on at will, but which never let me down.

'Has Moochie seen this yet?' asked Marla.

'No, not yet.'

'She's going to be thrilled with you,' grinned Marla.

'I hope so,' I said.

Moochie was Michou, Michou Bleu, large, untidy, constantly eating other people's tasties, mooching their ciggies, but so cheerfully and with so many laughing self-beratings that you couldn't get angry with her, nor could you refuse her. She always paid you back, in the end. Moochie in her moods of largesse was a bit intimidating, because she gave with a magnificence that reflected her affection for you and the inflated size of her guilt. Her sense of proportion was affected by her emotions; people she knew only casually were repaid what she borrowed and a little bit more – like four cigarettes for two. But someone she liked got tiny bits of jewellery, old old books or lace. Once she had given me the most exquisite tiny cup and saucer, probably made in 1928 or 1930, well over a hundred years ago anyway. It was a lovely clear yellow, fluted at the mouth, sprinked all over with deep blue dots and rimmed with gold. Apart from being incredibly difficult to find, it must have been worth a huge pledge.

The same sense that led her to such beauty worked with her selection of the music to fit the visual patterns of holovids. She could fit music to vision superbly, uniting the ear and the eye with a depth of meaning that flowered in the mind, lingered and grew long after the programme ended. Once, viewing a mix completed by Marla and Moochie, I hallucinated right back into Home. It was such a shock, being two places at once.

I hoped that Moochie could get on to this mix right away, but it wasn't certain. She'd been working on a special project with Berenice, which had started about six weeks before. I had an idea that the project was finished, but Moochie may have had to go off for a while, recharging. Special work was particularly draining. When Stella was fully trained, Moochie's work load would ease, but that would be some time yet. At fifteen Stella was obviously a natural for the work, but she was still too new to take off much of the load.

I left Marla to browse through the mix and went up to the Solarium to nab a dome. The Solarium was a huge room spanned by a synthetic glass dome as fine and clear as a soap bubble. Its toughness withstood the howls of prairie wind that came swooping across that enormous expanse of land, unchecked by tree or hill. Hail couldn't dent the dome, and ice or snow just slid off. The Solarium had been designed by a mind touched with magic, for it allowed smaller domes to spring out of the floor to encompass a space just right for the happening within. The sides of the smaller domes could be opaqued to two thirds of the way up for privacy; but in all of them the sense of space and sky was retained.

I walked down the centre of the room, feeling for the right spot. The choice of surroundings was varied, and I wanted just the right one for my viewing. The surroundings must be comfortable but not intrusive; if nothing was right, I'd have to dial it myself. Bamboo and palms – no, too casual. Velvet and silk – no, too luxurious. Bells, tiny mirrors and cushions big as beds – too ethnic. As I started over to a raining shade of pearl, one of the cushions moved and I saw Moochie, waking from a deep sleep it seemed. Her face was very white and her eyes wide with disorientation. She looked at me for a long moment, then buried her face in the crook of her arm and began to shake.

'Moochie, what's the matter, what is it?' I was suddenly alarmed. I'd never seen Moochie uncomposed before. I tried to hug her bigness as I smoothed her thick tumbled hair, feeling totally useless in my feeble attempts to comfort her, to stop her tears. Gradually she quietened and raised a swollen face.

'Thanks, Lydya,' she croaked out. 'Don't worry. There's nothing wrong really, I – I – I'm just a little drained after Berenice's project.' She blew her nose on an enormous square of turquoise and sniffed rapidly. 'Look, have you got a ciggie for me?' she said, with a laugh a long way back in her eyes, but there.

I smiled in return and pulled out my Candeez. 'Help yourself, honey chile; I'll just get a cold cloth for you while you puff; you look awful.'

When I got back with the towel, Moochie was once more serene, stretched out on her cushion, indigo against the plummy red, smoking intently. There was a look of singular concentration on her face, which she banished when she heard me. As I sponged her eyes and temples, she seemed to swing back to her normal exuberance. I knew that putting the music in did drain her, but I couldn't lose the feeling that something had disturbed her deeply, shaken her to the centre. And whatever it was, it seemed she had no intention of confiding in me.

By the time Cheva and I finally climbed into the flick and headed for home, it was midnight. I was both exhausted and exhilarated. The viewing had taken hours, as I expected it would, but they had been really good hours, with so much enthusiasm coming from the others that my energy level zoomed up and positively ricocheted round the dome. Moochie had kept waking Stella up. I was so involved in my own presentation that I didn't do more than spare a quick glance at her little pointed face. I could see she was in that space between sleep and waking that keeps all your faculties stretched into fantasy. Tiamat knows what impressions she'd had of the whole thing! Moochie had been fully in control, with so many wisecracks and jokes that, for a moment, I doubted my memory of the afternoon.

'If you let any other mind touch this mix, Lydya Brown,' she'd said to me threateningly, 'I'll personally find a way to set music to your nightmares!' I was delighted. It would have been easy enough for her to give the work over to a junior, since she had so recently finished Berenice's project. And as Senior in her field, she could pick and choose her projects. But I had never thought of anyone else doing mine.

Cheva's touch on my arm interrupted my musings. She pointed outside. We were flying high over still, black woods, and Luna rode in full majesty an armsreach away. Her light was streaking silver on the lakes and streams that wove in and through the furry blackness of the trees. Stars blazed and, in the far north, rippling lines of pink, green and primrose sang the dance of the lights of the snow. Their beauty was just one drop too much. I hallucinated Home.

2: Time-stream One

'Education Cuts Don't Heal' warned the poster, crookedly pasted to the wall of the building that shielded the Department of Social Welfare from the elements. Even through the swirling snow and her own cold-inspired hurry, Lillian was briefly tugged by Minnie's imagery, the sharp red scarf trailing across that body, the chill blues of despair. Should be a Minnie-inspired stew tonight, she remembered, and increased her pace so as not to miss the bus. The bus was very crowded. Lillian was soon packed tightly against other bodies which, she reflected, was ecologically sound since they were sharing a large pool of body heat. She hoped no one had a cold. And it wasn't comfortable. She could see nothing except the scarlet bobble on the toque of the woman sitting below her upstretched arm, and a bit of the steamy window behind, and that was all.

She hung on to the rail, swaying with everyone else. The rhythm was hypnotic. She began to rehearse her lines to its banal beat: sweet *lay*dee from thy *boun*tee hear my *plea*. She became aware of the hand on her leg.

At fourteen, Lillian had been five-foot-ten, skinny in the extreme, with mousy brown hair, glasses and slightly crooked teeth. Her pride, handed down with her father's blood and mother's milk, the pride of the Sicilians and the Dutch, kept her from hunching her shoulders as other tall girls did. That same pride kept her emotions hidden away, all the infantile hurts of teenage years taken inside and seemingly harming her not at all. By the time she was twenty-four, she'd blessed her height as the asset it was: she could wear clothes few others could wear and with a style that was truly her own. Her entry into the theatre had happened in college. She had dropped out in her second year to join a repertory company permanently. In the theatre she'd learned colour and texture and that indefinable something that is instantly recognised as style. And she was no stranger to the illicit groper, the breast fumble, the crotch touch.

The hand slid upwards from her knee. She tried to shift her legs, looking down. People were packed so tightly that she couldn't see below her own shoulders. A stab of anger pulsed in her stomach.

'If you don't take you hand from my leg this minute,' she said in a clear, very loud voice, 'I shall scream for the driver to stop and have you reported to the police for molestation.'

Heads turned. The hand snatched itself away.

'Sorry to shout,' she said to the faces about her, 'I just object to being groped.'

'Bastard,' said someone, 'leave her alone.'

'You just point 'im out, dear, an' I'll give 'im somethink to think about,' said a big woman with iron grey hair escaping from a yellow woollen babushka.

Lillian smiled and thanked her, feeling fierce strength coming from the woman's bigness.

'They take some learning, they do,' the woman snorted, 'fancy the cheek of it, and after that Duvalle case just bein' finished too.' She craned her neck, trying to spot the culprit. The bus lurched round a corner and stopped. People heaved and shoved. The big woman gathered her shopping bags, nodded to Lillian and forged a path to the back. The doors hissed, opened with a slam, hissed, and slammed shut. Lillian looked about for an empty seat, now that so many people had left. As she moved, she felt a sharp stabbing pain in her leg, where previously the hand had been. She cried out, looking down. An artist's scalpel, fixed to a pair of claws like those used to hold bandages in place, had been clipped to the inside seam of her jeans. As she moved, the scalpel had neatly slashed her other leg, about six inches above the knee. She looked at the contraption incredulously, pulling it off the seam. She glanced round at the people nearby. An old lady nodding, asleep. A man with a briefcase immersed in a paper. A couple whispering and laughing in their own world. A teenage boy picking his acne absently as he watched the streets roll by. A barrel-bellied man checking a betting book. No one looked at her. She felt very much alone.

She moved to the front of the bus, feeling blood turning sticky inside her jeans.

'Driver, I've been attacked,' she said in a low voice, grunting as the bus swerved violently, throwing her against his partition. The driver gave her a swift glance as he wrenched the wheel around on the icy road.

'Whaddya want me to do about it,' he asked sullenly. 'I'm ten minutes late, the bloody steering's going and the back brake's iced up. You ain't hurt bad, it don't look like to me, anyway. And you probably won't be able to tell me who done it or you'd 'ave him by the ear. So we spend five hours in the bloody cold – is that what you want me to do about it?'

She was taken aback by his vehemence, but he was right. She didn't know who it was, hadn't an inkling. And she was only three stops from home. She swore under her breath.

'OK,' she said grimly, 'but it really infuriates me that the bastard will get away with it – and how do I know that it's his first time? Or his last,' she added furiously.

'That's life,' said the driver, 'you win some, you lose some.'

The executive wing of American Vehicle Incorporated was Detroit upper-class comfortable, middle-class neutral and top-class intimidating. You could feel the power there. The walls were painted with it; it was palpably part of the chrome and smoked-glass furniture, the padding in the brown whalecord couches and chairs. Even the paintings sent out signals of power, power past, held by the heavy jowled faces looking stern and cold as befits leaders of men.

It was not a place to relax or be relaxed in. Meredith half expected a yellow-eyed lion to pad round the corner, given tangible shape from the raw energy in the corridors. He nodded to the men who came one after another into the foyer, each with his air of poise and camaraderie. What an odd group, he thought. As a relatively new boy from New York, this was his first 'brass gas', though he'd heard a lot about them. He recognised Max Lorst, head of the overseas department; he and his group 'kept an eye' on Japan, the European Continent and Britain, and were responsible for the success of the small cars pushed on to the market by the coquettish Lady Oil.

Lorst had with him his two lieutenants, each about six inches taller than he, but always a couple of deferential steps behind. A bit like bodyguards, Meredith thought. There was Stivell, Lorst's opposite on the domestic market, but why was he here by himself? And McKirdy from PR was here, with a couple of attentive acolytes; also Hunt and Jacobs from marketing, but where was anyone from sales? It was going to be a strange meeting, whatever the subject was.

As the second in command of Special Projects, Meredith expected to be called in on any sort of meeting, though he also knew that if Kendal hadn't smashed his car, he, Meredith wouldn't be at this one. He had known when he accepted the job that he hadn't a hope of getting to the top – in fact, he'd been surprised that he'd made it to where he was. Even after two years, Management still though he was unstable. The flicking remarks told him that. He knew these things travelled across from department to department, but even so, he felt the anger rise at the unfairness of it. Who had objected at the time to his 'removal' of the two men in Mexico? And his stint in Cuba had mainly met with their approval. Chile was the turning point. How was he to know that they wanted more information from that bloody group? 'Bring an end to the group's activities' – they couldn't argue that he hadn't done that. He shifted his weight in his chair and looked around the room.

Again he wondered what was up, why the designers, planners, engineers, union men were missing. They couldn't be late, because there was Farrimond and no one would be later than Farrimond. When he called a meeting for nine, you were there at five to, because once Farrimond had arrived (and he was always precisely on time) the meeting began. There were no interruptions. And no exceptions.

'Gentlemen, shall we begin,' said Farrimond. The words were spoken quietly, but in a voice that every ear had been alerted to catch. John Farrimond was a man who stepped quietly, spoke quietly: in short, a very big noise at American Vehicle. No one above him but God, thought Meredith, and God seems to approve. There at Farrimond's elbow was the financial whiz-kid Meredith had heard so much about during his two years in this department, but had never spoken to. At twenty-eight, already in charge of Am Vec's vast network of money. Stammering, shy and razor-brained Michael Carr, boy wonder of the auto empire.

Farrimond's voice gathered everyone's attention.

'This is not the first time we have sat here to discuss the effects of a train of events on our business,' he began, 'but I can say without hesitation this may be one of the most delicate assignments we've ever had.' The silence was total. 'Gentlemen, our long-term success, our levels of profitability, indeed the very fact of our existence, are based on that series of interactions we call free enterprise. Others call it capitalism. Both are correct, of course. Given the freedom to be enterprising with a little bit of capital, what can a man not do? In fact, look at what we've done!' A smile and a rustle circled the table.

'America, along with all other developed countries, has reached a significant stage in its cultural development, a point of no return, where the events of decades past, actions taken years ago, meet at a common point to shape our future.' Farrimond paused, looked around the table to meet all eyes. What's he leading up to, Meredith wondered.

'There's a third term applied to the American system of business, and it too applies to many more countries than ours. That is consumerism. It too is correct. We manufacture to have our goods bought – or consumed. It's that simple. And, for years, husbands and wives have been buying what we in industry have been selling: you might say it's the American way of life.'

Ecology, thought Meredith, it's ecology.

'Americans are excellent parents, gentlemen. We pride ourselves on it. My kids, say Mr and Mrs America, will have all the things that I never had. And Mr and Mrs America have not only been saying that for decades, they've been doing it for decades. For their kids. Better health, better education, better toys, clothes, holidays – the kids got 'em all. I got them, for instance, and so did you and you and you.' Farrimond nodded at the faces around the table. Meredith thought of his mother and mentally nodded. She'd never let him go out in a torn shirt or threadbare trousers; she'd worked as a cleaner at night to make sure he could go to college and, between them, she and his father had made sure he had a car when he did go. Hmm. He'd got them too.

'And while you were getting them,' said Farrimond, his voice very casual, quite gentle, 'so were your sisters.' He bent his head, touched the ashtray in front of him. A metallic glint sparked off his white-blond hair. The silence was a bulging wineskin. Farrimond's voice became even quieter, even more casual.

'The last thirty years have seen more and more women graduate from university, more and more women seriously going into business. It is laudable for American women to want a piece of the action. In fact, I'd be quite astonished if they didn't. But things are changing. The children of our sisters are a very different breed of women. A piece of the action is not what they want – no, they want the action itself.' Farrimond stopped. The tension was high and awkward, as if the big man had farted and everyone was afraid to laugh.

'They worry me,' Farrimond whispered in to the silence. 'They worry me a lot.' Carr coughed. As if at a signal, weight was shifted from cheek to cheek, legs recrossed and ears briefly scratched. Farrimond sipped water from a heavy, handcut crystal glass.

'Why? It's very simple. Because they are not interested in the shape of business or the shape of the community as we know it. Not only are they not interested, they know a great deal about it. And that's a rather terrifying combination, gentlemen.'

Women's libbers, thought Meredith. Holy shit, he's talking about women's libbers.

The big kitchen was steamy with rich cooking smells, beef stew mingling with apple pie baking and the instant coffee Min was pouring adding its fragrance to the rest. All around the walls were scraps of paper with sketches on them, fragments of hands, curves of hair around eye and nose, a cat dozing in the sun while a gull spread its wings to dive, doodles glimpsing half-remembered shapes. The walls also sported postcards from everywhere, some declared as official entries in the Worst Postcard in the World Contest. There were cartoons, illustrations pulled out of magazines, birthday cards, poems scribbled on schoolbook ruled paper and a vast expanse of telephone numbers on a huge sheet of green paper. Only one wall escaped the mass of paraphernalia. On it was a small glass case, inside which was an oil painting, not quite a miniature. It was the face and shoulders of a man, fleshy cheeks, large alive grey eyes, pupils dilated, fine floppy hair over ears and forehead. Behind him, faintly traced but supplying the tension and strength to the figure, were the formal masks of the theatre. Paul, Min's brother, actor and director. Min had painted his portrait a year ago, just before he went to England.

'Lillie should be home soon,' Min observed, handing mugs to Darlene and Shirley and sinking happily into the arms of a fat old armchair. 'What a bitch of a night.'

'Is it her bus or carpool day?' asked Shirley.

'Bus, I think' said Darlene.

'Because the queues at the bus stops were dreadful when I came by,' said Shirley. 'She could be quite a time getting home.'

'Well, the stew won't spoil, that's one good thing – are you two starving?' As Min asked, she was almost absently noting the slide of light on the twins' cheekbones, so similar yet subtly different, and that once-removed shade of blue that made their eyes different yet set in identical sockets, noses curving to the same nostril flare, lips almost a mirror image of the other. At the moment four blue eyes were beaming and Darlene was grinning her Snoopy grin.

'We bikies are always in need of a square meal,' intoned Shirley in her deepest John Wayne voice.

'Gannet guts,' said Min companionably. 'OK, go to it, but leave enough for us.'

Minnewanka Bell had been named after a lake in Alberta, site of the honeymoon revels of her parent lovers. She had seen the lake several times and painted it, or a suggestion of it, behind her own head in the one self-portrait she had finished. As a child, she had bitterly resented her name and the school-yard taunts it had caused. Now, her strongest reaction to a stranger's surprise was a rueful grin and a laughing 'Even the Stoneys thought it was a bit wet,' explaining where in Alberta the lake was, how it came to have its Stoney Indian name, and making a satirical comment about her athletic parents.

Minnie's work was well known among people interested in contemporary art. At the end of her university years she had had an exhibition, and one of her paintings had been bought by the Bank of Nova Scotia to grace its newest suburban branch. The money from that had given her enough to take a long lease on this big old house, which she now shared with Lillian Parelli, the Coral twins Darlene and Shirley, two cats and a fish called Fotheringay. The cats, Blinken and Nod, had long ceased to be interested in Fotheringay, who mouthed constant surprise at the activities the kitchen presented to his bulging eyes.

Now Minnie was pursing her lips in an unconscious imitation of Fotheringay as she listened to Hilary Shand's professional tones reassuring her tinnily through the telephone receiver.

'Look Min, she's a strong, healthy young woman. I've no doubt the infection in the wound will clear well, now that she's under treatment. When you first saw it, Min, what did it look like to you?'

'Just a slash across her leg, really, quite short and bleeding a little. I thought it would clear up very quickly.'

'Yes,' returned Hilary decisively. 'Well, I think there's no doubt that there was something on the blade of that little gadget, it's the only reason for it being so nasty. We've taken swabs – we'll have a look in the lab. But she's all right, Min, really. Pop in and see for yourself, why don't you?'

Min said she would and thanked Hilary. She put the phone down and turned to Fotheringay. 'Something in your line, Fothers, it seems to me. Something just a little fishy there.' As she tidied up the kitchen she unconsciously uttered little snorts of disgust at the sort of person who had fixed the scalpel to Lillie's leg. She put on her thick floor-length coat, jammed a rose wool toque on the back of her head and puzzled her way to the hospital.

'. . . for once in your life, not a worm. Unless of course you want to get another pair of lovebirds and assure them of a steady diet of fresh worm meat?' The acidity of the line was underscored by the control in Lillian's voice. Min applauded vigorously from the doorway, her Fair Isle mittens flashing as she clapped.

'Well done!' she said.

Lillie laughed at her from the bed, looking about sixteen in the blue and white striped T-shirt emblazoned with Cleveland Indians that she wore in preference to hospital starch.

'Do you really think it's OK?'

'Nah,' said Min, shaking her head. 'I think it's quite the worst thing you've ever read, and what's more, you'll have to do something about that whine in your voice.'

Lillian giggled. 'OK, OK, seashell, but you know – she's such a lovely bitch to play and I really want to do it well.'

'Well, all I can say is that I suspect you've been stealing vitriol from the nurses station, the way you spat that out. Anyway, how's the leg?'

Lillian screwed up her nose and shrugged. 'Hilary says it's coming along. They're giving me jabs about every four minutes or so. I dunno. It sort of throbs, and it's gone a crusty yellow. And look here –' she threw back the covers, 'see how dark the veins are all down my calf and up into my groin.'

The veins ran indigo across Lillie's pale skin.

'Yuk. Blood poisoning?'

'Mmmmn,' nodded Lillian, 'that too, Hilary says, though she thinks the major infection comes from something actually on the blade. But she says another four or five days should see it cleared up. And I can get out of here, thank Neptune! That'd be good timing, 'cause the play will start in three weeks and I'll have at least one full week of rehearsals.'

'Does she know what the infection is?'

'She's not sure – but she says it has to be something bacterial that's resistant to antibiotics.'

Minnie shook her head and tightened her lips. 'How could – ugh!'

'Never mind, Minnikins, it'll hurt him more than me in the long run.'

'Huh,' said Min dubiously, 'I don't know about that. But I do hope that this is one time when your blessed karmic law works. OK, ducky, I must run, I'm meeting the Gemini kids at the front door of the hall. Anything I can bring you next time?'

'Ooh yes, I've written out a little list – here,' replied Lillian, handing over a scrap of paper.

'Two fat joints,' read Min, 'a magnum of Dom P., three silk negligees, two amusing lovers and my blue slippers. Look, I don't know about the slippers,' she said, then kissed Lillian goodbye and plunged out in to the winter wild.

Meredith looked at Suzanne, a look that gradually moved from appreciation to calculation. She was unpacking a large brown bag of groceries. She was tall and well built, a big woman. Her thick brown hair gleamed with hints of red as it curved up into a bun on top of her head. Her size matched his own, perhaps one of the reasons why he enjoyed fucking with her more than most other women he'd known, he reflected.

'Hey, what do you think of women's libbers, Zane?'

'The what – oh, the feminists, you mean.' She turned to look at him. 'Why? What on earth are you, of all people, interested in feminists for?'

'Well, why not?' he challenged her. She looked at him steadily and he eventually shrugged. 'OK. No, it's just that a woman on the subway had this magazine stuck right in my face, and I read the same page about a dozen times. All about the oppression of women, stuff like that. Do you take them seriously?'

'Take them seriously? What a funny question. Take them seriously.' She dived back in to the bag. 'Well, sure, I guess so, they've done a log of good things for women, like abortion and things like that. Hey, and let's face it, it was certainly time someone did. But I don't go along with all the stuff they talk about. I think men have had a bad deal too.'

'What sort of stuff do they talk about?'

'Oh you know, men being the enemy, the oppressor, that sort of thing.' She looked round the sink, then began to pile dishes into it and run hot water over them. 'Honestly, you're worse than a kid, look at this mess.'

'I can't be bothered with dishes. I should have paper plates really, they'd be much easier.'

'Don't be silly! C'mon, you handsome hulk, get a towel and wipe up, then I'll cook up a thick, fat, juicy steak.' She leaned backwards to kiss him. He slipped his arms around her, bringing them up from her waist to squeeze her breasts.

'Mmmm,' she said appreciatively, 'I'll have a larger helping of that – later, please.'

They washed and wiped the dishes in a companionable silence. Meredith stacked the plates and said, 'Are any of your friends feminists?'

'What makes you think my friends are women?' Suzanne said lightly. 'Anyway, why do you want to know?'

'I'd just like to meet one,' said Meredith casually.

Suzanne gave him a long look. 'Would you now,' she said softly. 'What for?'

'I dunno. Just to see what they're like.'

'What, like giraffes,' she laughed, 'just to see what they're on about?'

'Something like that,' admitted Meredith.

'Well, sorry, big boy, I can't help you. You'll just have to find one all by yourself,' said Suzanne. 'I don't know anyone who calls herself a feminist.'

The hall was packed, which surprised Min, who had been expecting a smaller meeting. She hadn't been to this sort of thing before, but the twins had roused her interest in the clinic issue. She'd met Darlene at the door, but there was no sign of Shirley, and Darlene had told her that she thought her twin would be late.

'Are they all like this?' she whispered to Darlene as they took their seats in the middle row, saved for them by a young woman with a cloud of hair framing her pointed face.

'No,' said Darlene, 'but it's been on the radio a lot, and in the paper this afternoon.'

Several weeks previously, one of Toronto's newer housing suburbs had decided to improve its access to the downtown business centre of the city. They proposed and agreed upon the building of a double lane highway linking the suburb to the main motorway artery which would deposit motorists quickly in the city centre. But the path of the proposed highway ran right through the Cri de Coeur, a clinic and health centre that had been the subject of a stormy controversy when it opened three years before. Then, the clinic's avowed intent to include abortions in the list of the services it offered had caused a group of Catholics to attempt to block its opening. Their attempts had failed, mainly through the actions of five older Catholic women who had had the courage to organise a Speak Out, a public meeting to which the media had been invited, where woman after woman got up and told of her problems of incessant pregnancy, financial distress from huge families, contraceptive failures, nervous breakdown or refuge in alcohol to dull the weight of pain. They talked of self-induced abortions and backyard conspiracies, gin, quinine and knitting needles. 'Clinic battle won by cri de coeur' headlined a newspaper the following day, and gave the clinic its name.

A large map of the area had been pinned to the board on the easel at the side of the stage. On it, Min could see the proposed highway outlined in red. It was true that the plan appeared to take the most direct route to the main motorway, while giving the maximum number of accesses from the various suburban roads. It was also true that it cut through the heart of a park, nipped a large slice out of a children's playground and roller-coasted over the clinic.

The man on the stage, who introduced himself as Philippe Manet, was a representative from the firm of consulting engineers who had the contract for the job. He was fielding questions deftly, in an unflustered and friendly manner. Yes, he agreed with an angry father, the route did cut through recreational ground, but that had been done deliberately so as not to have to ask any family to move. The community wanted the road and indeed he could see why; the road would be achieved most easily by this route. If re-location of families came into the picture, the task would be much much harder. And there still was a lot of playground left, it wasn't as if the entire recreational area was going to be used. They planned a large bank and a very high fence, to protect the kiddies and cut down the noise. The bank would be grassed and topped on its ridge with ornamental shrubbery. Certainly, the community was to be fully informed before work began, he countered another query, it was only by pure chance that the news media had heard of the scheme before the community meeting took place.

Yes, of course it was regrettable that the clinic had to go, especially as it seemed to serve a wider segment of the population than actually lived there. But restitution could be made, and they could of course resettle somewhere else quite close. The costs had been investigated very carefully, and were markedly lower with this route than with all others, he assured them. There were, after all, the questions of sewers, electrical conduits and so on in settled areas, which did not apply as intensively to the proposed area, since the only building serviced by those facilities was the clinic. If the community wanted the highway – and it was certain that they did – then this was the most sensible and economically viable route to take.

The questions and protests flowed on. The man on the stage remained calm, smiling and controlled. Min could see his point of view very well.

'He does seem to have a point,' she whispered to Darlene, but Darlene only shook her head. Gradually, the mood of the hall became resigned, the voice of the man on the stage a fraction more encouraging. In a short time, he would get his vote of agreement, Min could tell.

'Excuse me, Mr Chair,' said a clear voice from the back of the hall. Min turned to see Shirley walking up the aisle to the stage, a roll of paper in one hand. She walked to a mid point in the aisle, then spoke to the seated people.

'My name is Shirley Coral. I'm sorry to be late to the meeting, but I've been checking some things out, and I wanted to have all my facts clear before I came. Today, I spoke to the Ministry of Works, to the Department of Transport and to St Helène du Pays Community Association. I'd like to tell you what I've discovered.'

'Carry on!' shouted someone. Darlene clutched Min's arm and grinned hugely.

'Yes, well,' said Shirley into the now silent hall, 'I was a bit upset about the rumour that the clinic would close, because I helped, in a tiny way, to get it open. So I thought I'd do a little asking about. I wanted to know what the cost of constructing this road was, and whether there was any other way to give the community what they needed without building the road. And I also wanted to know how the St Helène du Pays community would feel if they didn't have the motorway entrance.' She paused for breath and looked around.

'To start back to front, the Community Association executives can't recall that the motorway access was really discussed at their meetings until a representative from a construction company approached them. Each of the Board members assumed that the request had been made by one or more of the other members; and the idea was a good one, insofar as it appeared to be concerned about commuting hassles experienced by the residents of the community.'

A ripple of whispers. A large man stood up.

'Most of you know me – Whitlaw, from the Community Association. I just wanted to say that what Ms Coral has told you is, as far as I'm concerned, factual. The Association's executive feels both embarrassed and annoyed. A special open meeting will be held in the community hall next Tuesday, should all of you want to attend.' He sat down again. The whispers increased to a loud buzz.

'If I could continue?' Shirley said loudly, glancing at the man on the stage, who had taken a seat near the map. He made no response, but the buzz of voices died away.

'When did she do all this?' hissed Min to Darlene, but Darlene didn't answer, only nodded in Shirley's direction and flashed another wide grin.

'I went to see the Ministry of Works who eventually gave me an estimate of one-and-a-quarter million dollars for the construction of the highway proposed, including the reconstruction of the entry road's aprons, the central divide and access and exits along the three-quarters-of-a-mile length of the road. This, I'd like to stress, is only an estimate and may well be wildly inaccurate.

'The last piece of information is quite simple: I wonder if you'd allow me to demonstrate it from the stage?' she said to the man by the map. He nodded. She ran up the aisle and vaulted on to the stage. She unrolled the paper she was carrying, which proved to be a map with a clear Kodatrace overlay, which left the map underneath visible while showing clearly the lines on Shirley's new one.

'I contacted the Department of Transport, and asked them to plot for me a series of one-way streets within the community, together with interlinked traffic lights that would allow the speeding up of community traffic at peak periods during business days.' She traced the route with one finger. 'This is what we came up with. If this, this and this street is each made a one-way east, and the interleaved ones are made one-ways west, and these four streets going north and south are each made one-way to complete the flow, what we'd be left with would be a vastly speeded-up network of roads that led directly into the motorway. With their help, this exercise has also been roughly costed. That estimated figure is about twenty thousand dollars.'

What followed was virtually a shouting match. Shirley's actions had given the audience the support – and the answers – they needed. Though the man on the stage pointed out that Shirley's solution was only a short-term one, and would need to be thought about carefully in terms of the community's growth, he'd lost his case. The audience preferred Shirley's solution, that was clear. And even if that didn't work, as one man pointed out, at least they now realised there were other solutions possible.

It took some time to get home, because the reporters for the papers and radio stations who were at the meeting all wanted to talk to Shirley. In spite of her protests that they really should speak to Mr Whitlaw, it was she they wanted, and they wouldn't be put off. When the women finally got through to their own front door, the phone was ringing.

'I didn't give them our number,' called Shirley as Min hurried to answer it.

'Where have you been,' squealed Lillian. 'I've been calling and calling – wasn't Shirl tremendous, well done, oh, I wish I'd been there!'

'How are you calling us at this time of night,' cried Min, 'it's after midnight!'

'I'm at the nurses' station, of course. We've all been listening to the radio. Shirl's final bit was broadcast, they'd got a tape back by then!'

Min handed the receiver over to Shirley. Darlene bent her head to hear.

'Look, the nurses just think you're marvellous, Shirl, and I keep telling them you *are*. That was a goodie – how did the bad guys take it?'

'They were not happy. The one on the stage definitely looked a trifle pissed off.'

'I'll bet he did. Anyway, I've decided you can borrow my red sweater, just to celebrate in!'

'Oh, that's good, because I'm wearing it!'

Lillian shrieked down the line 'My sweater – she was wearing my sweater – my sweater's famous!'

'Yep – inspired me to all those good deeds, this red sweater. I'm going to ask if it can be admitted to the Feminist Hall of Fame, along with Emmeline's hat, Susan's handbag and Mary W's second best pair of shoes . . .'

Min and Darlene motioned to Shirley that they'd make some coffee and disappeared into the kitchen.

'Naturally,' said Lillian, then added, more seriously, 'You OK? Is it OK?'

'Yes, it seems to be fine. They weren't expecting anything. I'll be in the papers, though, which is a bit of a pity, but–'

'Can't be helped. Oh, I want to *be* there,' Lillian wailed, 'I wanna come home . . .'

'Don't you come home with a rotting leg, Lillie P,' said Shirley mock sternly. 'You go get tucked up in your nice white bed, I'm going to have a cup of coffee. I'll come and see you tomorrow, 'K?'

'Aww,' protested Lillie. 'I wanna be *there*. I feel left out! I wanna cup of coffee too . . .' she sobbed away from the phone then put it down. Shirley laughed softly, for Lillie's child act was not only funny, but real too. You could see exactly what she'd been like as a little girl. She hung up, pausing a moment in the hall, the light from the kitchen a clear swatch of yellow in front of her. Because that was the only light, what was, in the daylight, a perfectly ordinary hall thronging with coats, became a nearly mysterious place soft with secrets in the corners.

She was still buoyant from the mood of the meeting, and from winning the battle. She knew it was won, because the community people were determined to keep their park, and had grown accustomed to the clinic. In fact, they even took a pride in it being there, realising it gave them a sort of cachet, a degree of sophistication in the eyes of other communities which they now enjoyed. And thank the goddess for the team, she thought. Ever since they'd first come together, they had been melding into an efficient unit, a team of people who asked no questions but with immense speed and reliability did what had to be done.

Darlene came from the kitchen, slipped an arm around Shirley's waist and the so-similar bodies merged into one shape.

'Not bad, Toby,' she murmured into Shirley's neck, 'not bad at all.'

'Close one though, Jess,' whispered Shirley. 'The fuckers nearly pulled that one off.'

Meredith liked this Canadian city, even in winter. As a place to live, he reflected, he would choose it over New York any day in the week. New York was terribly adult, thoroughly neurotic and mingled the scent of fresh bread with the smell of bad teeth. This city was like champagne served in a child's brightly painted tumbler, the picture a crude representation of the shrine at Lourdes.

He'd been here a week, but viewed with satisfaction the accomplishments of those days. An apartment rented, a car leased. Mail had arrived at his new address. He'd chatted to people on the same floor as his apartment, beginning to establish his identity as a sociologist on a year's sabbatical, doing some type of research, knowing that only another sociologist would care to question him minutely. He stared out of the window thinking of Farrimond and that meeting. Privately, he thought the whole thing a bit far-fetched – sure, women like Jane Fonda and Angela Davis were stirrers and no wonder they were on Nixon's list. But the women he knew actually never thought much about the real side of life, if at all. He'd found himself surprised by the sorts of things Farrimond talked about – groups of women hassling employers about pay and the places they worked. And now women being nosy about politics – what a pity. Why couldn't they just be content with what they'd got? It didn't seem like such a bad deal to him. As for his being here – was Farrimond jumping to conclusions about the oil information leak? Why should he assume the women had anything to do with it? There were plenty of hungry bottom-rung politicos who'd be more likely suspects, surely. Oh well. His not to reason why. It was a pretty cushy number, after all.

He turned from his view of cathedral spires fretted by snow and resumed his study of the pile of newspapers. Nice looking woman, Shirley Coral, small neat head and a firm tilt to it that made her look both self-assured and slightly arrogant. Good brain too, from what the papers said. A computer engineer – yeah, a good brain. And a feminist. He flipped over to the women's page, looking for announcements. He skimmed the story about a nurse in Nepal, the revolution in wedding garments. Ah! Yes, this was more like it. The Wilfred Laurier YWCA group was having a series of meetings to explore the role of women in politics, starting, tonight, with the Conservative Party. Guest speaker Mona Cullard, a candidate in the last election. At 7.30, admission $1.50, coffee would be served.

3: Time-stream One

The day was ice white and blue, pale winter sun spangling through the ice-thickened branches of the stoic trees. Darlene took a minute to absorb the day, the tinge of peach and smoke-blue the sun had brushed on to snowdrifts, the clarity of the air making the children's coats blaze against the background of white. Living with Min had sharpened her ability to see, she thought, and made a mental note to tell Min so. Strange how difficult she found talking when she wasn't with the children. She could talk to Shirley, but that was different, for their talking was based on all the years they shared, and Shirley knew almost without words what she was saying.

Lillian was easy too, and their loving togetherness filled some space in her, a space born she didn't know when, but it was connected with always being half, always being (until they were adults and adopted their own hairstyles and clothes) mixed up with Shirley, always being compared, and everyone's property somehow, because she was a twin. The joy of Lillie! The joy of finding a smile that answered her own, a chuckle that pulled hers into life, a matching leap of laughter that whirled them into dancing in the middle of a dark, rain-bouncing street. A smile curved from her lips into her eyes as she hurried forward into her working day.

'Bonjour M'zelle, good morning Miss, hello Teacher.' The greetings were a familiar part of the pattern of her mornings. The children looked too fat for movement in their bulky parkas, thick scarves, heavy boots, but they darted and rolled and wriggled nevertheless. Darlene stepped inside quickly to avoid being run into by a group playing tag.

A small hand slipped into hers. She looked down at Yvette with affection. You weren't supposed to have favourites, but every teacher she knew – except Viner – did. This tiny-bodied child was hers. A delicate olive-skinned face, soft dark hair clinging in small curls to a wide forehead, tiny little ears. Watch it, she cautioned herself, don't go overboard – she'll be on her way into someone else's class next year; crying for them as if they were your own was silly. But still she squeezed Yvette's hand in a special hello and laughed as they slipped into the school.

The staff room was a wide, untidy and attractive room, with seats running under the windows on one side, plants in odd corners and hanging from the pelmet, books and papers everywhere. There were three very comfortable chairs, seven moderately comfy ones and ten that were distinctly severe on the derrière. The Marie Curie School for Girls was long on learning and short on funds, and its teachers had an unspoken roster system for the chairs. If you had your period or were in a crisis, you automatically got one of the three; if not, you took one of the ten three days in five. The school had an outstanding record of Junior Matriculation passes. Darlene had been delighted when, three years ago, she'd got the letter of appointment here.

'Hello, chérie, how's your wonderful twin today? She was superb on the radio!'

Darlene struggled out of her thick blue peajacket, smiling at Lorae, a teacher her own age who had become quite a close friend.

'Fine!' she replied, 'went out with so much energy that someone should warn the computers or she'll short-circuit them.'

'Of course you're discussing your clever sister,' drawled Adele Viner as she walked through the door. 'I suppose last night was a good work ploy, if a trifle epic.'

'What do you mean?' asked Darlene.

Adele shrugged her elegant coat off and hung it carefully on a padded hanger. 'Oh, defender of the community and all that. Caring for the rights of cabbagy housewives and squally brats. But very good for the computer business, I should think. Sounds so right when someone like that seems to care for home and hearth.'

'I think that some people think that everything is done with an ulterior motive,' snapped Lorae. 'Perhaps they've got one of those mirrors that only reflect themselves.'

'How very unsubtle you are, Polski,' said Viner.

'Is that why you would have done it, to look good at work?' asked Darlene, the genuine curiosity in her voice robbing the words of insult.

Adele looked at herself in the small furry mirror and patted her hair. 'Got to look after number one, haven't you?' she replied lightly, and strolled to the door. She paused, her hand on the handle. 'I'll ask my Ethics class, and let you know what they think – Ethics being so important these days.' The door swung to behind her.

'That woman drives me nuts,' exclaimed Lorae, perching herself on the arm of the best chair. 'I can't figure out whether she's deliberately bitchy, just acting superior or is so obscurely clever that my overworked brain can't spot it!'

'My trouble is, I don't really care,' answered Darlene. 'Now move your ass, we've got to go to work.' She gathered her belongings and went down the long chalk-scented corridor to her classroom. She liked her home room with the score of pupils' drawings on the walls, the mobiles they'd made and hung, and the odd things they had on their own desks.

She glanced at her watch. It was already twenty minutes to nine.

Damn. Five more minutes of solitude, five minutes to get something on the board.

Meredith approached the meeting hall with a slight air of expectation, which he identified, then smiled about. Well, well, thinking something different might happen, old cock, now why is that. And he realised it was because he didn't know what to expect. He snorted at his own naivety. The woman on the door was about fifty, with one of those determinedly cheerful expressions, contrasting sharply with the alcoholic flush spread across her cheekbones and a nose like a new and painful sunburn. Tonight, at least, thought Meredith, she's sober, but I wouldn't give odds on her staying that way if they serve a bit of sherry later on.

'Would you like to make a donation to the cause,' she asked as he dug in his pockets for the admission fee.

'I thought this . . .' he gestured.

'Oh my no,' she shook her head briskly, 'this pays for the coffee and the hall and for the speakers. That's why I mentioned it. Lots of people make the same mistake, and are only too happy to help when they do.'

Meredith reached for his wallet. 'You pay the speakers?' In his experience, any political party was happy to speak any time, anywhere, under any aegis, for free.

'Of course we pay the speakers,' she said with a touch of asperity. 'We've long passed the time when we expect women to give of their time and energy for nothing.'

'Well, in that case, do keep the change,' said Meredith, laying down two dollar bills. There was just a shade of sarcasm in his voice.

'Thanks very much, we appreciate it,' she called after him. There wasn't a trace of sarcasm in hers.

He found a chair halfway along the room near the wall, took off his sheepskin-lined jacket and draped it over the chair back. The hall was about three-quarters full, the audience predominantly women; Meredith saw with no suprise that the sprinkling of men were the slender, wispily bearded types that instantly said middle-class, educated, liberal left. He thought he probably looked very conspicuous and wished he'd arranged for a woman to accompany him. He decided to sit in the middle of the row, to bury himself. As he made his way down the row, he trod on somebody's toe. He was a big man and the toe gave out a decided crunch at the same time as the woman gave out a decided gasp of pain.

'Terribly sorry,' he said to her contorted face, 'are you OK?'

'No, of course I'm not OK, you clumsy fool, would you be OK if an elephant trod on you,' she said jerkily. A tear edged its way down her cheek. Her face had whitened. The women on either side of her were shooting him angry looks. One bent down to ease her shoe off. Meredith apologised again and took the seat he'd been aiming for.

Mona Cullard turned out to be surprisingly youthful. Meredith didn't think she could be much over thirty-five. She had thick springy dark hair, cut short, a clear skin delicately made up and sharp eyes behind large round glasses. She was slim, well dressed, in a conservative but expensive outfit of kelly green. Her voice was cool, precise and carried very well.

The role of women in politics was, she said, one that her party had long recognised. Women had a deeper understanding of the needs of the community, and therefore were best placed to advise on the stringent changes that often were needed at grassroots level. Projects such as the cottage hospital scheme were an example, for who better than a community's women to advise on maternity? The whole atmosphere of the hospitals was to be one of joyous enthusiasm, with mothers welcomed in an atmosphere of celebration as they came to give birth, and their friends and loved ones allowed free access to mother and child.

Well, that's not a bad line, thought Meredith. Encourage babying and for those who won't, keep 'em at the grassroots level. He glanced down the row and noticed that the little group of women were concentrating intently and taking copious notes. He smiled. Mona Cullard ended her speech with a declaration of intent from the Conservative Party that said briefly the Party pledged its support of any woman who felt like joining in the battle that would play an active part in shaping the nation's future. She sat down to strong applause. The chairwoman invited questions. There was only a short pause before the first one.

'Ms Cullard, I was very interested to hear that you are encouraging grassroots activity for women. I wonder if you could outline any help your Party might be prepared to give to women who are interested in standing for local body offices, that sort of thing.'

A stooge, thought Meredith, glancing at the questioner, who in her dress and age group bore a marked similarity to Cullard herself. Top marks for technique, he awarded silently. The little group to his right kept on making notes through the whole course, but none got up to ask questions or comment on Cullard's speech.

At the end of another fortnight, Meredith was pissed off. He'd attended all the meetings at the YWCA, and tried to attend others that seemed interesting and in the feminist arena, in spite of the 'Women Only' injunction at the bottom of the poster. At the door of the hall he had been stopped by two women who said, politely, that the audience was restricted to women only. When he'd said he was sympathetic and supportive of the feminists, they'd smiled and said in that case he'd understand why they wanted all the seats to be taken by women. He wouldn't like to think that a woman was denied a seat that she could have, would he? There was no plausible reply to that. He had left.

Now here he was again. He tried to get into this meeting saying he'd be happy to stand against the wall, but the women were firm. Women only, it said, and that was what it meant.

'But send your wife along!' shouted one of the women as he turned and walked off. He made no reply, but went back to his apartment, thought for a moment, and picked up the phone.

'Hello?' Her voice sounded so close, its richness in his ear flicking straight through to his balls.

'Zane? How are ya, honey? Missing me?'

'No, I'm having a bath. Where are you?' The warm chuckle under her words made him smile.

'Still in Canada.'

'How much longer do you think you'll be there?'

'That's just it, sweetheart, this one could take a long time. I was wondering whether you could come up here, live with me for a couple of weeks. Take some time off without pay. I'll fund you for a while.'

'I can't do that!'

'Why not?'

'Well –' He could hear her breathing quicken as she grappled with all the reasons.

'Well what?' he said, dropping his voice to its warmest. 'If it's the apartment, just get someone to look after it. Or, better still, find someone who needs a place for a spell. If it's your job, I've already said I'd fund you. Look, chuck the damn job in, you can always get another. What the hell – you only live once – and I need you, baby.'

'But –! Oh hell. This is er – sudden, isn't it?' The honesty in her voice made him wince a little, and he was flooded with the realisation that she loved him. He deepened his voice a little more.

'Zane. I want you here with me. Come. Please come.'

A long pause. He held the receiver tightly to his ear; it seemed very important now that she do as he wanted.

The silence stretched a little longer. Then very low, hesitatingly, she said 'OK, Joe Blow, I will.'

It was another week before she arrived, falling out of the train into his arms, the snow curling to make a miniscule white room of privacy around them. He had used the time to get a double bed, some more dishes and pots and pans. But not too much. He wanted her to have to buy things for the apartment, make it more like her place too. He talked to the people in the apartment across the hall, the apartment below. He told them she was coming, wanting them to welcome her. And he rented a small room downtown, just big enough for a filing cabinet, a desk and a phone. He lugged all his files down there, and put three bottles of whisky in the bottom drawer of his desk. She was delighted with the apartment, spending ten minutes absorbed in the misty snow-crystalled view of the cathedral spires, trees, houses and the spread of the river in the distance. She turned from it and came into his arms. Her thick hair flew round his neck as she buried her face in his shoulder. He drank in the smell of her, a fragrance of perfume, shampoo and Suzanne. He wondered how much he could tell her, and how long it would be before he could put her to work.

Min regarded Fotheringay severely. 'And don't you tell me that it's all right, young man,' she said, 'because I've got feelings like every other woman, and I know that it's not.'

Fotheringay said nothing, being a fish of permanent discretion. He watched as Min stirred her coffee, put an orange and two biscuits on a plate and disappeared through the doorway in the direction of her studio.

The canvas on her easel was about a third done. She regarded it with vexation.

'How can I be expected to pay you any attention when they're in trouble?' she asked it. But the painting only continued to show its own point of view. She turned away from it with a grunt and went to the window seat. She looked out over the city. Her eyes flicked and flicked again, seeing shapes and patterns. She sometimes wondered what other people saw when they looked, knowing with her head that it was different; but she was unable to look without *seeing*.

People told her she was absent-minded, and she knew now that she was. But so many things seemed incredibly trivial beside this compelling urge that was so seldom stilled. When Darlene and Shirley and Lillian had come to see the house she had liked them immediately. She had asked them what they wanted a house to be, and was satisfied when Lillian immediately said 'a sanctuary', and the twins had said 'no, a home'. As they all went to the kitchen to talk about money, Shirley had told her there was one other thing that Minnie had to know, that they all wanted it to be straight from the start. Min glanced at her, surprised slightly by her stern tone. The three stood there almost defiantly, she thought; they told her they were lesbians. She, whose sexuality flickered fitfully, taking great rages that lasted for a few weeks, then not thinking about sex or feeling its itch for months, just smiled.

'OK,' she said gently, 'it's OK with me.' And it became as important as the fact that Lillian had a scarlet sweater and Shirley had a Rosa Bonheur on her wall.

Goddamit, she thought now, they of all people should understand what it's like to worry about friends. They were friends, the four of them, close friends, though it had taken some time for it to happen. When she first saw Darlene and Shirley, Min was immediately fascinated by their visual challenge. She kept staring at them. They were used to being stared at, because they had discovered that twins are much more visible than ordinary people. But it wasn't until Min showed them her studio and made an oblique reference to their 'twinness' that they began to ask her questions about her work.

When they moved in, Min asked them almost immediately if she could paint them. Their eyes flew to each other and they laughed.

'We wondered how long it would be,' said Darlene.

'I said a week,' added Shirley, 'and she said two days.'

'Was it that obvious,' Min apologised. 'I'm sorry, it's just that . . .'

'It's all right,' interrupted Shirley, 'we decided when you asked we'd say yes.'

'Sort of to get it over, you know?' offered Darlene.

'Oh, it won't be that bad,' replied Min vigorously. 'Were you thinking of hours of sitting still and things? No, it's not like that at all. I just want to take lots and lots of photos of you, no poses, nothing like that. It's the definition of angles that fascinates me.'

She moved them to chairs as she spoke, then darted round the room examining them and staring at them intently. She was clearly deep in her own world, they were almost objects to her. They sat quite still until Min came out of her ramble, refocussed on them.

She looked at them, horrified, but before she could say anything, they burst out laughing. After a bewildered minute, she smiled. The twins hugged her.

'You take all the photographs that you want to, Ms Minnewanka Bell,' said Shirley, 'it won't bother us. Only let us see the final piccy, won't you – the one you'll paint, I mean.'

But it did bother them a little, in the end, because when Min said lots and lots of photos, she meant it. She took shots of them eating, sleeping, laughing, walking, chatting, coming out of doors and going in them, showering, fighting, sulking and tired. For nearly two weeks, everything they did seemed to be accompanied by the click, zizz, whirr of the Polaroid. They became quite edgy. Just when they were getting to the point when they thought they'd have to say something, Min stopped. And since then, she'd not alluded to their sameness. She'd dived into the pool of it, then stepped out, shaken herself and understood it. The paintings that resulted seemed to the twins to have very little relevance to them and they were glad about that. But Min had, for their mother, done a portrait of the twins. She had painted it at their request for their mother's birthday. They'd offered to pose, but she'd shaken her head, muttered something inaudible and gone away. When it was finished, they were astonished by it.

She had put them into the 1600s, Shirley as a highwayman in plumed hat and velvet doublet, black cloak swirling behind. Darlene was his lady, royally dressed. They looked out of the painting, Darlene on the horse, Shirley at its head, giving allegiance to each other and no one else. From the time they were five or six, and inspired by nothing that they could remember, the twins had been entranced by the highwayman. It was their favourite game, holding people to ransom for the gold to serve the higher good. Sometimes Darlene tried to be the highwayman, but it felt wrong. Shirley was Toby, the highwayman, and Darlene was Jess, his lady. And here was a painting by someone who had known them only a few months, giving substance to the game they had not played for years.

'What's the matter?' asked Min, alarmed by the look of their faces. 'Don't you like it?' She had been pleased by the painting, by the delight she felt as it began to burgeon under her hands. It had come quickly, finished in a couple of weeks. In spite of the oils and the richness of colours, it had a lightness about it that gave her an inner grin of satisfaction each time she focussed on it.

'Min, we love it,' said Darlene quickly, 'we really love it. It's just such a surprise.'

'We've been playing highwayman since we were kids. What do you think of that?' said Shirley gravely, but her eyes danced.

And what Min thought of that took several hours of food and talk and laughter. The friendship between them all was cemented during those hours.

But there was a side to them which they kept from her and which drove Min to distraction. All three women, Darlene, Shirley and Lillian, would drop a subject when she came into the room. Not often, but often enough even for absent-minded Min. It wasn't connected with the fury between the twins, which seemed not to affect Lillie at all, Min seeing what she meant when Lillie finally told her she reckoned it was identity battling, nothing serious. It was all three of them, preoccupied with something that she knew nothing about. Something outside. And now it was wrong, and Min couldn't concentrate properly until she knew what it was. She marched back to the easel, regarding it with softening anger.

4: Time-stream One

The women had been working all evening, since the last of them had assembled in the Place at 7.30. They had discussed the advances in Project Pollution, which was a study they were doing in conjunction with Friends of the Earth about domestic recycling. They had reviewed the position of the Crisis Refuge Centre, planned a money raising venture, revised a work roster. They had discussed even more thoroughly the increasing amount of data they had on federal and provincial politicians, material they had been amassing over the eighteen months since the last election, data which Shirley honed down and transferred to tape. They were profiling each politician, starting with a brief biography; then in depth from campaign speeches, activities that were public, and many that were private. The growing files kept tabs on federal and provincial politicians for Ontario.

Their original idea had been to provide the press with reminders of campaign promises as each one was broken; but the kind of material that they discovered, and the quantity of it, had led them to the idea of a book, which they planned to publish just before the next election. They had begun to concentrate on the cause and effect relationship between political actions and business activities. Together, they had begun to strike all kinds of gold.

Lillian was leading this meeting. They took turns at leading, a decision made at the very start of the group's formation to give each of them experience in leadership. It had been possible to get to the heart of the clinic crisis quickly, simply because of these long months of work, and the facilities opened to them.

Because of their combined areas of work, they got leads into activities behind many business doors. Two of the women worked for newspapers, one for a radio station. One sold CB units, and one real estate. Several were secretaries, the long history of invisibility this job gave them working to their advantage. There were teachers and nurses, a gardener and a taxi driver, a travel agent ticketer, two from the banking business, one in general finance and three in social welfare. Cora was training to be a veterinarian and Amanda was a tour guide.

One of their continuing activities was to attend and take notes at every politically slanted meeting in the city. Groups in other cities were doing the same, and a series of exchange meetings swapped information across the country. At the last meeting they had covered, just a couple of days ago, some papers had been found under a chair. They were computered statistics on women in the workforce, relating to Toronto in particular, but generalised against the country's employed women, and seeming to concentrate solely on women in positions of responsibility; men weren't covered. No one knew who the sheets belonged to; there had been no inquiries for them.

'What do you make of the papers, Shirley?' asked Lucy.

'I don't know what to make of them,' declared Shirley, 'but sure as hell, someone somewhere is as interested in women's activities as we are. The question is, who?'

Lillian pulled the papers over the table again and went through their contents once more. They were very clear, in black and white, with red underlining and graphs to illustrate further the area of interest. This was obviously part of a statistical and written report on women in the workforce. The section it related to dealt with the increase, such as it was, of women in positions of secondary or prime authority. The profiles of the companies they worked for were included, plus a sketch attempt to relate the personal political stances with those of the other members of the company executives, the financial position of each company and its relationship to the economy of the country. By several of the names were green and red asterisks.

'What was the meeting again?' Lillian asked Lucy.

'It was put on by NOW – sort of a follow-on from those political party ones a few weeks back. This one was Women and Leadership. Beryl Mikovich was the speaker – you know, she's the woman's credit union lady.'

'And how did you find them?'

'I didn't,' replied Lucy, 'Margo did. She was sitting about four rows behind us and was waiting till the crowd left to join us. As she got out of her row, she saw them under one of the chairs.'

'And I don't remember who was sitting there,' said Margo hurriedly, 'it was near one end of the row and I was nearly at the other.'

'Who was recording?'

'I was,' said Lorae, 'with Cora and Lucy.'

'Any of you notice anything different – anything at all? *Think*.'

The silence spun out etched by the spurt of a match, a cleared throat, the swish of legs being crossed. Lillian looked at each face in turn and her gaze kept returning to Lorae. Lorae finally answered the pull of her eyes.

'I'm sorry, Lillie, I can't,' she said. 'I just can't remember anything, any comment, anything which niggled me. I've been over my notes, too. Nothing.'

'Me neither,' said Cora.

'They could easily belong to a woman who's doing sociological research, couldn't they?' asked Amanda. 'I mean, that's exactly the sort of stuff that they love.'

'Sure,' said Lillian. 'What's got me a little worried are those bloody asterisks. They're a bit fishy, in fact they stink like a groper's graveyard.'

'Would you mind if I took them home with me?' asked Shirley quietly. Two dozen pairs of eyes looked at her.

'No – why?' Cora said finally.

'I'd just like to study 'em a little longer. They're really just a computer printout – and that's my field. Maybe I can get something more out of it.'

'Terrific!' said Lillie, and everyone agreed, thankful to have someone in charge. 'Sheesh, I could sure use a coffee – anyone else for a coffee?'

The tension of the group dissipated as Lillian stretched hard, wrapping her arms around Darlene who was standing behind her chair. Several conversations broke out at once. The large room suddenly seemed warmer, cosier. Around two adjacent walls were bookshelves and filing cabinet, a fireplace breaking the line on one side. The other two walls were given over to maps, one huge map of the city and several maps of individual areas in the city, greatly enlarged. The long table parallelled the long wall, running into the front room from under the maps; it was cluttered with books, two cameras, files, pens, paper clips, scissors – the collective clutter of working materials. There were two phones at the wall end of the table, a green one and a white one, separated by mounds of paper and manilla files. The smaller room created by the angle of the table and the long wall was full of cushions, a couple of easy chairs and an old rocker with wide, carved arms and leather seat.

The whistle of the kettle brought women to the little kitchen, where Lillian and Darlene were filling cups and passing them out to those at the door.

'Look what I've done,' said Lucy's soft voice from behind. They turned to see her holding out a pair of date loaves.

'Aaah,' squealed Lillie, 'you little darlin', elope with me, tonight, tonight, anything for a taste, a tittle, a jot – one crumb of your wonderful cake!'

'You're so fickle,' smiled Lucy, holding the cakes away, 'just so fickle, Lillian Parelli, that you'd leave me for a pastry cook, I know!'

'Oh, I can't stand it,' cried Lillie, arm to head, 'spurned, rejected yet again.' Shrieks of laughter, skeins of conversation, then the slow move home.

The white van was fitted out with a little kitchen, and a long bench ran along one side which, together with a couple of crates, supported a double mattress for trips longer than a day away. The streets were nearly empty, the lights of the traffic signals lambent in the cold, wet dark. No one had spoken since leaving the Place. Darlene's repeated glances at Lillian had failed to break Lillian's concentration. Shirley glanced over at Darlene, who met her eyes.

Lillian drew air into her lungs, pushed her hair back behind her ears and let her breath go. 'That fucking file worries me,' she said flatly. 'I don't know what to do.'

'Well, I've been thinking about that too,' said Shirley musingly. 'I just might be able to find out – or at least get a bit of a lead – on who did it.'

'How?' asked Darlene and Lillian together.

'Because it's a computer printout. I might be able to suss out the pattern. That's why I wanted to have the file with me. It's possible to tell quite a lot from the page code. Maybe I can take it further than that.'

'It would be good if you could,' said Lillian slowly, 'because I get a really weird feeling every time I concentrate on it. I can't define it – it's like being dizzy in my guts.'

Darlene shifted uneasily. She put her arm along the back of the seat, around Lillie's shoulders. Shirley missed double-declutching and crashed the gears into second, but even that failed to draw a comment from Lillie. A mile slid by.

'Lillie,' said Darlene a little later, 'there's something else. Shirley and I figure we're going to have to say something to Minnie. She knows something is wrong or, at least, that something is going on. It's worrying her.'

'No, we can't tell her,' said Lillian positively. 'We can't put that on her – she's an artist, and a real one too. It's a different world.'

'We think you should let her make that decision,' said Shirley. 'Look, we all know she's really one of us, pollywog; I don't think it's fair for her to be upset without knowing what's going on. She's too sensitive.'

'Pollywog?' drawled Lillian. '*Pollywog*?'

Shirley laughed. 'It's Fotheringay and you getting to me. He thinks Darlene's a right young pollywog, and so do you!'

'A fish of perception, Fothers,' said Lillie. 'Must come from living in a fishbowl.' The others groaned.

'And we live in her house,' said Darlene, coming back to the point. 'When it comes right down to it, that alone means we should be straight with her. Don't you think?'

'Oh – trout spawn,' said Lillian ferociously. 'Eelturds. Shrimpshit. Oystersnot.'

'Lillie!' the twins protested simultaneously.

'Well, I don't want to. She's a nice person and a splendid artist. She'll be upset. She'll worry. It'll interfere with her work.'

'But I think it's doing that now, Lillie,' said Darlene seriously. 'I really do. She keeps looking at us with such puzzled eyes. She sees we're preoccupied, cut her off in certain areas. We have lots of inexplicable phone calls. I tell you she's *worried*.' The van sped along, lights eating up the blackness. Shirley and Darlene exchanged glances over Lillian's head; Darlene nodded imperceptibly.

'Oh – all right,' said Lillie finally. 'So how much do we tell her?'

'Well, at least that we're involved in some serious feminist work, something like that,' said Darlene.

'She's not going to be satisfied with generalities like that,' said Lillie scornfully.

'I think we should tell her the whole thing,' said Shirley, 'from beginning to now. I think we owe it to her. And I think we should offer to move out, so she can see our dilemma too.'

Shirley swung the van round the switchback up into the hill road, and deliberately crashed the gears. She smiled as Lillie drew in her breath, and waited for the explosion, which broke over her head immediately. Lillie was ragingly scathing for several sentences, ending with a request that Shirley use her next paycheck to take driving lessons.

'If I was a Pisces like you, dear heart, I obviously would be able to drive as well as you. But we Taureans just bull our way around. You must try and overlook it in your usual generous fashion,' said Shirley in a to-a-child soothing voice.

Lillian snorted, then grinned. 'OK, OK. When do you want to do this talking to Minnewanka Bell?'

'Now?' said Shirley.

Lillie considered. 'Why not?'

'Let me get this completely straight,' said Min. 'The three of you and a couple of dozen other people are part of a national network of feminists who believe there is a deliberate backlash against feminism, a move to try and destroy it?'

'Right!' nodded the three approvingly.

'But – uh – I can't quite – what do you do?' she said, unable quite to put the immensity of this new angle on her flatmates into its correct place. The three exchanged glances, grinning slightly. Darlene got more comfortable at Lillie's side; Shirley rubbed her cheek.

'Well,' she said to Min, 'you've got to be in charge of your own life, haven't you? We just sort of – keep an eye on things. And when we see the need for action, we act.'

'Yeah,' said Darlene consideringly. 'It really is that simple.'

'I see,' said Min thoughtfully, drinking her coffee. 'As in the clinic!' she exclaimed, light dawning.

'Uh-huh,' drawled Lillie. 'You got it, seashell. As in the clinic.'

'Well!' said Min, draining the last of her coffee and putting her cup down. 'Seems like a good idea! Maybe you'd better tell me about it.'

5: Time-stream One

Suzanne hummed as she spooned runny white yoghurt over the muesli and fruit. She put both bowls on the tray in front of her, added a jug of milk and the sugar bowl to the toast, coffee and orange juice already crowding the tray, and carried it into the bedroom. Meredith was a still mound in the bed. Suzanne put down the tray and got into bed, very deliberately bouncing and jostling. When that had no effect, she put her feet in the middle of his back. As they felt about twenty degrees colder than he did, she wasn't surprised at his yelp and jerk away.

'Breakfast,' she said cheerfully, 'and in bed too. Aren't you a lucky boy!'

Meredith groaned. 'I never eat breakfast at midnight,' he croaked.

'Your inner clock's just a little slow, darling, it's nearly seven o'clock.'

'Nearly?' said Meredith, rolling over in alarm. 'You mean it's not even seven o'clock?'

Suzanne smiled, and blew him a kiss. Meredith slumped back and pulled the covers over his head.

Suzanne smoothed her covers down and plumped the pillow against the wall. She brought the tray on to her knees and with appreciative smacks and gurgles, drank her orange juice and started on the muesli. Slowly, Meredith's head emerged.

'You'll get crumbs in the bed,' he complained. In answer, Suzanne handed him his orange juice and threatened him with a yoghurty kiss. 'Yeech,' he recoiled. He drank the juice and poured coffee, leaning back against the wall as if the task required supreme effort.

'Zane, why are we awake at this disgusting hour of the night? I mean, what do we need to be up at this hour for? Are you part of an organisation that specialises in tearing the fabric of American life apart by killing its manhood with kindness?'

'Oh, well done,' applauded Suzanne through a mouthful of muesli. She swallowed and nodded. 'Yep, that's right – didn't you know I was really MataSu, the Manchurian mistress spy? Here, let me show you what I mean by mistress,' she said throatily, reaching under the covers.

'Watch the tray!' shouted Meredith, grabbing for the coffee pot. Suzanne laughed and straightened up. 'Anyway, you interrupted a gorgeous tête-à-tête I was having with a mermaid,' he complained.

'Tête-à-tête's all you'd get with a mermaid! Now you take me, a living breathing woman – go on, take me.' she laughed, rubbing his arm with her shoulder.

'Later, love, later,' said Meredith, grumpy still. Suzanne rolled her eyes to the ceiling and poured herself another cup of coffee.

'Well,' she said, leaning back on the pillow and holding the cup between her breasts, 'I though we could forget your work for today and go up to the hills, see if spring is coming.'

Meredith propped himself up on one elbow. 'Do you mean to tell me,' he said, spacing the words, 'that you woke me up before seven AM to take me on a hike?'

'Uh huh,' nodded Suzanne.

'You're nuts,' he said flatly, and slumped back on to his pillow. Suzanne sipped her coffee. 'Besides,' said Meredith, his voice muffled by the edge of the blanket. 'I'm a working man. I can't take the day off and go cavorting in the hills, just like that.'

'Let me help you, then it'll be done that much quicker!' She put the cup down and lay down beside him, slowly drawing the blanket away from his face. 'Huh? Pul-leeze, Mr Meredith, can this be done?'

Their eyes were only six inches apart. Meredith could see the darker flecks of brown in the amber of her iris. Through her eyes came a warm stream of love and affection, and a clear honesty that gave him a sudden pulse of guilt.

'No, honey,' he said gently, 'I want you to have a good time, not get stuck in a whole batch of dry statistics.'

'Oh yes, that's what I wanted to ask you,' she said, moving away and propping herself up to look at him. 'Why did we go to that meeting last night?'

'Just part of the research, crowd behaviour and things,' he said casually.

'Oh yes?' she said, with a glint of irony. 'I noticed the audience was almost all women and the topic was women in politics. And don't I remember you talking about feminists back home. Were you trying to meet a feminist at that meeting, John Meredith?'

Meredith seized the chance. 'Yeah, sort of I am,' he said casually, 'it's more like see how they operate – I'm doing a study on them for AmVec.'

'What on earth is AmVec interested in feminists for?'

'It's all market research, babe. If we don't keep abreast of the changing interests of our market, we can't communicate with 'em. And if we don't communicate with 'em, we lose sales to the people who do. See?'

Suzanne put her head back against the wall. 'Oh – yes, of course. Yes, I see that. It feels funny though – what exactly are you doing?'

'Just compiling statistics, mainly. How many live where and do what for a living.'

'Is that what your briefcase is full of – statistics? Anything that heavy has to be – boring! That's what it is, boring with an overtone of voyeurism. Not pleasant.'

'Did I say it was pleasant?' he said quickly. 'Wasn't I the one who said you shouldn't get stuck in that pile of statistics?'

She smiled at him, stroking his chest. 'So you were,' she murmured, 'and as always, you were right.'

He reached up and pulled her down on to him. 'Now is later,' he said into her neck, and she giggled happily. He began to kiss her under the thick scented fall of her hair. Happily he slid his hand around her breast. She brushed her lips along his shoulder, her fingers scratching his back lightly. He kissed down her shoulder to her breast.

'Meredith,' she said slowly, 'why are you doing the study here – I mean, there are plenty of feminists and feminist groups in New York City. Why do you have to study here?'

'Because, Susie Snoops, someone else is doing the New York scene and the California scene and the New Orleans scene and the Fairbanks scene too, for that matter. Now can we change the subject?'

'Sorry,' she breathed, and slid her mouth on to his.

The muscles in her thighs were beginning to ripple and her whole pelvis lifted again and again, waiting for him to enter her. But he knew well how to make the minutes last until that point of desire for his thickness and weight broke through into a vocal plea deep in her throat. Their bodies slid on one another until she lost all consciousness of her own outline and form, and they merged into a single unit of sensation.

'I wonder how long it takes us to climax,' she said lazily a little later. 'Now there's a survey I could do without any hassle at all, John Meredith. How about putting that up to old AmVec?'

'What, and give away all my secrets,' he growled. 'I don't want to be pestered to death.'

'Arrogant sonofabitch,' she said affectionately. She stretched and yawned. 'Maybe I'll just have another little snooze before I head for the hills.'

'Do. You'll need it.'

'Come too,' she said through a tremendous yawn.

'No, baby, I've really got to work.'

'Suit yourself.' she said sleepily, 'I'll take some photos.'

'Do,' he said. They slept.

As he unlocked the office door and stepped inside, the stale-smoke aridity of the room made Meredith envy Suzanne's trip into the sharp cold air of the hills. The room was dim, a little grey winter light came in through the window that looked out on to a grey wall. He flicked the light on. His desk sprang into focus, thick with papers, his briefcase lying across them. He swore softly, and made a cup of coffee before sitting down.

By noon, he had transferred the contents of most of the papers on his desk on to little cassettes, which he would drop in the overnight bag a little later. The data he had came mainly from the Department of Statistics, the electoral roll and the Registry of Companies. He was cross-checking those names against the sheets from AmVec, with priority on the ones with red asterisks. Those were the troublesome ones. It was slow and tedious work, but already he could see the strength of the base he was laying. He stretched, thought about going for a sandwich, then decided to tackle the briefcase first. After that, he'd treat himself to hot soup and French bread at the restaurant across the street.

Halfway through, he realised that a couple of sheets were missing. He had a quick flash of Suzanne holding his briefcase gaping open, half-dropping it, recovering it and snapping it shut, with a quick guilty look at him. Yesterday. Outside the post office. Fuck. He never thought to check if anything had fallen out. What a fucking nuisance. He'd have to go through it all over again. He drafted a request for a copy, saying the first one had been snow-damaged and was largely indecipherable.

At quarter to five, his office door flew open. Suzanne rushed in with the tang of winter freshness surrounding her. She wrinkled her nose as she shut the door.

'Pee-yew, it stinks in here. How can you stand it?' she exclaimed, coming over and kissing him. 'Hey, are you glad to see me – are you ready to go?'

'D'you realise you lost a whole pile of statistics out of my briefcase when you were lugging it around yesterday?'

'Oh hell, did I? I'm sorry – but it's not my fault anyway, your briefcase keeps falling open!'

'Didn't you see anything drop?'

She shook her head. 'Nope. Anyway you've got a nerve telling me off – I was only doing you a favour by carrying it, and you were the one who insisted I carry that – I wanted to carry the box!'

He got up and stretched. 'I'll know better next time to keep you from training as a good woman's libber.'

'Ah – that reminds me, I met this really interesting woman up there. You would have liked her, she was very beautiful, slim with long blonde hair. You'd have been asking her over for a drink in no time.' He caught her slight edge of sarcasm and she giggled. 'No, actually she wasn't like that at all. But she was very pleasant.'

'Did you get her address for me?' he asked sweetly.

She threw him a dirty look. 'No, I'm not a pimp. But anyway, you might see her tonight.'

He finished putting things into his briefcase, and she held his coat for him to slip into. They went out, snibbing the door behind them.

'Why will I see her tonight? Did you invite her round?' Meredith asked as they stood waiting for the elevator to creak through the terrible distance between the ground and the second floors.

'No, no. She was telling me that tonight there's a Reclaim the Night march, sort of to protest about unsafe streets, rape, violence, the whole thing. She asked if I was coming to it. When I said I didn't know anything about it, she wrote down where it starts and told me to be sure to come.'

They gasped as the wind outside hit them, and ran for the car across the street, slamming the doors.

'Phew!' she said. He wiped the snow off his eyebrows.

'Are you going to go?' he asked casually.

'What, in this weather? You must be joking. I'm going to cook us a nice thick beef stew and you're going to buy a bottle of red wine, and we're going to be cosy in our little concrete tree house, that's what I'm going to do,' she said as he pulled out into the lane of traffic. 'Besides, it's a women-only march,' she added, as if that concluded the matter.

Is it by God, he thought savagely. Well, now's the time to circumvent that little rule.

'We can do that any night,' he said, turning to smile at her. 'Go on, go on the march, see what it's like.'

She took her arm from behind his seat in order to draw back and look at him. 'You're not joking, are you?'

'No, I mean it – and afterwards, we can go to a late night restaurant and I'll treat you to a good bourguignon while you tell me all about it. You never know, it might come in handy for my research.'

'Ooh,' she said, thrusting her hands around his arm and snuggling close to him, 'now there's an offer I can't refuse. OK, I will. Look out feminists, I'm coming to join your ranks!'

Meredith was taken aback to see a huge crowd of women gathered at the meeting point. He had expected a hundred, perhaps two, but in the throng on the car park were at least a thousand women. As he stood watching them, he realised for the first time that his employers were not underestimating the feminist phenomenon. The car park bustled with young women, children and grandmothers, at least in years. Some women carried guitars, stroking out little sprays of music that mingled with the laughing and greetings that also hung in the snapping air. Suzanne gazed at the crowd.

'Ooh,' she said, bemused. 'Oh, Meredith, there are so many of them – oh, I don't know – maybe I shouldn't go tonight – let's just follow behind.'

Before he could speak, a loud hailer boomed out, used by a woman who had mounted a box of some kind in the centre of the mass of women.

'Hello sisters,' she boomed out. 'Bonsoir, mes soeurs!'

'Hi,' the crowd roared back.

'Marshals, take your positions,' she bellowed. 'Repeat, Marshals take your positions. OK now everyone listen closely. This is a peaceful march. Repeat, this is a peaceful march.' She repeated the sentences in French. 'Are you all with me on that?' Cheers and yells reverberated. Meredith brought the camera up to his eyes, with its long action night lens. She was a big woman, part Indian he thought, looking at the flat planes of her face. He took three shots of her.

'Go on,' he urged Suzanne, and gave her a little push.

She hesitated for a moment, then seemed to get caught up in the exuberance, pulled into the crowd like a minnow caught by an ocean's current. He saw her head moving towards the woman with the loudspeaker, then lost sight of her. The messages from the loudspeaker caught his attention. The woman was singing the song that obviously was to be the theme of the march:

> Reclaim the night, the night's our right
> Reclaim the night, tonight's the night!

She sang it once, and then again, motioning them to join her. Hundreds of voices lifted to accompany her. The crowd sang it through four times before she shouted 'You've got it! Now remember where we go, and that the march ends in the park. And it's a peaceful march. What is it?'

'A peaceful march!' the crowd roared back.

'OK!' she beamed, and brought her arm up in a huge arc, then pointed off down the road. 'Women, hooo!' she cried. Immediately women began to stream on to the road. Meredith realised he was going to be at the end of the march unless he did some quick manoeuvring. He started to walk very quickly down the road, when suddenly Suzanne was there beside him.

'I've talked to her – the one on the hill,' she said rapidly. 'We didn't say where we'd meet?'

'At the park gate, I should think that's best.' She nodded urgently, and dived back into the fray.

Meredith walked rapidly, skirting the edges of the throng. He turned the corner and with a few more minutes' rapid walking, estimated he was about a third of the way up the march. He stopped and took some photographs, but kept moving slowly ahead. There were some stunning looking women, one group in particular seemed to consist solely of exceptionally beautiful women, all of them singing and holding arms. The resemblance between them was strong. Meredith wondered if they could possibly be quads. Or perhaps two sets of twins. He took two shots of them, close-ups of two at a time.

By the time the march had been under way for twenty minutes or so, he had worked his way up to a little past the midpoint. There were police everywhere, walking at the side of the march, walkie-talkies to their mouths. People lining the sidewalks watched, some with blank faces, some with smiles and some with sneers. He caught snatches of comments as he moved past:

'– bet they're all on welfare –'

'– but I couldn't, I like men –'

'– teach them a thing or two –'

'– they're beautiful, isn't it exciting!'

In an unexpected pool of quiet, he heard a wistful elderly voice say 'I wish I could join them.'

He glanced at the speaker, a tiny wisp of a woman who was watching the march from a wheelchair; a younger woman – perhaps her daughter – was holding the handlebars.

Another few minutes gained him a position near the head of the march; he looked round for a vantage point. He spotted a bus shelter, heaters going, but it was crowded. Then he saw the perfect spot, a trio of steps set at an angle to the street. He pushed his way to it and waggled his camera at a man at the front of the group. Grudgingly, the man made him a little space.

The march was streaming by. He could see hundreds of placards waving, wildly exultant laughing faces, groups of women chanting STOP RAPE, another passing a joint back and forth, several women sharing the contents of a thermos flask. He took photos of the women carrying placards, those with guitars, and those whom he thought looked to be militant. His film finished, he just leaned back, watching, then stepped down and made his way towards the park gate. He felt a touch on his arm and heard a gentle voice say 'Oh, excuse me, can you help me?' He turned to see a young woman with a fine-boned face framed by a cloud of Preraphaelite hair. She was looking at him beseechingly, a camera in her hand.

'What's the trouble?'

'My darn camera – I saw you had one too, and I thought perhaps you'd know what's wrong with it. It seems jammed. When I press the button, nothing happens.' He caught the drift of her perfume.

'Here, let's have a look at it,' he said, taking her camera and giving her his. The camera was a very nice Nikon. He pressed the shutter release. It depressed, but there was no shutter click. He turned the film advance lever, and it went round. He pressed the shutter again; it clicked across with a satisfying thud.

'There's no film in it, is there?' he exclaimed, looking up. And gaped because she and his camera were gone. Rage filled him, clamouring through his body. He wanted to shout with frustration. His ears were surging with the din of the march, which somehow inflamed his wrath. He spotted a policeman, made his way to him and told him the story. The policeman wasn't too interested, particularly as Meredith was still clutching the Nikon. The policeman directed him to the station tersely, his eyes constantly scanning the crowd. Meredith swore and made his way to the park entrance, hoping Suzanne would be there. But it was nearly an hour before she arrived, full of exuberance, cheeks scarlet with cold. She soothed his anger and said, as the policeman had, that at least he still had the Nikon.

At the police station, he reported his camera stolen. The desk sergeant asked him to describe it, though Meredith was sure that there were not many Leicas around. When he'd finished his description, the sergeant reached under the counter and produced Meredith's camera.

'Just sign here, sir,' said the sergeant. Meredith signed.

'That the young lady's camera, sir?' asked the sergeant. 'She said to tell you she was very sorry, but she got pushed into the crowd. And she asked you to leave her camera here, so she can pick it up tomorrow.' Meredith handed the Nikon over, pleased to have his Leica back, and in a queer way relieved that the gentle-looking woman hadn't, after all, turned out to be a thief.

When he processed the film, all the shots were disappointing. Most of them were far too blurred to tell anything from them other than that they were of people. There were three excellent shots of the placards, but he must have been shooting high, because the faces of the women holding them couldn't be seen.

6: Time-streams Two and Three

I rise up through the singing dark, floating up through luminescence of acqua, rising, rising to primrose and peach and glowing white. My selves are scattered and distinct, waving through my light with clear bellness, till I chime. I gather my light, weaving the pattern of admittance until the tapestry of colour limns sharp and clear and, at the moment of perfect pitch, the great Seal parts and I am Home. Through the merging comes the dissonance of theme unfulfilled. I signal my response, aware of the prismatic blend interfered. I strike the chords of colour to leave the little that I've learned, with a contrapuntal request for a time with the source. Slowly the affirmation drifts through, though still with that undeniable element of dissonance that lingers reprovingly as the melody dies.

Crystal it flows, limpid, irridescent, clear. At one, the pattern reappears, my thread of colour pulsing softly. I align myself and the lotus balms. Swift are the themes renewed. Where goes the dark but to light, for nothing exists alone. Every circle turns. I follow down the light, down from glowing white, down down until the barrier is reached, and I lose myself once more.

'Joy it is to see you, soeur, and sorrow when you go.'

'Sorrow fills on leaving you,' *I acknowledge, coming to myself and greeting Chula. My eyes focus wholly and behind her shoulder I see Jacinthe, merry yellow eyes sending warmth.*

'Joy it is to see you, soeur,' *I say warming to Jacinthe. She increases the light so that I fairly sparkle.*

'Have you been Home?' *Chula asks me, a soft touch recapturing my attention.*

'Yes,' *I reply,* 'but only briefly. I was somewhere Else, forgot myself in joy and before I knew it, I was rising.'

'Grief hurts,' *replied Chula mechanically. I was captured by the nothingness in her tone, unusual even for the response. I centred on her.*

'Where is your pain?' I ask her, holding her eyes with mine and seeing the pupil stain.

'Here,' she said, and gave it to me.

The pictures flashed and blended and faded and swelled, till the story was done. Chula had been far away, to the time where Sappho was flowering her love and in the course of her learning, Chula had been to the island where that wellwoman lived. But her tarrying had led her to experience the brutality of hand to hand combat, for when the rage of the warriors shadowed the time, she had no defences up and had been drawn in. She was dismembered with repeated hacks, her brain spilling from her skull in shaking clumps, the veins of her arms stretching white and snapping at the bone. Her womb saw the sun with horror. Her teeth lay like nacrous shells in the sand. Finally her blood turned brown, crackled and drifted with the wind. I shuddered as I withdrew from her, but her eyes were now clear violet and I could see I had been the final drain.

'Sister, you give me room for pleasure,' said Chula thankfully, and with a touch of her hand on my wrist, she turned and moved away, down to the grove by the river where the labour of the flowers healed.

I turned to Jacinthe and opened my arms. Her earthwind hair tumbled over my arms as we hugged.

'Yaleen,' she whispered into my neck, 'Yaleen. Give me your mouth, my soulmate, or I think I shall burst with despair.' She turned her face up to mine, yellow eyes the deepest gold, skin of bronze, taut over knowing bones. I put my lips to her, drinking her in, and letting her drink me. The feeling spun higher. I knew that if I didn't pull away, we'd merge, and once again I'd lose my way. With a sigh, I took my lips from hers. She had understood my thought; there was no reproach, only a faint underleaf of amethyst regret.

'What's happening here?' I queried, accepting the globes of drink from her and settling back against the warm wall.

'You aren't very welcome at the moment, dear heart,' she chuckled, 'and I was almost sure you wouldn't stop. But Chula was in need – so. You must go back as quickly as you can, though, for the crisis is soon, I gather. Can you recall what that Now is like?'

I fell back, mouth full and swallowed before I shook my head.

'No. Cold, I think, and no colour. A sense of urgency. I could be wrong.'

'I doubt it – you're the best Impressionist among us.' She hugged me.

'And you?' I searched her eyes. 'Do you have a goal?'

'No, I'm still resting. But I don't think it'll be long – my energy level increases with each day.'

'Save some energy for me – that is, if you're here when I next come. One quick melt –'

I put my arms around her brief slimness, sending what I could to that place that had been nearly emptied at her last going. She turned her face to me, and our lips held each other for a moment. Then she thrust a small object into my hand, saying, 'I give you this energy link. When you need it, it will be what it needs to be.' She stepped back and put her hand behind her to the key.

Vaguely, I watched her fade from my sight.

'Lydya, Lydya,' I heard a small voice saying, and became aware that the tossing of the boat that I was in was actually a hand shaking my shoulder. I came to myself, realising that Cheva was trying to rouse me.

'I'm here,' I muttered, pulling myself up. The flick was coming to our settlement. The dawn flushed pearly gold and rose and the hills stood greenly behind the colours of our homes. Cheva said 'Buckles', her hands busy with punching the co-ordinates. I pressed the button and the soft grey webs slid over us. In another few moments we were drifting up to my doorway. Cheva leaned back against the seat, regarding me sternly.

'You are pushing yourself too hard, Lydya Brown. It took me several minutes to rouse you. And you went out like a light – one minute you were star gazing, the next you're like a three-day-old lettuce leaf.'

'I'm all right,' I smiled. 'It's just that I was on an emotional high for most of yesterday. That kind of stretches me. Did I miss anything?'

Cheva shook her head. 'No, absolutely straightforward, though very beautiful flight. I did run through your jogger – Vemare is due today at three.'

I made a face, which I always seem to do at the mention of Vemare's name. It wasn't that I hadn't tried to like her; it was just that she had a way of putting my back up that either was a genuine indication that our vibrations couldn't mix, or me using her as a catchall for my own negativism. I couldn't decide which.

'What's she coming for?'

Cheva gave me a strange look. 'I'm just telling you – you set up the meeting, didn't you?'

'Did I?' I said blankly, having no recollection whatever of asking Vemare to a meeting.

'I'll soon see,' she replied, getting the recall button to slow reverse. And in another minute, there it was, green on black: LB–VP–viz 1500TMST.

'Yes, I did,' I said, staring at the little screen. 'But I can't remember why.'

'Well,' said Cheva briskly. 'I suggest a nap and then a nip of zip. I'll give you a click at two – or get Meriol to if I'm out – that'll give you time to pull yourself together. Now, out you get, I want to go home!'

Vemare Puce was the Speaker of our Settlement. There was one for every place of habitation. The Speaker's job was to act as a central point for information. Vemare excelled at it; I'd received notification of various events in good time since she took office and three times I'd wanted something arranged myself. It had been done with efficiency and dispatch. But I knew very little about her except that she was a little older than me, and had many Accolades from the Sector for her work efficiency. I had seen her once entering the Dome, and saw that in one of the notices of meetings she had been named as guest speaker on the Universal Inversion Truth, so I knew she was part of the First Church of the Profound Principle – the Twopees, we call them – that religious group whose god was mathematics. What on earth had I arranged a meeting with her for? I went straight to my workroom, to consult my memovid.

The memovid confirmed the meeting, but flipping back through its frames, I came across a memo from her to me, asking for a meeting, and a note to myself to ring her and arrange another time. I breathed a thankful sigh that I'd not lost a piece of my mind, and went off to shower and eat.

Vemare arrived promptly at three. Thanks to Cheva's two o'clock click, I was feeling very much better. I had dressed in the soft yellow and green that I felt so good in in the afternoon light. I set the drink dispenser to varied. My receiving room was gratifying to each of my senses, the movements of light and sound mingling well with the solidity and spaces I had created by the placement of my lounging blocks, tables and paintings. The well water soothed and wound its sound through the music of the air.

Vemare, I noted warily, was wearing very severe shapes in shades of purple and olive. Just the clothing was enough to set my alarm bells ringing. I gave her the greeting hug, trying to infuse her with some of my lightness. Her bodyscent was strong and harsh, though not unpleasant, a little like the scent of pines as the saps well in spring. I picked a little sprig of myrtle from the inner garden and fastened it to her shoulder, then led the way to the receiving room. Vemare wanted orange and ijua, a mover combination that I quite liked myself, so I dialled two. We sipped leisurely, chatted superficially and I waited for her to begin. I could feel her winding herself up to the point of her call. She cleared her throat.

'Lydya Brown,' she began formally, 'the Centre has received enough complaints about you as a resident to warrant your dismissal from this Settlement. It falls to me, as Speaker, to inform you of the Settlement's feeling and ask you when you'd like the Discussion Day set?'

I was stunned. Never had I thought of dismissal as something that could happen to me. Dismissal was usually the result of violence or mindblocking or something equally heinous. My face must have registered my shock, for she threw her hand out in my direction, asking me if she could get me something. I shook my head. She kept talking while I struggled for self control. This was the reason she had wanted to see me all those weeks, she said. The thing had been building for a long time. She was sorry to have to be the bringer of the news, but that was part of the Speaker's job, and so –

'But why, sweet sunrise,' I blurted out, having regained enough control to speak. 'I can't have offended – I'm scarcely here enough to make friends, let alone offend.'

'You've put your finger on the nub of the complaint, Lydya. Many of the other Settlement members feel that you should be living nearer to Comnet, where you spend so much of your time, doing your no doubt taxing but stimulating job. It has been pointed out that several people could benefit from the use of the premises you inhabit – Malee could have her parents for instance, and Jayrel speaks of having the older children with her, if she had the space.'

She watched me closely for a minute. I could feel her eyes trying to gauge the degree of my distress. She seemed curiously – avid, somehow.

'You can't be forced to go, of course,' she said slowly, 'but you know what happens when one lives in a Settlement where one isn't welcome. . .'

And of course I did, who didn't? No services given quickly and those very patterns it depends on goodwill to spin never begun – or if started, soon to wither under the blight of rejection. I'd have to go

– but my heart darkened at the thought of leaving this tranquillity centre of mine. I felt an insistent urge to cry.

'Excuse me,' I said hurriedly to Vemare, 'please wait here a moment.' I went out into my inner courtyard, away from her line of sight. The satin bark was like a lover's skin. Its delicate leafy fronds swayed around me, the murmur of its leaves soothing. Behind my eyes, pictures flipped of the parts of my house I most loved, the corner of the stair where my statuette slid silver in the shadows, the bowl of the rest room filled with huge cushions of green and gold and plum and grey. My study, with its ruddy firewood desk, the shelves of holovids and reference material spaced with touchstones that I'd picked up on beaches everywhere, bits of twisted waterwood and seaglass that swelled with the power of the waves. I let out a silent scream of sorrow, feeling the pain all the way through its depth. Then I drew myself together and went back to Vemare. She was still in the receiving room, pacing. She turned at my step, and I was quite startled at the look on her face, a compound of defensiveness, curiosity and an odd tinge of triumph.

'Why do you look at me so?' I blurted out.

'Look at you? What do you mean?' she asked, startled. I shrugged one shoulder. I couldn't summon the energy to describe the look. Vemare came towards me.

'Are you all right?'

'Yes, I'm centred,' I said impatiently, not wanting comfort from her. 'I've decided I don't want a Discussion Day. I accept the decision of the Settlement. I'll leave as soon as I can find somewhere else. Or have there already been discussions on when you all would like me to go?'

Vemare shook her head, short sprays of black wisping across her cheek. 'No, no – we didn't expect –' she broke off, embarrassed.

'Me not to contest it?' I finished for her with a touch of iron. 'Yes, well. Would you arrange to have all the transcriptions of the complaints against me, together with one of the final decision, sent to me at Comnet.'

It was my right to have them, but I felt a strange tinge to the room, a false note chiming. She nodded once and turned to the leaveway. 'Of course. They'll be ready by the time you go.'

'I should like them tomorrow,' I said quickly.

'Tomorrow?'

Outside a cloud moved and inside Vemare's head was inked blackly against the wall.

'Tomorrow,' I repeated, holding the doorway open. Without another word, she left and for the next few hours I kept flashing to her leaving when, as the sun caught her eyes, I thought for one moment I saw in them again a distinct pulse of triumph.

The transcripts arrived the following afternoon. I was surprised at how small the bundle was, how streamlined my ejection from my Settlement looked to be. That annoyed me. I realised my sense of my own importance dictated the annoyance. That annoyed me even more. But being rational wasn't going to ease the hurt. So I gave myself wholeheartedly to a fit of very bad temper.

When I calmed down I felt restless, wanting to do something. I turned that into the planning of the move, but within a short time had so enraged myself again that I could see clearly it was fruitless. When the veeyou went, I answered it with grim heartiness. Cheva's face was concerned.

'How are you Lydya? I just heard.'

'How do you think I am. Furious.'

'Would you like me to come over?'

'I'm in no mood to be socially convenable.'

'Tell you what, dial a Cocaine Split for me and a Tiger's Eye for yourself, and I'll be there.' She broke the connection. I was pleased she was coming, even though I knew I was in a vile mood. I dialled the Cocaine Split, but didn't press for issue till she'd arrived. I wondered how it was that Cheva hadn't heard of my ejection before, and why she hadn't warned me. She arrived a minute or two later, giving me a long greeting hug, then holding her arm round my shoulders as we went to the dispenser. I asked her if she hadn't heard the rumours before.

'Yes, of course. I was asked if I thought you were a desirable resident for this Settlement. I said –' The Cocaine Split was coming down, the spiralling curves of the green glass it was served in now being outlined by the gentle fall of white flakes and crystals. We both watched this little ritual, for a moment nothing mattering except the completion of the mover.

'That looks so good, I'll have one instead of a Tiger's Eye,' I said, and press the button, 'anyway, we should be moving in the same direction.'

'You're quite right,' she said with a quick smile, and we watched the whole thing again, green glass filling with exquisite flakes and crystals; then slowly over them, misting delicately so as not to destroy the shapes, slid a pale golden liquid. When the glass was full, a slender sipping tube was attached to the rim, and the mover presented to me on the dispenser's foreplate.

I motioned Cheva to the little inner courtyard, under the silver birch. We settled on the accomocushes.

'So what did you say when they asked you?' I really wanted to know.

'I said that as far as I was concerned the Settlement ought to be proud of having you here and that they should understand your need for solitude in the light of the intensity of your work. And what you did for people all over the world, not just residents of this Settlement.'

This so accurately expressed how I felt that a lump formed in my throat and incriminating tears sprang to the corners of my eyes.

'But it's not enough,' she said bluntly. 'You can see that too, once you get to your objectivity space. You have the best place here, plus transport and my services, which of course are impeccable –' she cocked an eyebrow at me, mischievous, and I saluted her with my mover, 'and people never see you. They say you're arrogant, conceited and think you're too good for them. My explanations of your work and time schedules couldn't hold any sway against such envy and spite. And they haven't forgotten we were lovers, so that weakened my words.'

'Why didn't you tell me?'

'I didn't know if it would happen, for one thing, and for another, you just were too involved to stand another bit of stress.'

I nodded slowly. We sipped our movers and the sun gently approved of the day. 'I wonder why she should look so pleased with herself,' I mused out loud.

'Hmmn?'

'Vemare. She –' I turned to look at Cheva. 'Open up, I'll give it to you the easy way.'

'OK,' she said, and opened to me. We locked together and I played her the whole thing, running the image of Vemare as she left a couple of times to stress it, then query. Cheva painted fear of my power. I was dubious. Cheva painted lust. I was even more dubious. Then she threw up an image of a transcript, and I flashed immediately to those sitting on my table in the receiving room. We broke connection and I got up to get them.

'You've got them quickly, haven't you?' called Cheva after me as I went, and I flung back a rude remark about Vemare to explain why. Once again I was struck by how slender the pile actually was. I broke the seal as I walked back, flipping through the pages. There were thirty-one pages in all. I handed Cheva half the pile and began to read what people had been thinking and saying about me. Couched in the neutral terminology the Dismissal Form required, the words were careful, but the meaning was not. My job, my money, my taste in clothes, not to mention the artifacts I'd brought home from my worktrips, had all aroused the envy, and therefore the enmity, of several people. I didn't share them as I should – I was not communally minded. A muttered exclamation from Cheva made me look up.

'What?'

'Me. Listen to this. "The Settler seems to prefer the lighter associations of bonding, rather than those more usual in a stable Settlement of this sort. While it is reasonable to expect so busy a person to wish to avoid the stringent duties of Mothering, there is little indication that she is genuine in her desire to become a deep-rooted, long-term member of the community. This is indicated by her continued interest in ephemeral contacts with Settlers not of her equivalent financial rating." That's me – a light person not of your equivalent financial rating.'

'Who signed that bit?'

She flipped over the page. 'Vemare Puce.'

'What a disgusting mind she's got. And why should she object to my not taking a permanent bondmate – it's not against the law.'

'Maybe she really does fancy you.'

'Don't be silly.'

'Maybe she's been pining after you all this time and you've turned her sour by ignoring her.'

'To the point where she'd conspire to have me thrown out? That's a little far fetched!'

'Conspiracy? That's a strong word,' said Cheva.

I just shook my head and sipped my Split. The words on the pages in front of me suddenly seemed far far away and exceedingly trivial. I felt a bubble of laughter rise in me – at the thought of Vemare lusting after me. The mover, I thought sternly, and directed my thoughts elsewhere.

'I've got to go, I've accepted that,' I said slowly, my tongue pleasantly obvious in my word shaping. 'I'll be gone in a couple of days.' Then, out of need for her, 'Cheva, come too!'

She finished the last of her mover and put the glass down carefully. The mover was obviously beginning to push her too. 'You've forgotten about Meriol,' she replied dreamily.

'So I have,' I apologised. Meriol would find it much harder to leave than either Cheva or I, for her homefolks were still alive and she'd been Mothering for three years now. She was pretty fixed. 'That going well with you?' I asked her.

Cheva nodded dreamily, love liquefying her eyes. 'She's wonderful, Lyddie, just a sweet wonderful woman.'

'Not even the bond we've forged will make me accept "Lyddie", Cheva Rose, and don't you forget it. It makes me sound like a label on a disinfectant dispenser.'

She snorted into giggles as I said that, so infectious that the mover had its way with us, and for the next two hours, we had, gloriously, the best kind of moving you can get from a Cocaine Split.

The following day, I veeyoued Comnet, requesting Berenice. Her strong face filled the screen, black eyes alert. I told her of the Dismissal notice and of my decision. She agreed at once to find me temporary quarters in Regina, ready for my arrival in a couple of days. She would tell the others, and reschedule the commencement time of my project. In a surprisingly short time, I had packed and sent off the things I wanted to keep, my touchstones, paintings, statuettes and precious books from long ago. The holovids and reference material belonged to Comnet anyway, and I had them teleported all in one space so that I need waste no time looking for them when I wanted to consult them.

By mid-morning two days after the visit from Vemare, I was ready to go. Cheva would be with me in a few more minutes. I walked through the space of the house, but couldn't summon up any more than a thin feeling of sadness. And that, I realised, must be because without my own things, the house once more assumed that feeling of passive waiting. In the courtyard, only the silver birch touched my heart. I slid my arms around it, feeling its cool skin on my cheek. I thanked it for all the times it had pleasured my eyes and spirit, and wished it well in its long life. Then, vibrating through its slenderness, I heard the whirr of the flick. I kissed its silver body and went away.

The worst part of my Dismissal from the Settlement was the procedure I'd have to go through to find another place to live. A hundred years ago, in 1995, the Earth Council for Organised Housing (ECOH) had been set up by popular global vote through the United Countries of the World. Its final formats were reasonable and simple, but they did require a lot of form filling. The forms were on computers and could be filled from any terminal, but the questions were tedious and time-consuming. Because I was from the Work Sector, my requirements had to be filled quickly. It was very likely that would get a stern rebuke from ECOH, who considered it a 'failure' if a Settler of my standing had to be resettled.

There had been a time when I had debated joining the Discovery Sector, particularly when I'd finished my seven years. But I thought about the things I could do on my own, as opposed to those I could do almost instantly through the better funding of the Work Sector, so I had opted to stay. I had had my spacious home in recognition of my status as a Senior Worker, and that status wasn't consonant with receiving a Dismissal Notice. It would take some time before the difficulties would ease and let me find somewhere else as pleasant to live. Following an extremely tedious series of talks, I finally found myself free to look for another home.

But the urgency of my project lay on my mind. I decided to find somewhere close to Comnet just to tide me over until it was completed and I could take a longer break. This particular project called for the most complicated mix I'd ever done. Because it was destined for senior learning centres globally, creating it had been an exacting task. No area of contribution that had a major effect on now-time could be overlooked.

I'd spun the strands of knowledge as deftly as I could. The faces of the people at the World Summit Meeting held over that Christmas Time in 1995 were my starting points, and slowly I'd layered the children, the explosions, the huge lighted trees, the torture rooms, the exuberance of dolphins, napalm stroking fire, a baby's head emerging from the pulsing vagina of the mother, rockets arrowing the blue, blood-filled oceans, the glowing world hanging in the dark. As the new facets presented, I laid wider images, star maps and reindeer herds, gleaming statues under Grecian suns, commuter jetbelt terminals, the tiny perfection of silicon, charters in glass cases. These and all the others spun, until I'd reached the final facet links, those most difficult of all, bringing me back in full circle to the Summit through the starving bellies and the blazing symmetry of holography.

I turned off the projector with a sigh of satisfaction. It had been several days since I'd looked at it, and my mind had been away from it completely. It still stood strongly. I felt a thrill of pleasure at recognising what I'd done. I veeyoued Moochie, and arranged for our next days to be spent going over it, having her absorb it before we went into the long process of adding the final message of music.

7: Time-streams One, Two and Three

All I need to do is think, Meredith realised with a small shock. I just need to sit down and think it through. Why the fuck haven't I seen that before. And thinking it brought the recognition that Suzanne was the reason, the amount of time he spent with her. She had become so central to his private life that she now influenced how he spent his hours. He'd not allowed anyone to know much about his private life before, a habit he'd got into following his father's advice: decide what you want to do, and do it, kid. And don't get too buddy-buddy with anyone until you've made it. A guy wants ta do you, he's most likely to try through your gut. Keep your work out of your house and you keep a lotta trouble out of your life.

And there she was, the private side of his life, running into his office every day, ringing him up to chat, coaxing him with her laughter into lunches, long nights of talking, eating out, seeing plays, going to hockey games. She even helped him in a way at his work, taking the stuff over to the computer to process and picking it up for him, just to cut down on the time he spent at work.

He looked down at the telex again. Its meaning was unmistakable. ARRIVING 1120 HRS PAN AM FLGT 402 TUES 25 KENDAL. He got a cup of coffee and sat down at his desk. Carefully he put the coffee cup in line with the top edge of the telephone and took the phone off the hook. He loosened his tie. Then, putting his elbows on the desk, he made a cradle of his hands and put his head into them. He closed his eyes and began to think.

Presently he reached for the coffee and took a long swallow. Then he went to the stack of newspapers in the corner until he reached the one that was headlined NEW ROAD BLOCKED BY CRI DE COEUR. He noted down two names: Philippe Manet, Consolidated Earthworks Ltd., and Shirley Coral, Independent Data Control.

Philippe Manet was small and his movements were quick. He spoke rapidly, making darting gestures to punctuate his points. Above his thin lips was a moustache, crisp as a stroke of Chinese caligraphy. His eyes were very pale blue, bulging slightly. Around them, lines that emphasised his tan also emphasised his self-assurance.

'But it was just one of those natural mistakes, M'sieur, where interests are confused. No harm done – we just invest elsewhere.' His slim hand gave a little wave, indicating the breadth of their choice.

'So there's no truth in what the girl implies,' said Meredith bluntly. 'You weren't trying to get at the abortion clinic.'

Manet's eyelids drew together slightly; the pale blue eyes turned hard and grey. 'What is your interest, Mr Meredith?' queried Manet softly. 'Who pays you the salary that lets us eat in Rochelle's oh-so-pleasant restaurant today?'

'American Vehicle Corporation,' said Meredith evenly. 'Special Projects. We're concerned with events outside the marketplace that might affect our business.'

'Like our new highway?'

'Yes,' replied Meredith, 'like your new highway.' There was a small pause. Manet plucked a silver cigarette case from his inner pocket and proferred it to Meredith. Meredith shook his head, noticing the cigarettes were Black Russians. What an affectation, he thought. Strong rich smoke blossomed. Manet reflected. Meredith waited. Then Manet rose quickly.

'I think we should carry on our talk in my office,' smiled the little man. 'Please accept my invitation for coffee.'

The two men threaded their way through the tables, paid their bill and left. They didn't talk again until they were inside Manet's large, well furnished office.

Meredith left an hour later with much to think about. After they had checked each other's 'credentials' out, Manet had given Meredith a lot of information. Manet had had five brushes with a group of women who'd brought his companies' operations to a halt, or stunted them ludicrously. The group obviously had access to a great deal of information but Manet didn't know how or why they got it. Communist fanatics, or ecology freaks. But he'd find out.

One of his woman friends taught school with a woman who was part of the group. And, he assured Meredith with a small smile, his Adele liked money enough to have become very interested in helping him when he pointed out that her own land investments could be threatened.

Darlene hurried through the slush, wanting to run because she was so late, but unable to because of the crowded sidewalk. She muttered excuse me's as she dodged, and felt some exasperated looks from the people she didn't quite miss. Should have gone to bed sooner, she thought, but couldn't have left before it had all been talked out. She was late for school, but it was worth it.

To her surprise, her classroom door was shut and there was no pandemonium from the other side. She opened the door, greeting the thirty-six pairs of eyes that swivelled to watch her entrance.

'All right, all right, just because Miss Coral's a bit late doesn't mean everyone has to stop', said Adele Viner. 'Carry on with your assignment, please.'

'Thanks a stack,' said Darlene in an undertone, hurriedly taking of her jacket. 'I was sure they'd have the room into bits by now.'

'Forget it,' said Adele in the same undertone, 'I had a free period anyway.'

'How did you know I'd be late?'

'I didn't. I was waiting to catch you before class, and when you didn't come, I just gave the little darlings something to do.'

'What?'

'Well,' drawled Adele with a hint of humour, 'I couldn't think of anything else so I asked them to write an essay on being a teacher.'

'They must have loved that!'

Adele shrugged. 'Who cares?' she said lightly. She picked up her bag and closed the book she'd been reading.

'What did you want to see me about?' said Darlene, sliding into her chair.

'I wanted to know if you'd like a ticket to Bette Midler. I've got two but now my date can't make it.'

Darlene stared at her. 'I think the Goddess must have sent you,' she said finally. 'Do you know that I had a ticket and lost it, and couldn't get another for love or money? I was going down on the offchance, but –'

Adele looked slightly embarrassed, red tinging her cheekbones. 'Well, see you down there then, about a quarter to. By the ticket office?'

'Yeah. *Yeah*. And thanks Adele. Thanks very much. For the kids too.'

'It's nothing,' she replied airily. 'Don't let the brats get you.' And with a swirl of grey skirt she was gone.

Midler owned the stage. Though not long in her possession, it was indelibly hers, a tailor made negligee, a sumptuous satin mirroring her voluptuousness, wise, female and wickedly knowing. She strolled across it as positively as a cavalry of Indians coming over the hill, her feathers flying. She mocked her audience, drawled insults at them, spoke innocently in hesitant half sentences to them, elongating every mood until even the slowest knew what was going on. Then, with a finale that equalled for triumph Cleopatra's entrance into Rome, she left.

Midler withdrawal symptoms are high-pitched giggles, shakes of the head, pale parodies of her movements, sentences incoherent with laughter that try to retell the script. The cafe was full of them. Darlene, Shirley, Adele, Min, Lillian and Lucy sat round one table glancing at the people who'd been equally infected, exchanging the comprehending smiles of companions in combat. They talked the show through again and again. As their chat slowed and the mood calmed, Adele asked if Midler was a feminist.

'Do you mean, is she political?' Darlene asked Adele.

'Aren't all feminists political?'

Lillian laughed. 'Not by a long shot, ducks. Lots of them are just strong, independent women who know where they're going and go there. They're supportive, but not active and definitely not political.' As anyone should know, her tone implied.

'Are all of you feminists?' asked Adele.

'I'm just getting there, I think,' said Min. 'What about you?'

'Don't think so,' said Adele, 'I think I like men too much ever to be a feminist.'

'Hang on there,' cried Lillian, 'Whoa and hold your horses. If you haven't put your toe in the water, don't tell us about its currents!'

'Well, you know what I mean,' said Adele, 'you are all lesbians, aren't you?'

'So – what's that got to do with anything?'

'Not all lesbians are feminists,' interjected Darlene, 'and not all feminists are lesbians.'

'Are you all feminists?' Adele said again, looking round the table and seeing agreement in their faces, 'and aren't all of you lesbians?'

'No,' said Lillian evenly, 'not all of us – what about you?'

Adele looked at her coldly. 'No,' she replied shortly, 'I like fucking men a lot.'

'Good on you,' replied Lillian sweetly. 'You have to start somewhere.'

'Hey, hey,' protested Darlene.

Adele turned to face Darlene squarely. 'What about you?'

Darlene laughed and shrugged. 'Sure,' she said easily, 'both lesbian and feminist. Does that make a difference?'

'No,' said Adele lightly, 'it's just that you're the first lesbians I've ever met, at least to my knowledge.'

'Make you feel nervous?' demanded Lillian. 'Did you wonder which of us would fancy you?'

'Lillie!' said Shirley with such a wealth of command in her voice that Lillie laughed at Adele and apologised casually.

'Lydya, come and look at this.' Moochie's voice was pitched high with excitement. We were in the archives, deep below the Comnet building. All around us were stacks of tapes, sound tapes, video tapes, films and microfilm, all labelled with their source and contents. Moochie turned the can she was holding to the light. The can was the deep green that meant folk material, and the label read: *Drumming: African: various*. Below the title were all the track-titles and times, in code.

'Some of this is ages old,' said Moochie reverently, 'rhythms and styles not changed for hundreds of years.'

'Do you want to use it?'

Moochie nodded, attention on the can. 'Mmmmn, I can hear beats, these kinds of drumbeats.'

'Right,' I declared, taking the tin from her and depositing it on the wheeled tray, 'in it goes.'

Moochie's eyes followed the can, a half-smile of anticipation on her face. She watched me deposit it, then turned eagerly to the waiting sounds on the shelves. We had been over and over the mix so many times that, once, I saw it as the most clumsily assembled piece I'd ever done. I told Moochie the whole project was off. She, having seen this syndrome before, kept me away from the project, made me go to the Playroom to find my perspective again. But I couldn't stay away long.

Watching Moochie at work was an experience I had half forgotten. She took riffs from electric guitars, twined them around trills of flutes, underscored them with violas, fretted them with brass and ARPS and laid the sound against four sclonas tuned to an atonal resonance, contriving a depth and mood expression that perfectly complemented and enlarged the visual action. She could remember a single note made by an instrument she'd heard only once long ago on an obsolete tape. And she would search it out, saying it was just exactly. . . and it would be.

She had asked me in detail what key scenes meant to me, why I chose that visual image, what I felt. Then she'd play eight bars of a piano concerto by Brahms, three notes of Andromedian Hystras, nine bars from the finale of Kiel's eleventh, or one massed crescendo from the caverns of Killarend, each making a connection with the visual image in a way I'd only glimpsed. At the end of each session, I felt both elated and drained. The mix was about an hour long. After two weeks, we had completed to Moochie's satisfaction about four minutes of music. I quelled impatience, for I knew that all of the music we'd listened to, the hours of talking and feeling and hearing, were damming up inside of her; soon, the flood of her vision would crash through in a gush of work that would immerse the whole mix. The four minutes we had was just the first trickle. The little trolley was now bulging with brightly coloured cans, red for martial music, the folk green, yellow for children's music, classical whites, and the blues, pinks, and lilac of religious, rock and jazz.

'We can't heap another can on here, Moochie. Let's take this bunch up and go through them?'

She grinned at the piled trolley, a little shamefaced. 'I do get carried away, don't I? But,' she added, staring at the cans, 'I don't think I want to do without any of them.'

'You be as carried away as you like, I don't care, as long as the result is super-brilliant.'

'Well. It'll be as good as your mix is,' she said cheerfully, helping me push the trolley to the dispatching mouth.

'Oh dear, I was hoping you could do better than that,' I said. She just flung me a look and reached into my pocket for the Candeez there, lighting it as we fed cans slowly into the mouth.

'It's a good mix,' she said reflectively, blowing the smoke out in a long greenish plume. 'Classical and commercial stuff are completely different areas, I know, but honestly Lydya, this is the best mix I've ever worked on. The seamings are –' she waved the hand holding the Candeez about, making green swirls of smoke dance '– well they're splendid.'

I didn't know what to say, so I just grinned at her. The tone peremptorily demanded the last of the cans. We piled them in neatly, then went up to my office. By the time we got there, the cans had arrived and were adding their brightness to the confusion all around. The sun was morning fresh, stretching out across the wide flat greens. Huge white clouds paraded grandly, with the silver flash of flicks needling their flanks. I suddenly felt like being outside, running across those green flats under the lumbering clouds.

'Sometimes, Moochie-mine, work is woe,' I observed, 'look at that day.' I turned from the window to see her kneeling beside the cans, so lost in sorting out her precious sounds that she hadn't heard a word.

'Lydya, do you think that we could have another machine up here?'

'Another? We've got three. . .' I began, and saw impatience run across her face '. . .and that's only the beginning,' I finished hurriedly. 'Of course, I'll get it now.'

'I really need it,' she said half defiantly.

'I'll get you the waterfalls of Uhuru if you want them,' I said to her.

'No, no, just another machine – and perhaps the teeniest little snack?' she smiled mischievously.

'An eight-course meal, I know,' I nodded. I veeyoued facilities and asked them for another machine, the newest they had, as quickly as possible. Moochie had returned to her tapes, but she acknowledged my action with a brief smile as I left to get some food. On the way back, Berenice stopped me in the corridor.

'Going well?'

'Yes, but slowly,' I said.

'Looks like Moochie's hitting her stride though,' she said, eyeing the fruits, nuts, cheese and biscuits in my arms. 'When she gets hungry, you know the whole thing is starting to gel.'

'Hope so,' I said. 'I've never felt so strongly about a mix before – silly, isn't it?'

'I hope not,' she laughed, 'I feel that about most of mine! Anything I can do?'

I shook my head. 'No – except perhaps to make sure the food supply never dwindles!'

'Everyone knows about Moochie,' she assured me. 'She's a special favourite there. Oh, by the way, I've had a query from ECOH about you – are you settled permanently, do you seem content. Are you?'

'Who has time to think about it?' I said, juggling the food in my arms.

'That's what I thought,' she replied, 'so I gave them a non-committal answer. How long do you think it will take now?' I knew she meant the mix, not the housing.

'Optimistically, about a decade,' I said, edging down the corridor.

'Mmm. you can't rush Moochie. What about Stella, has she been any help?'

'Sweet sunrise!' I had forgotten all about her. Moochie had asked me if she could sit in on this mix, and I'd agreed. But until this second, the child had gone completely out of my mind.

'I'll fix it now,' I promised Berenice and headed for my office.

Ten days later, I blessed Berenice once again for having reminded me of Stella. The girl was the only way I could get through to Moochie, who was working at fever pitch, sleeping very little and muttering under her breath as she dived wildly between the machines. Stella was a child – slender, not very tall for fifteen – with no noticeable development of her breasts. Her amber skin, her beautiful bones, the grace with which she sat, walked and ran all appeased my inner twitches for beauty. She was a joy to look at. With growing thanks, I discovered she was also a joy to work with, for she instantly became a bridge between Moochie and all other realities. Moochie was functioning somewhere else, heedless of time, other people, everything but her own inner orchestra. Stella's voice seemed to be the only thing that could penetrate to that place where Moochie was. She also seemed to know in advance what Moochie wanted, going unerringly to the right group, and shuffling the cans till she got the tape.

Stella seemed to watch Moochie with one part of herself, and work with her with another. She would murmur and point as they reviewed and reviewed the mix. Moochie would nod vigorously or shake her head with scorn. Moochie moved quickly, in spite of her bulkiness; Stella flowed from place to place, counterpoint to the major melody.

I pushed my chair away from the machine. 'I'm too tired. I can't think clearly. I feel as if every single cell in my brain has shorted out.' Stella glanced at me with understanding. 'Do you think she'd stop?' I asked her.

Stella looked at Moochie, then shook her head. 'Not for a while yet. She's right in the middle of a sequence.'

I smiled as I got up. 'Well, I have to have a break. I'll go down to the Playroom, have a massage. I'll be back in an hour or so. Veeyou me if you need me.' I didn't ask her to come, because we'd agreed days ago that one of us would always stay with Moochie. 'Would you like me to bring you back something?' I asked her, 'a mover, some food – juice perhaps?'

She shook her head, russet hues appearing under her cheekbones, glowing brown neck a delight in its delicate turning.

'No, Lydya. I'll go when you come back.'

Gratefully I headed for the Playroom. When I got there, I could see through its door that there were very few lights on, the huge room was almost empty. In one corner under a pool of soft light, a woman only days away from birthgiving was relaxing herself, two other women helping her movements. I recognised Sarni, from her pregnant bulk and the coil of her hair. I waved at her, but headed for the massage area on the other wall. Only one cubicle glowed. At this hour of the night, there would be few people wanting massage. I hoped the cubicle was empty and smiled with relief when I saw Trina sitting reading and eating an apple. Within a few minutes, she'd stripped me, rubbed me briefly and escorted me to the sauna, promising to rescue me in a few minutes. The heat seeped into me hesitantly; I let my muscles go, one by one. The hum of the electric rocks and the dim red glow of the single lamp soothed me into near sleep. I was shivered into wakefulness by the cold airstream from the door Trina opened. I followed her back to the cubicle and sank face down on her table, blissfully embracing the hard mat. Her hands took my foot, her fingers sought my muscles and I fell deeply asleep. I woke up with Trina shaking me.

'I'd like to let you sleep, but I'm sure you're working on something important, so I thought I'd better not.'

'How long have I been here?'

''Bout an hour and a half, I think,' she replied.

'That's OK.' I slid off the table. 'But you're right, I must get back. Oh, I do feel better!' Trina smiled delightedly as I flexed my arms, shook my body. I left, warning her that I was sending Stella down next and Moochie after that if I could manage it.

Of course she was still at the machines, totally indifferent to the chaos around her or to the glimmer of orange light scrabbling at the blackness on the horizon. Stella was sound asleep, one arm a pillow for her dark head. I thought about waking her and sending her home, but decided to leave her until Moochie was at her breaking point, then all go home together. I covered Stella over with my coat and slipped a cushion under her head. She smiled in her sleep.

Moochie didn't acknowledge my presence, just gave out terse instructions. 'Three to six-oh-four, hold, two to nine. To the frame please and release on cue.' She opened channels on the board, lined up reels, started, swore, and cued everything up again. Bits of image hung in odd places in the room before dissipating like smoke. We made progress, moment by moment. There was an underlying rhythm to the work, the images flickering soundlessly, the sound pulsing without vision, the gradual merging of one to the other until they began to blend together, live and breathe of themselves. A fall of flute notes rippled with muscles under skin, a burst of sonic wind lifted arms. Rockets sang in brass blazes. With the last note right, we finished the finale of the twelfth sequence.

Moochie took off her head monitor and laid it on the console. As she reached forward to flick down the switch, she slumped as if her electricity had been cut off. She fell half under the console, rolling a little to one side. I bent over her, wondering, with my own heart hammering, if she was dead. As I touched her, I got a terrific jolt, shock waves shuddering through me. The walls of the room swayed, flat weeds in deep water. I was beside myself, marking time in two places. Air streamed through the spaces between my pores.

'Yaleen, Yaleen,' whispered Jacinthe, *'the waters move and I am with their going. Yaleen, I melt with you.'*

I shook terribly, caught and held by equal times. In my left ear, Moochie began to moan, great gusts of air grunting from her lungs. Her movements half held me aware of here. A voice was gulping out a stream of words: *'Hot, so hot don't fight smoke drink smoke Cassie remember fuck blood hot oh hurt. . .'* I was surrounded by heat, smoke in my hair, my mouth, flames licking wood and flesh. Than I felt a coolness on my arm. I concentrated on it. I became aware that someone was shaking my arm. I heard an urgent voice and listened hard to its words:

'Lydya, Lydya. What's the matter? Lydya!'

The urgency in the voice solidified time. Lydya. I was Lydya. Slowly I came back into myself, recognised Stella. With the smell of smoke still strong and my flesh shuddering from the flames, I turned to her, seeing eyes wide with fear, mouth open and little gasps of air quivering her lips. I shook my head to clear the lingering feelings, trying to make myself alert. I knew who I was, and where.

Moochie was lying very still, face oyster grey and dry. The skin around her eyes was a deep purply charcoal. Her breath was coming in shallow gasps. I had no strength, but whispered to Stella, 'Put your arms around her, give her warmth.' I moved out of the way as Stella put my coat over Moochie, struggled to get her young arms around Moochie's bulk. Weak and dizzy, I crawled over to my desk, pulled open the bottom drawer and groped in it for one of the small Reviver packets I kept there.

I pinched one into my mouth, feeling the cold stream of energy slip down my throat. I took a couple over to Moochie and managed to get enough into her mouth to bring her halfway round. She struggled against the second one, but her eyes opened and I saw recognition in them. She shut them again, leaning against Stella, sobbing weakly. At that moment, I remembered the time in the Solarium. She'd looked just the same. The three of us were quiet for a long time. Finally, I dialled a flick and got it to take us to Moochie's house, by which time she had enough presence of mind to be able to hold her head up to the doorglow and speak her opening words.

With Stella and me holding her, she made her way to the bedroom. The three of us lay down on her enormous bed. I had time just to see Stella closing her eyes, her slenderness even smaller next to Moochie's dugong body. Then time spun and I was rising.

Cinnamon hair and grave golden eyes, Jacinthe watching the entrance, tawny delight gleaming as I arrived.

'I knew you'd come,' she cried, 'I felt you so strongly, I was talking to you.' My hand pulsed, holding the link she'd given me before.

'I heard you through a bad time. You spoke of the waters moving.'

'I am rested and must leave,' she explained, 'and I wanted you to know, wherever you were.'

'Sorrow fills,' I replied, my soul aching a little. We looked at one another and saw the same things, and the colours moved like rainbow mists as we merged. She filled me with before and after, and I gave what I had to give. Soon came the murmur of other harmonies and we

sang as the colours did. Descending, firming, slowing, forming, separating. Perhaps for many Times. But once more knowing, one became two again.

The scent of coffee roused me. Stella came into the room, a tray of steaming cups in her small brown hands, the cups surrounding bowls of fruit. Moochie was nowhere in sight, but from the far side of the room I heard the gurgle of water.

'Lydya!' exclaimed Stella. 'How are you?'

'Tired,' I said slowly, rolling off the bed to my feet. I went to the windows, pulling aside the heavy coverings. The bright sun of noon streaked into the room. The bedroom window looked out into a large green arbour; birds trilled. I opened the window, letting the fresh cool of the outdoors flood in.

'Lydya!' Moochie came across the room, looking absolutely radiant. She'd washed her hair and wore a loose flowing robe of deep plum, scrolled over with pink and beige. She looked as if she'd had no work for weeks, and was on her way to a celebration. She took my hands and searched my face.

'You look awful,' she said. 'Have a shower, a bath, whatever you feel like. I'll find something else for you to wear, you'll feel better for clean clothes.'

'No, have something to eat first, it's all ready,' protested Stella softly. I looked from one to the other, unable to make a decision. Moochie laughed at my expression, drew me over to a trio of chairs and installed me in one. She put a bowl of fruit and a cup of coffee on its arm and motioned Stella to sit down. The two of them watched me as I picked at the fruit, sipped the drink.

'Stella, tell me what you saw,' I said abruptly. Moochie leaned back. She looked at Stella, clearly inviting her to begin. Stella looked into middle space, collecting the scene.

'Moochie was under the third machine and you were on your knees beside her when I woke up. You had your hands on the floor, your head was hanging down. At first I thought Moochie was dead and you were crying, but then I heard you talking. I went over to you, to help, and that's when I discovered you seem to be in a trance or something. The words you were saying didn't make any real sense. You seemed to be in pain.'

'What was I saying?'

'It was only words – smoke and hot – you said them lots of times.'

Far away I heard a small sound. I shook my head.

'And then?'

'There wasn't much more; you mumbled and screamed a little when I touched you. Then you leaned forward and seemed to be listening. Moochie was groaning. Then you came round and told me to keep her warm.'

Stella sat on a small footstool midway between the armchairs Moochie and I were in, a dryad perched for a summer second before winging back to darker enchantments. I shook my head again, remembering that she was an astute and responsible young woman; this was no time for poetic reverie.

'Do you remember anything, Moochie? I'm astonished by you, you look so very well.'

She laughed and made an airy gesture. 'That's the beauty of having a bit of flesh on your bones, you are insulated against the unexpected.'

'Do you remember anything at all?'

'Not much. A sort of swimmy feeling, like I was falling, and a tremendous rush of heat. That's all.'

'Has that happened to you before?'

She looked across at me, raising her lips in a kissing moue. 'Don't play the circuits, Lydya. You know it has!'

'The Solarium?'

She nodded. 'But that's the only other time. I wasn't nearly as tired, but it gave me one hell of a fright.'

'What I want to know is, why did it happen,' said Stella, her arms propped on her knees, the inner curve of pink of her palms outlining her chin as she rested her head in her hands.

'I don't know,' I said slowly, then, drawn out from the force I couldn't resist, 'I think I was called,' I added.

'Called? Who called you?' Moochie asked curiously.

The answer flashed through me, but so fast I couldn't hear it, and I felt weak with the trying. Suddenly all I wanted was to bathe and have some hours of peace. I thought longingly of my bedroom at the Settlement, cool silvergreen walls, the whisper of the leaves of the young birch tree.

'I don't know,' I said again, 'but I do know I must rest. I declare today a holiday.'

'A sound decision,' Moochie said impishly. 'C'mon, I'll run you a bath. Stella, you pick some rosemary from the garden to put in it. You just sit there, Lydya Brown. We'll look after everything.'

Moochie's bathing room was warm and welcoming. She had

chosen yellow and russet red as wall colours. With the room full of steam, lying in the bath felt like total security. Afterwards, I slid into her bed, which she had remade, slipping some fresh lavender inside the airpillo. The sheets were smoothing, soothing, slowing. I slept.

We resumed the following day, both of us approaching the project with renewed zest, and Stella positively leaping with energy. A few hours later we had almost finished. Moochie seemed just as wild-eyed and dishevelled as before, but I conserved my strength and took regular breaks, making Stella do the same. We were now beginning the final linking process, the most delicate of all. Now was the time that we had to move everything down to the projection suite off the Transmission room. We had to have all the facets of the visuals in front of us for the final circle linking this process.

Stella and Moochie took down the completed vids and the remaining linkers. I paused and dialled Berenice, asking if she could get someone to come and re-route all the rest of the sound-tapes back down to archives and generally straighten my office. Berenice was delighted to hear that we were only a couple more days from completion. She promised to detail someone to look after things and wished us luck with the ending. We had been working about three hours when Moochie pulled her monitor away from her ear and looked at it distastefully.

'What is it?' I asked her, prepared for white noise, cut-out channels.

'Voices', said Moochie frowning at the monitor. She shook it slightly and handed it to me. I put it to my ear. The voices were far away but distinct: '— can you confirm all ready?' A clicking sound overlayed with a buzz as the reply began then, startlingly close, the words '— in an eight three two, with zero confirmed.' Another click, very loud, then Moochie's music came flooding back. I listened for a few moments, then gave her back the gleaming shape.

'It seems to be fine now. It must have been a leak from next door.'

We both glanced into Transmission, enough of the huge area clear behind the narrow brown window. People sat at the major console; the receiving points blinked steadily. Moochie shrugged and regarded her monitor as if it had betrayed her. Gingerly, she fitted it once again into her ear.

Hours sped by, our spirits rising as note after note chimed true, fitted into place with the precision only classic structuring can bring.

Stella slipped in and out with coffee, piles of fruit, protein nibbles, tapes we'd needed at the last minute. In between, she sat on Moochie's left, murmuring as she absorbed. I kept my notes hurriedly as the mix grew.

Midnight – and I coaxed Moochie into a short break, a stroll to stretch our cramped muscles. The Transmission room was calm, only one operator keeping the programmes beaming out to those places where time was called another name. Moochie was almost monosyllabic, her mind clearly on her work. We went back to the projection suite, her relief evident. She adjusted her monitor into the curve of her ear and swore violently, snatching it out.

'It's that leak again, voices all over the place. I can't go on with that one, I don't trust it.'

'No, of course not,' I soothed. 'Stella, nip next door to Facilities and bring back a better monitor, would you? Then you'd better run along home.'

She nodded once and was gone. I put the monitor's cold slender shaft to my ear, thinking that I'd note down enough words to identify the programme and therefore the leak for servicing.

'Sectors report by sequence and number action,' intoned voice one.

'One at four nine six, zero confirmed,' answered voice two. I thought it sounded like a child's programme, which would narrow down the leak.

'Two at five one oh, zero not confirmed, repeat not confirmed,' said the third voice. The voices were all thinned out and metallic from the equipment, but quite clear.

'Two to report in sequence five, confirm.'

'Confirm.'

'Three?'

Stella came back, gave Moochie a black box lined with Selafirm, from which six brand new monitors pointed silently to the ceiling.

'Three at seven seven eight, zero confirm.'

I was suddenly very alert, for I thought I knew that voice. I listened attentively, but there was only the reply.

'Confirmed, and a query for four.'

Then, as suddenly as it had begun, it stopped. Moochie was looking at me impatiently, the replacement monitor already in her ear.

'I haven't got all day, Lydya, unplug and let me get back to it.'

'Wait a minute, wait,' I said to her, taking out my monitor, but preventing her from linking in.

'Lydya, the leak doesn't matter. I'll use this monitor – let's get back to work,' she protested.

'No, no, you don't understand. I think I know one of the voices.'

'Do you? Who – which programme?'

'No – not a programme – it just sounded a lot like Vemare's voice – you know, the one from my old Settlement.'

'But so what,' said Moochie, 'So she's involved in some sort of communciations link-up, so what?'

I groped for the words that could adequately describe my vague unease. 'I don't know, Moochie, but it *feels* wrong. It feels – off key – that's exactly it, off key.'

She stared at me, then shook her head, once. 'OK, Lydya, I don't know much about anything, but I do know you. If you feel something's not right, then it's probably not. So what do we do?'

'Listen some more? And perhaps we should call Berenice?'

'OK!' Moochie replied cheerfully and put her monitor in. 'Not a sound now,' she said.

'Keep listening. I'll get Berenice.'

I veeyoued Berenice's office, but there was no reply, and I remembered with exasperation that it was very late. I punched Comcen for her home co-ordinates and they flickered through. When she replied, she kept her screen blank. Her voice wasn't sleepy and there was an edge of hardness to it.

'Berenice. Who's there?'

'Lydya. I'm sorry to have broken your rest.'

'Lydya. One moment.' My screen glowed and she appeared in close-up, her sleeping room dimly discernible behind her and a long shape in her bed. She'd been loving.

'What is it?' she asked calmly.

'I wouldn't ask if it weren't important,' I apologised, which she acknowledged with a short nod. 'I think you should come to the Centre. And bring Marla.'

'Can you explain?'

'No-o. I mean yes, there's something, but it's too – too tentative. But it *is* there.'

She gazed at me steadily for a long moment, then nodded decisively.

'All right. As soon as I can.' The screen blanked.

'Now what?' said Moochie.

'We both listen,' I said, feeling a little foolish. We attached the auditors and for several minutes listened to blankness. Moochie began to shift restlessly.

'Look,' she said, 'I've just thought – why don't we open all the channels and record?' Her hands got busy as she spoke, throwing channels open and patching each one through to the massive tapers. 'Let's be smart for once,' she added wryly, 'yes?'

'Smart lady,' I said approvingly. Then, 'Would you like a ciggie?'

There was a wealth of meaning in her glinting reply, and she pulled hard at the pale tube that I put in her mouth. Suddenly she sat very still. Her eyes scanned the board and she turned up the controls. Faintly, almost indecipherable, I heard a babble of voices. She spun the knob to full volume. The voices were only marginally louder. I caught odd words, numbers mainly, but Moochie was ramrod straight with concentration. The sounds faded. Moochie turned to meet my eyes.

'Thirty minutes from Waskana One and moving. Confirms from Two, Three, Five and Eight. What do you suppose that *means*?' she whispered.

I shook my head and opened my mouth, but she held up a hand. This time, the voices were much louder, every syllable totally distinct.

'Last contact to zero. All confirm twenty minutes from zero. Confirm to 0300, adjust per zone. Count confirm.'

'One. Two. Three. Four. Five. Six. Seven. Eight. Nine. Ten.' One after one the voices came through, the levels varying, but the clarity holding. Then 'Complete Confirm. Out.'

And the whole thing went dead, not even a faint zizz of white noise. Every alarm bell I had in my mind was ringing. Although only one word, I was sure now that it was Vemare who had said Three. My mind raced. Moochie spun knobs, shook her head. She closed the channels, took off her auditor and put the tapes on rewind. A babble of noise and she flicked it to play. Tinnily, the words clipped out: Thirty minutes from Waskana. Confirms from Two, Three, Five and Eight. Then the noise of the ether. The noise in my head was quite loud, and as I puzzled over the words, they quietly slid into place, made some kind of sense. Waskana was the name of the little creek that had once flowed through Regina. I had seen its watercourse a thousand times, children running across the grey concrete bottom where once mud and tangled weeds had enticed a vagrant swan. Whatever else, Waskana One could only mean here. From the militarism of the countdown, I was sure that somebody or another was on their way to Comnet. I relayed my thoughts to Moochie.

'But why should they be coming here?'

'Don't be silly,' I said impatiently, 'what is there of importance in Regina but Comnet – from here we transmit to the globe, to the entire world.' I saw realisation flood alarm through her eyes as I pushed myself out of my chair and ran for the door. My instinct was urging me strongly to shut the doors.

'Shut the front doors, Moochie, secure the building! Sound the alert – do something, quickly!' She was dialling as I left the room.

Outside, in Transmission, only one person was working and she gave me a startled glance as I raced for the door, threw the first one open, tripped the switch which locked the outer doors, then urged the inner doors shut against the pillow of resisting air. The doors clicked to; I rammed home the bolts which groaned in their steel shafts as they went.

'What are you doing?' asked a voice full of curiosity. I turned to the technician who had been working at the console.

'What's your name?' I snapped.

'Pink,' she said easily. 'Bonita Pink. And you're Lydya Brown, I know. What's going on?'

'Something a bit odd, Technician Pink –'

'Bonita,' she said aside.

'Bonita,' I affirmed, 'there might be an attempt to take control of Comnet in about fifteen minutes. I think.'

'Take control of Comnet?' she repeated incredulously. 'Are you serious?'

'Look, I know it sounds crazy, but please, just do as I ask for the moment?'

'Sure,' she said wide-eyed, 'I'm not off till six anyway. What do you want me to do?'

'Just . . . keep your transmission going, keep things normal.'

'Hey, Technician,' called Moochie from the doorway, 'how many regions have you got?'

'What for?' asked Bonita Pink.

'I'll fill her in, shall I?' I said to Moochie. 'Look,' I asked Bonita, 'does your board need you at the moment?'

'No. It's a while before this mix ends.'

'OK, come with me for a minute. It's OK,' I assured her when she looked at her board doubtfully. 'Senex Bleu will watch it, won't you?'

I took Bonita into the projection suite, explaining about the voices leaking through into our channels – or something similar happening. I played her the tape. Her head turned sharply when she heard the voices.

'That's Borda,' she said urgently. 'I'd know her voice anywhere.'

I made a mental note of the name. 'Do the numbers mean anything to you?' I asked.

'Sure,' she nodded, 'it's like Senex Bleu says – there are nine satellite centres to Comnet – and your tape counts to ten. If that means anything.'

Connection. A lazylight burned in that dark room in my mind.

'Are we patched into them all?' I asked as we simultaneously turned for the door and went back to Moochie.

'Uh huh,' she replied, 'and the codes are on the console.'

'What happens if we open all channels, can we speak to everyone at once?'

'Yes – but the scrambler can only handle up to eight languages at one time.'

'Don't need languages,' said Moochie quickly, 'There's the emergency tone, send that out on all ten.'

'It's not enough,' I said, 'we need to warn them to secure all their stations.'

'I know,' cried Bonita, 'put on the attack vid. It's faceted for all receivers.' She scrabbled in a red-fronted drawer, emerged with the ten-sided cassette. She slotted it into the centre of the board, snapped circuits open, pushed buttons. The map in front of us blazed. Overhead, a red light began blinking furiously. The warning sounds blared out; Bonita hurriedly cut the studio sound. The veeyou buzzer erupted into the new quiet, Moochie touched its reply button, bringing the gaze of the guard at the front door to our eyes.

'Two persons requiring admission,' he said stiffly, 'and orders to admit no one. Advice required.'

'Sweet sunrise, Moochie, you forget to tell him about Berenice and Marla,' I hissed as a large grin travelled across her face. Struggling to order her features, she solemnly had the guard request identification from Berenice and Marla, then ordered them to be admitted. She told the guard to double lock the door and put on the deadfall. No reponse to her words appeared on his face, but her orders were acknowledged by his brief shoulder salute. The screen blanked.

I opened the Transmission doors to let in Berenice and Marla. Berenice wore a scarlet warm against the night air and its colour throbbed under the blinking alarm light. She and Marla listened attentively as I told of my Settlement incident with Vemare, what I'd felt. Then Moochie played the tape of the leaking noises. I kept feeling foolish, as if I were paranoid, but I couldn't get away from that false note chiming in my head.

'There is this,' said Berenice. 'Even if your suspicions and feelings had nothing to do with this, this is definite proof that a group of people are on some kind of tactical exercise in this vicinity. And any such activity, we would know about. Or should know about, either in full or through Stratcom restrictions.'

Her black eyes and the flat brown planes of her face gave her an outward look of impassivity at the best of times, but with a hint of anger in her voice and her eyes metallic, she looked positively dangerous.

'Exactly,' said Marla, running fingers through her thick white hair. 'So who – or what – is going on?'

'I'm sure that Vemare Puce was one voice – and you thought you recognised another, didn't you?' I asked Bonita.

'Not thought,' she said, swinging her head to one side, the skull-stars gleaming through her inch-long scarlet hair. 'Knew. It was Borda. I'd know her voice anywhere.' She paused as we looked at her. 'We were pleasure-givers for quite a while,' she explained.

'Who is Borda, where does she Settle?'

'She's at Larisha – at least she was a six-month back. She's an Agmin, third rank.'

Larisha was the Food Depot for Region Two. Set in the green pine-treed hills of Ethiopia, the place administered the movement of food for its entire Region, which went in a broad band down from Settlements in the Arctic, across the Great European States, through Africa and up to the newest Antarctica Settlement of Hakiami. When magnetic pulsing became the moving energy for vehicles, and after the world summit in 1995, Food Depots had been set up in each of the ten regions, just as each Region had its own medical, settling and training depots, all in their own separate centres.

'You trained together, I suppose?' asked Marla.

'Yes,' Bonita said with a tiny gasp, 'but she wanted outdoor work, which pretty well means Agmin, and I wanted communications, so we loosened bonds when we left training. That was two years ago.

But we always kept in touch, or did up until six months ago. She just stopped answering my callsign.' Bonita's head was down and her voice low.

'Did she ever say anything to you about –' Berenice began, but the veeyou buzz interrupted. I touched the button and the guard's face appeared.

'Lydya. Yes?'

'Two persons report a damaged flick and injuries that need attention. They request admission and help.'

Marla snorted, flashed a glance at Berenice.

'Can you see the damaged flick?' I asked.

'It is some way distant, I am informed,' he replied.

'And are the people at the door wounded?'

'I am unable to say. They appear distressed.'

'Offer them the co-ordinates to one of the flicks. Tell them we shall inform the Medicentre at Sweethills to expect them. Monitor their flight. Do not give them entrance. Repeat. Do not give them entrance. Understand?'

He acknowledged and blanked.

Berenice was already at the field console and had opened the screen. Two people appeared, walking slowing towards the line of flicks nestled into the holding dock. They walked wearily.

'Perhaps they are genuinely hurt,' said Bonita.

'They'll be better off at Sweethills then,' replied Marla crisply. At that moment, all the lights went off. The Transmission board whined as it died, and only a red glow behind my eyes reminded me of the furious blink of the warning light.

8: Time-stream One

Every other day or so, Shirley's words came though Min's head: you've got to be in charge of your own life, haven't you? She found herself paying more attention to newspapers, to television, to the way people spoke. She wished she hadn't. She realised just how much ignorance can be, if not bliss, at least equally as strong a buffer. Sayings she had known for years took on new meanings – master of your own fate, shaping your own destiny. She felt as if she had spent her thirty-two years as a teenager, concerned with embroidery while bombs fell at the bottom of the garden.

She couldn't paint. Her days were spent planting and weeding, the damp spring earth responding happily to her attentions. Her nights were spent in talking, talking, talking. The size, the scope and the levels of activity of the women's movement took her a little by surprise. Set against that, the group her three friends were part of made sense and became reduced in size. She felt over-privileged and selfish. She made plans during the day to take in a dozen girls, a half-dozen elderly women. She discussed the plans at night and slowly came to the recognition that the structure of society should be able to cope more humanely; prevention is better than cure was another truism in which she saw more of the truth. But how to teach prevention to blind eyes and bitter ears?

Shirley took her to the Place. Min met the mainstay women, and Boadicea, the proud young Alsatian who slept there at night. Eventually, Min asked to be put on the roster. She took phone messages about abortions, from women who'd been bashed around, from women who needed somewhere to stay, from women who were broke, drunk, drugged, crazy. Her newly bountiful compassion was tempered by learning of the artful dodgers, the swingers, the lazy radicals, the rip-off contortionists who stole anything from anyone on the excuse that it was tearing down The System, a type of truculent criminality that in the end she also recognised as being part of the problem. She began to paint again, full colour portions of women's bodies, limbs crowding against the frame, flesh bulging with the pressure of its bulk against the rigidity, tissues oozing. She wondered what the gallery would make of her 'new style'.

Easter holidays. Spring solstice, in her new parlance, she learned, and that gave her a ribbon of pleasure somewhere deep inside, that feeling of being connected to the pagan rituals, the sensible, joyous, pagan rites. The three were going to the Lake District for a week, with several other women. They urged Min to come, promising clean air, the scent of pines, tranquillity, fun. She gestured to Fotheringay and Blinken and Nod. Within the hour Lillie had commandeered the services of a friend, a nurse who had to stay in town and was delighted to spend a week in someone else's home, the sort of pleasant change that took the edge off having to work the holiday week. Before they left, they stocked the fridge for her, left notes for her on plants and animal habits, filled the van with the paraphernalia camping requires, and headed north to the lake-filled woods.

Min had never experienced anything remotely like it. Her painter's eyes were blitzed by the beauty of fifty or more women wandering through the trees, many naked or nearly naked; by the circles of women that sprang up to discuss, argue, sing or be quiet together. Tension-filled arguments were soothed over by laughing understanding. Smudge pots drifted blue haze, shrieks of laughter filled small boats, glittering fish spattered in hot pans. There was dancing, storytelling, singing to flutes and guitars. When the rain came, they curled up in one another's tents, talking, talking, talking. Comparing notes from other centres, recognising the same problems, listening to each other's solutions.

They returned to the city late on Saturday night. Min was more rested than she ever remembered being, and felt more alive. She'd begun to understand the phrase 'women's energy'. Fiona the nurse had left that afternoon. By the telephone was a long message: 'Dear Famous Four: what a fab and funtabulous residence! Your fairy folk didn't object to my presence, nor did Fotheringay, a fish of distinction I have discovered. Many burbles came over the ear-ringer, some of which were eminently repeatable at a later date and others that insisted on being inscribed. I herewith incribe! Lillian will be furious to learn that her rehearsal has been brought forward a day, and she's called for ten o'clock. The dynamic duo will be contacted once more by Douglas Warren of the *Sunday Mirror,* who wants to do a bio bit and rehash Shirl's clinic coup. And to top it all off, the electricity people were threatening the Big Cut Off if you didn't instantly pay them $56.17, so I paid that and will wait for your suitably grovelling cheque. Love and burnt toast, Fiona.'

'What about the *Sunday Mirror?*' asked Darlene.

'Fuck 'em,' said Shirley brusquely.

'But it might help!' cried Min.

'Don't you believe it,' said Shirley. 'The papers only say what the papers want to say.'

'But . .' started Min, and stopped at the look on Shirley's face.

'I said no, Min. No. There's no point.'

'But you'll ring them at least?'

'Yes. To say no.' She looked at Min challengingly, but Min only put up her hands, laughed, and assured Shirley that she was sure she knew best.

As Fiona had predicted, Lillie groaned at her rehearsal's coming forward. Darlene seemed reluctant to go to school, but Shirley went off to her computers with a little whistle, and Min couldn't wait to get into her studio. She seemed bursting with ideas and happily immersed herself in sketches, littering the floor like a summer snow. Later in the week, just as it began to drizzle the soft misty rain of late spring, Shirley arrived home in the thickening twilight. She looked tired, but gleamed at the others, saying with quiet triumph 'I've got it!'

'What?' asked Lillian absently. But Darlene just looked at her twin carefully and said at the same time, 'The list?'

Shirley nodded. 'Yep. It's got a dozen names on it.'

Lillian whooped.

'I don't know what you're all talking about,' complained Min.

Lillian explained about the finding of the computer print-out, then turned to Shirley. 'Who's on it?'

'Give me a break,' Shirley said good-naturedly. 'How about a cup of tea for this poor working heroine?'

Darlene put on the kettle, Min piled a plate with food and Lillian got a towel, took off Shirley's wet socks and began to rub her feet.

'This is just so I keep you captive till you've Told All,' she laughed up at Shirley.

'What's the list of?' asked Min.

'Companies who use time on the computer that produced the sheets we found,' replied Shirley. 'Most computers do the same thing, but because there are so many different computer firms selling their own systems, you can spot a system and trace it back to the source.'

'OK, so give us the names,' demanded Darlene, handing Shirley a huge mug of tea.

Mutual Benefit Insurance was the first name, followed by Fruit and Vegetable Food Ltd., Marine Savings and Loan, Great Prairie and Eastern Meat Company, Snodoos Unlimited Ltd., The Belmont Trading Company, Automotive and Aerial Insurance Ltd., Gable and Garbo Gear Company and the Track and Dog Magazine Incorporated.

'I wonder what the Belmont Trading Company trades in,' mused Lillie.

'Trust Auntie Shirley,' chided Shirley. 'I've been checking them all out – that's why I was so late.'

'How did you find out?' asked Min.

'Company register,' said Shirley. 'Anyone can have a look. Tedious, but accurate.'

Now I knew that, thought Min, but I've never had to realise what it meant. The Belmont Trading Company was a construction supply company, dealing in cement, wood, bricks, concrete blocks, and sand. It had been established in 1959 and had done very nicely since. Gable and Garbo Gear turned out to be a clothing factory; Snodoos Unlimited manufactured skidoos and imported skis, as well as handling a comprehensive line in motorised sleds. The other companies were as their names described them. All used the same computer system as displayed on the sheets discovered at the meeting.

Shirley had also noted the registered owners of each company. Only six of the companies were wholly Canadian. Money was present from America, Germany, Bermuda, Argentina and to her surprise, South Africa. They discussed the list at length, speculating wildly on each company and its possible reason for compiling statistics on women. Eventually, Darlene pointed out that all the others should know, and Lillian said she would call a special meeting.

'I'd like to come,' said Min. Three pairs of eyes regarded her with surprise.

'Just try and stay away,' declared Lillian. 'We'd show you a thing or two!'

The Place took on a different air for meetings, thought Min. There were over twenty women there, sitting cross-legged on the floor, perched on the table's edge, leaning against the wall and lounging in the chairs. There was a feeling of determination, she thought, no – a sense of purpose, that was it exactly. There was much chatter and exchange of holiday experiences. One or two of the women had been at the forest camp and greeted Min. After a time the room fell quiet. Shirley recapped the last meeting for those who hadn't been there, then read out the list of companies she'd compiled, together with their parent or affiliated companies. She explained that it was certain that the computer sheets in their possession had been done by the same computer system that handled work for these companies. It was possible that one of these companies' employees was using his company's free time for his own ends. It was equally possible that one of the companies was sub-contracting its free time out to other companies. Their immediate task was in narrowing that down.

A serious and rapid discussion followed, with two suggestions finally adopted for action. One was to get the Society for Research on Women to send a letter to each company, requesting any statistics they may have available to help them complete some of their own studies. The second idea was similar, but not linked wholly to a women's organisation. Amanda had a contact she could trust in a market research firm. Some kind of approach through that firm was suggested, perhaps a letter describing the increasing lucrativeness of the female market and offering to consolidate their statistics with any of those the company already had. The group agreed to Amanda making the approach.

'What else could we try?' said Lillian.

'I know someone who works for Gable and Garbo,' said Felicia, 'so I could gently check that one out.'

'Maybe we should check up on the man taking photographs,' said Lucy, 'the one on the march who didn't check out.'

'Have you got his address?' asked Lillian, her voice curious and a smile hovering.

Lucy nodded. 'Uhuh. I asked the desk sergeant if I could have it so I could write a thank you letter to the nice man.' She tipped her head to one side, her masses of curly hair half sliding across her face. Her voice had gone very demure and she gently lowered her eyelids with a little flutter of their lashes.

'Hollywood's been robbed,' crowed Lillian. 'OK. Tell all. Who is he?'

'Well, he's put down here, John Meredith, 219 Grove Poplar Drive, City.'

'Grove Poplar – that's on my route,' said Alice, '219 – that's the apartment block across from the Rehab centre, you know. Does it give an apartment number?'

'Alice is a postie,' whispered Darlene to Min.

''Fraid we're not that lucky,' said Lucy, shaking her head.

'Never mind. I'll dummy up a parcel and deliver it in person,' said Alice.

'What will you put in it?' Min asked her, curious.

'Oh,' shrugged Alice, 'one of the freebie books, Condensed Book Club, Time Life, one of those. There's always something lying around. Don't worry, it'll look real.'

'I'm sure it will,' said Min quickly. 'It wouldn't cross my mind that it could be any other way!'

Alice looked at the apartment house with fresh eyes. Quite swank. Money. Well, of course, they knew that all along. She went into the foyer, ran her fingers along the buttons looking for Meredith. Apartment 1210. She pressed the buzzer. A women's voice answered. Married, was he?

'Parcel, ma'am, may I bring it up? It won't fit in your mailbox.'

'Oh, sure,' said the voice, and the buzzer went.

Alice pulled open the foyer door as the buzzer sounded. She took the elevator to the twelfth floor, pleased the woman hadn't told her to leave the book with the caretaker. She got out of the elevator, found the apartment door, then went back down the corridor. She checked that there was no one about, then took a nail from her pocket and pulled it up her calf muscle, hard. With the blood oozing, she went back to the door and pressed its bell.

Suzanne opened the door, seeing a wiry tanned women, very short hair, in an old green T-shirt and shorts, looking down at a bleeding wound on her leg.

'What on earth have you done?' exclaimed Suzanne, bending to look at the leg.

'It was a nail,' said Alice truthfully. 'It hurts like hell.'

'You poor thing,' said Suzanne, 'look, come in, do. I'll get a washcloth.'

She ushered Alice into the apartment, put the parcel Alice had given her on the table, dumped Alice's bag by the corner of the couch and piloted her through to the tiny bathroom. As she was helping Alice sponge the cut with disinfectant, she noticed a tiny silver circle with a cross on the bottom in her ear. She's a feminist, thought Suzanne.

'I think that's quite clean now – how did you do it?'

'On a nail, outside,' said Alice who didn't like to lie to women. 'Thanks very much, it feels much better.'

'Would you like a coffee?'

'Yes,' said Alice with a swift smile of pleasure. 'I would, very much.' She followed Suzanne into the kitchen and sat at the round white table. I wonder if she was on the march, thought Suzanne, getting the coffee cups out.

'Nice place you've got, Mrs Meredith,' said Alice.

'Not Mrs anything,' said Suzanne, 'just Suzanne. I don't quite believe in marriage, I think. It doesn't seem to work all that well, does it?' She put a cup of coffee in front of Alice and proffered a plate of cookies.

'No, it doesn't,' replied Alice, taking a cookie, 'but people keep trying it, think they'll be different, I guess. Have you noticed how everyone thinks their set of emotions is special, not like anyone else's in the whole wide world?'

Suzanne laughed and nodded. 'Yeah! Hey, were you on the Reclaim the Night march?'

'Wasn't everyone?' queried Alice rhetorically.

'Wasn't it wonderful!' said Suzanne, warmth beaming from her. Eager, thought Alice, and new to it all. But a nice women. They discussed the march for a little, Alice being careful to enthuse as much as Suzanne.

'How come I haven't seen you at other things?' asked Alice, taking a shot that the march was the first thing Suzanne had been on.

'Oh – I'm an American,' said Suzanne. 'The man I live with got posted here to do some research. When he found he was going to be here for a while, he suggested I come. So here I am. It's such a nice city. I love it, I love it! I almost don't want to go back!'

'Maybe your man will get a permanent posting here with – who's he with?'

'American Vehicle.'

'With American Vehicle, and you can stay. Or maybe you could apply to stay anyway.'

'True,' nodded Suzanne, 'and I do like Canada – or at least this particular bit of it.'

'We can always use another good woman,' replied Alice. 'Look, I've got to go – I've got half my route to finish. Thanks for the medical aid and the coffee – I really did appreciate it.'

'You take care now,' said Suzanne as she escorted Alice to the door.

'And you,' said Alice, meaning it. 'Thanks again.'

9: Time-stream One

Today I'll take the kids on a nature walk, decided Darlene. I don't think I could bear to be inside. The air was still and warm and moist, with that clarity of light that only comes with spring, making trees, houses, flowers, even the roads look freshly rinsed. Delicate, luminous young green hazed the trees over. Across the road, under the long line of maples, Yvette came running, slender body clad in kingfisher blue overalls, olive cheeks flushed tawny with exertion. She ran into Darlene, hugging her legs fiercely, gazing up at her with pure love. Darlene chuckled, grinned in return, took Yvette's hand and together they ran in and out of the trees that marched up to the school.

Her class was waiting outside, some gathered into squabbling groups, some vying for nomination as Best Child. Darlene rounded them all up, told them about the nature walk, asking who needed to go home to get strong shoes or rubber boots. None volunteered, but several were told to go by Darlene, who could see the walk muddying the little patent shoes, staining the spotless skirts. Within the hour the children had returned and the group set off. Being outside seemed to calm the children. While they spun here and there, ran, jumped, wriggled and rolled, they were obedient to some greater sense of harmony.

She took them to the woods at the edge of the city, climbing up a hill where crocuses and little white daisies with yellow hearts dotted the thick grass. She flung herself down in the grass; the children sang and shouted. For a time, the whole day seemed suspended in a bright gauzy irridescent bubble. They ate their lunches on top of the hill, sitting in a scattered circle on the grass, munching happily as the spires of the city shone. Darlene told them the story of the city's beginnings, pointing out the early settlement places near the banks of the great river. Then, reluctantly, they made their way down again, Darlene feeling unaccountably depressed as they got closer and closer to school.

She realised there would be little point in trying to make the children spend the last half hour inside, so told them to play in the yard until the bell rang. In the empty classroom, she wandered up and down the aisles of desks, straightening books, peeking into scribblers, putting away the scattered scraps of paper, card, scissors and glue piled on the art table that ran across the back of the room.

A cursory knock on the door; Lorae poked her head round.

'Ah, you're back. I though I saw Yvette outside. Good trip?'

'Mmmn,' nodded Darlene. 'I didn't do anything instructive, really.'

'Good thing, probably,' said Lorae briskly, 'they probably learned much more than you realise. I'm here as a messenger. Miss Proust would like to see you when you've got a free minute.' She mimicked Miss Proust's crisp tones.

'What about?' Darlene asked.

'Dunno. Have you been a bad girl?'

'Not that I can recall. I only swiped one box of chalk.'

'Curtains for you,' laughed Lorae as she went away. 'Let me know how many lashes you get!'

'Yea, sure,' called Darlene after her, 'thanks a stack!'

She gathered up her bag, looked once more round the room, closed a window, then made her way up to her headmistress' office.

'Ah, Miss Coral, come in,' Miss Proust greeted her as Darlene lifted her hand to knock on the half open door. Gisele Proust was a small, neatly built woman with high cheekbones and a strong nose. Her brown hair was now sprinkled liberally with light grey, but her face showed few signs of ageing. Her light grey eyes were clear and steadily appraising. She gestured to a comfortable chair at the edge of her desk and asked Darlene if she'd like a glass of sherry. Darlene nodded. They made small talk as Miss Proust poured the sherry from the tall glass decanter into two discreetly small glasses. Darlene sipped the sweet ruddy liquid, trying not to grimace. She preferred beer. Miss Proust placed her glass directly in front of her and looked straight at Darlene.

'A most unpleasant thing happened this morning, Miss Coral,' she began.

'Oh? What was that?' said Darlene.

Miss Proust hesitated, seemingly at a loss for words.

'There have been some innuendos before, now that I look back on it,' she said obscurely, 'but you're an excellent teacher and I ignored them. I make it a rule to respect the privacy of my teachers' personal lives.' She took up the sherry glass, had three tiny sips and returned the glass to the polished wood. Darlene felt a little stab of fear in her guts.

'Today,' said Miss Proust rapidly, 'I received a strongly worded complaint about you. An official one, unfortunately. It says that you are an admitted lesbian, and it makes some pointed remarks about you and one of your students.' She met Darlene's eyes only as she finished the sentence. Darlene felt nausea rising. 'Will you refute this complaint?'

Darlene looked at Gisele Proust's strong face, her rain-clear eyes. She glanced round the office, the thick green carpet, tall oak bookcases with the warm old colours nestled in them, the pleasant Berthe Morisot print returning a small radiant patch of green to the swaying tree outside the window. She looked back to her headmistress, who was regarding her with a mixture of compassion and formality. She shrugged.

'No,' she said shortly. 'I am a lesbian. I am not ashamed of it. And as for my students, the mind that thought that one up is sick.'

'Perhaps you don't understand the seriousness of this, Miss Coral,' said Miss Proust. 'If you deny the accusation at this level, I can quash it. But to admit it – well, it'll mean going to the Board. That's almost certain dismissal.' Darlene thought Miss Proust's eyes begged her to reflect.

'I might as well deny that my eyes are blue, or that my heart beats,' said Darlene. 'It's not difficult to substantiate for anyone who really wants to.'

Miss Proust sighed. 'I understand. And I respect you, my dear. But I don't want to lose a good teacher. Why let them have the satisfaction?'

Darlene drew a breath, shrugging, her hands out. 'Because it never ends, I suppose. I know it so well. The more you try to hide it, the more stress you're in, the more you fear. I don't think it's wrong, I think public attitudes are wrong. If you're not in the wrong, hold your position – isn't that what Boadicea said?'

'Something like that,' admitted Miss Proust, pouring them more sherry. 'I admire your courage,' she added in a low voice. Their eyes met. Worlds of words were there. Gisele Proust acknowledged what Darlene read there with a brief nod. 'I've only five more years to go,' she said apologetically. Darlene nodded her understanding and got to her feet.

'I'll bring you my resignation in the morning,' she said quietly.

'No, no, I don't think that's necessary,' protested Miss Proust.

'See the term out. I'll fix it from this end. You must think of your future.'

'Thank you,' said Darlene simply. At the door she turned back. 'Oh – who put in the complaint?'

'Yes,' said Miss Proust, 'you should know that. Adele Viner. If she'd just made a verbal complaint – but she seemed extremely determined. It's a pity her own record is unblemished,' she finished bitterly.

'Adele Viner. I see,' said Darlene. She looked at Miss Proust as though numbed and closed the smooth brown door.

Shirley, Lillian and Minnie were furious. Minnie in particular couldn't remember being so angry: she slammed doors and frying pans, scowled at Fotheringay and evicted Blinken from the old fat armchair in the corner. Lillian folded her arms round Darlene and rocked her silently, then told her a series of excruciatingly bad jokes, going on and on until finally she pulled a smile from her, even a tiny chuckle. Shirley said nothing, but her eyes blazed. She mixed a large Benedictine and brandy and gave it to Darlene, indifferent to the expectant faces of the others. Minnie began to cook furiously, producing a stream of delectable dishes: asparagus soup, chicken with cream and tarragon, fresh beans in drawn butter, Chantilly strawberries. Shirley stayed close to Darlene. After dinner, she spread the massage cloth on the floor, turned on a heater and brought in her scented oils. Then, while Lillian and Min talked desultorily and Joni Mitchell sang, Shirley dug in to her sister's muscles, rubbed and rolled and kneaded until, presently, the tears coursed quietly down.

The phone started ringing very early in the morning two days later. Minnie woke with a start, hurrying to answer the urgent summons with heart pounding and all the premonitions of doom clanging.

'Is Lillian or Shirley there, Minnie? It's Lucy here.'

'Yes, sure, but they're both asleep, Lucy. Is it urgent?'

'Yes, it is,' said Lucy in her soft voice. 'Please could you wake Shirley up?'

'OK,' said Min reluctantly. 'Hold on a sec.'

The dawn chill lingered on the floor as she padded upstairs to Shirley's room. Shirley lay sprawled, skiff of dark hair tousled over white cheeks, years reduced with the intense blue eyes closed. Min hesitated, loathing to disturb her, but touched her shoulder lightly and called her name. Shirley woke instantly, eyes vague.

'Sorry, love, but Lucy's on the phone. She says it's urgent.'

Shirley stiffened, came out of bed quickly, wrapped a deep plum jacket around her naked body and ran down the stairs. Min followed, worried and cold. She went past Shirley into the kitchen and put the kettle on. She could hear Shirley's side of the conversation which was not very informative. Shirley hung up, came in to the kitchen. One glance at her face was enough to alarm Min, for her face was dull angry red.

'What?' said Min with a gasp, 'what is it?'

'There's something nasty in the paper about Darlene,' said Shirley tightly. 'I'm going to get a copy. Min – would you wake up the others?' She got the doorway. 'Tell them what happened,' she said, half hanging on the door jamb, 'I'll be as quick as I can.'

'But I don't know what . . .' began Min, then stopped as she heard Shirley take the stairs in doubles, run along the corridor, then, within a very few seconds run back down and slam out the front door.

Min made a large pot of tea, took three cups upstairs. Lillian woke quickly, but was not talkative. In her room, Darlene was curled on her side, covers thrashed wildly and spun tightly about her. It took several moments of shaking and talking to get her awake. Min called Lillian to come into Darlene's room. She handed the tea cups around. Lillie wriggled her way into Darlene's bed, put an arm around her. They looked at Min expectantly. Min sipped her tea and didn't know what to say. She began to tell them of Lucy's call, then heard the front door bang and called Shirley up.

Shirley burst into the room, her face grim, her anger an electric coat enveloping. She threw several copies of *Straight Talking* on to the bed. Even from where she was, Min could read the headline: LESBIANS IN GIRLS' SCHOOL it shrieked in 96 point.

'Oh my God,' moaned Darlene.

Min pulled a paper towards her. 'A top city school for girls, The Marie Curie School, has accepted the resignation of a woman teacher,' she read. '"Personal reasons" is the only statement given in explanation for the resignation, although it is know that the teacher freely admits to being a lesbian and lives in an all-lesbian household somewhere in the eastern suburbs. Apparently, the school did not know of the woman's lifestyle until a few days ago. A number of parents have been in a closed meeting with the School Board today, and the meeting was still underway as we went to press. The teacher who resigned from the school has held her position for three years. A Department of Statistics survey, completed in 1980, shows that eighty-three per cent of the country's teachers are women, nearly half of whom are unmarried.' The article went on, putting totally irrelevant facts against one another to make an implication that they couldn't print outright. Min felt sickened, and her head swam from anger.

'How did the paper get on to this, that's what I want to know,' said Lillian grimly.

'Adele Viner, probably,' Darlene replied. 'She's really got it in for me.'

'Yeah – but why?' said Shirley abruptly. 'What's she got to gain? She's got a senior teacher's job, so it's not that she's after yours. What's she got to gain?'

There was a little pause. The new light of morning slid past Darlene's crowded windowsill and timidly fingered the intricate bedspread.

'Money,' declared Lillian into the silence. 'Has to be. What else could it be?'

'How much would the paper pay for a story like this,' cried Minnie angrily. 'What are today's rates for this kind of filth?'

'Couple of thousand, maybe,' shrugged Lillian.

'She dresses very well,' said Darlene. 'Expensively, I mean.'

'It'll be money, seashell, you can bet your weed on that,' answered Lillian.

The next few days tumbled around them. The phone went constantly, friends, the parents of the girls Darlene taught, and the press. Darlene thanked the friends, dealt with the parents as gently as she could, and said nothing to the reporters. The persistent ones who besieged the house saw no one, except two cats blinking in the noon sun. She had a long conversation with Gisele Proust, both of them having realised she couldn't come back to school, and worked out her final pay details on the phone. Darlene asked Gisele if her own position was threatened but, in a burst of uncharacteristic frankness, Gisele Proust revealed that she was very close to three of the Board members, and that her own position was secure. Adele Viner seemed not to care about anyone else's sexuality. She had seemed determined to get at Darlene.

Darlene couldn't say so, but she felt a little sorry for Gisele Proust. To have lived for so long under such secretive conditions:

that almost made it look as if she agreed with the unthinking majority that lesbianism was disgusting, perverted, immoral, unnatural. Darlene knew in her bones that the way to make society look freshly at lesbianism was for all lesbians to be open and unafraid of social attitudes. Easy to say. She'd ducked out a few times herself, under the harsh hammer of money. Not that she felt you had to make a point of it before you needed to; just so you didn't deny it when it became relevant. She should have said something to Miss Proust when she was hired. But damn it, it made no difference to her ability as a teacher. Then she corrected herself – yes, it did make a difference! It made her a better teacher, she was sure, for the love and protectiveness she felt for the girls, as well as the insights she had gained from constantly being aware of herself, these all made her a more understanding teacher. She didn't think many people would listen tolerantly to her opinion. She supposed they thought she taught young girls so she could 'interfere' with them. Her quick rush of angry nausea was followed by relieving tears.

With her days now unstructured Darlene spent more time thinking about the computer sheets and the problems they seemed to pose. She went to visit Alice.

Alice wasn't back yet from her post round when she arrived, but two of her flatmates were. They invited Darlene in, gave her coffee and a huge slab of carrot cake. She hadn't finished it before Alice came in and soon the flatmates drifted away, leaving Alice and Darlene in possession of the big, untidy but cosy kitchen. Alice gently drew from Darlene the last of the details of her leaving.

She studied Darlene's face. 'Not letting the bastards get you down, are you?' she said lightly.

'A little,' admitted Darlene, and her throat closed momentarily. 'But the worst thing is I'll probably never be able to teach again. No way the Department will give me another school.'

Alice poured them both another cup of coffee, Darlene protesting that her kidneys were floating already. So Alice added a dollop of brandy, to give Darlene's kidneys something to do. She then beckoned Darlene into her own room.

Alice's room was a corner one, an odd kink in its walls forming a tiny V-shaped alcove. In the alcove was a table, a scrap of beautiful fabric and a dazzling collection of delicate little shells. On one wall was a gallery of photographs of women gardening, marching, singing, pulling faces, talking, holding snakes, hammering beams, eating, kissing, swimming, dancing. Darlene knew everyone on the wall and featured in three of the photos herself. She checked to see if there were any new photos since she'd been here a few weeks back.

Alice turned on the radio and settled into one of the armchairs. She watched Darlene go over to the photographs. Kid looked a little strained, thought Alice, sipping her brandy-laced brew. Not to be wondered at, but must try to give her a laugh or two. Her eyes crinkled as she thought of her morning; she looked down at her leg, and thought hearing about Suzanne might just cheer little Darlene up.

Lillian had had a good day, her anger on Darlene's behalf making her delivery at rehearsal spirited and real. The director was very pleased with her, hugging her as the cast sat around drinking coffee before the slow dispersal.

'Just do that on opening night, darling,' he cried, 'and I'll find you a dressing room with diamond-topped taps!'

'They'd probably drip,' said Lillian dryly, 'and anyway, I prefer my diamonds neat. For now, could I borrow Thor?'

Thor was the theatre's station wagon, an old old vehicle that roared and clattered its way around the town. Her director waved his hands as if distributing largesse. Lillian collected her things and headed across town for the Marie Curie School for Girls. She arrived a few minutes before school was dismissed, walked along the wide curve of the drive, and found a spot to sit under one of the big maples, which the afternoon sun was making a radiant umbrella. She kept her eyes on the front door as she thought about the woman she was playing in *Tartuffe*, the fragile daughter's companion, full of commonsense.

The children burst out of school, jellybeans erupting from a paper bag. One by one the teachers came, and there was Adele Viner, tall and slender in a pale orange chiffon blouse and grey skirt. You look lovely, thought Lillian. What a pity you're a bitch. She stepped out of the trees as Adele came abreast of her.

'Hello, Adele,' she said pleasantly, 'I've come to have a talk with you,' and she linked her arm firmly with Adele's and positively marched her to the waiting car.

'Get in,' she said. Adele looked mutinous and started to protest, but one glance at Lillian's face and she climbed in.

'Put your seat belt on,' Lillian told Adele.

'What for? I've got an appointment in ten minutes. If you want to talk, talk here.'

'Ten minutes is just not enough time, Ms Viner, I'm taking you to a place where we can chat undisturbed. And I'm a very bad driver, so I advise you to put your belt on.'

Lillian watched her until Adele reached for both ends of her seat belt. As Adele brought her hands together to lock the ends, Lillian grabbed them and manacled them together. Adele stared unbelievingly at the hand cuffs.

'What the fuck are you doing?' Adele spat out at her.

Lillian snapped her own belt together, started the car and glanced round to check the traffic before she pulled out. 'Oh I'm playing the heavy,' she said lightly, 'I'm an actress, remember? I have a taste for drama, you might say. I want your undivided attention, so I've made you a captive audience! That's every actor's dream, did you know? A captive audience. I've had that a time or two, myself actually – held my audience captive. Makes me feel – good – to do that.' She looked in the rear view mirror then changed lanes.

'It's to be a tear jerker then,' said Adele with heavy irony.

Lillian stopped at the red lights before them. 'Possibly, sheshark,' she admitted with the gentlest of smiles. 'It's quite possible that tears will be shed.'

She drove rapidly through the city, reaching and leaving the city's suburban limits before the rush-hour traffic snaked its way through their streets. The trees waved leafy hands in their direction, the sun turning their green to gold. Thor's open windows rattled, but through them came the heavy scent of hay.

'You know, I've thought about you a lot,' Lillian said conversationally. 'In fact, I've tried to put myself in your place, which is what I do with my characters, actually. I thought to myself, I wonder what it's like to be Adele Viner.' From Adele's quick stillness she knew she had her attention.

'I thought about how you looked, and I said to myself, well, I've got taste, I like expensively simple clothes. And I'm ruthless – I can dump eelshit on a colleague without a qualm. So I probably fought to get up here – probably had some screaming life as a breadline child, or maybe ninth kid in a family of twelve?' She turned her head in time to catch the small tightening around Adele's eyes. 'Yeah,' she said softly, 'not exactly Enid Blyton's version of growing up.'

'Tough from the start, eh kid,' she said in a deeper, gruff tone, sitting up straighter at the wheel, trying to be a Gary Cooper playing

James Cagney. 'But you made it, yessiree you made it. Good job, good clothes, bet there's a good boyfriend with some dollars on him somewhere in the picture too, eh? Gooood stuff!'

She dropped the role to concentrate on passing a huge furniture van that was winding its way up the country road. SMOOTH MOVES TRANSPORT CO, Lillian read as she passed its length, and gave a brief grin.

'But what I can't figure out,' she continued, with a return to her conversational tone, 'is what happened between then and now. I mean something must have happened, to make you the woman you are now – what was it? Poverty, incest, pregnancy – what?'

There was a tiny clink as Adele's hands moved in their shackles.

Lillian frowned, then shrugged. 'I would like to know,' she said quietly, looking at Adele. But Adele's head lifted; she turned and stared out of her window. Around the next bend appeared a road-sign. 'RITCHIE'S ESSO SERVICE 2 miles', it proclaimed.

'This'll do,' said Lillian and pulled on to the shoulder of the road just behind the sign. She turned the car off, then reached in to the back for a brown paper bag that was on the floor just in front of boxes of old costumes, bits of stage set and some small props.

'What are you going to do?' said Adele quickly.

'Well,' said Lillian, bringing out a roll of wide surgical tape, 'when I said captive, I meant truly captive – I don't even want you to make a sound during my performance.' She tore the tape open to six inches along its length and cut it off. Then she cut the strip in two. She put the strips across Adele's mouth, ignoring the thumps Adele delivered as she did so.

She leaned back, viewed her handiwork, then tore off a long piece of tape and wound it about Adele's hands, binding them together. Adele glared at her furiously. Lillian beamed at her, started the car and pulled back on to the road. Within a short time, the houses of a small town's suburbs came into view. Lillian drove through the late afternoon streets until she found what she was looking for: a supermarket with its wide parking lot, the last few cars of family shopprs leaving its flat breadth. She drove past the store windows, seeing the clerks tilling up, a tardy shopper having the door held open for her by the bored attendant, because the automatic doors were already switched off. She went to the furthest end of the lot and pulled up beside a lamp post, shutting off the engine. White backs of warehouses were behind them.

She reached into the back again, bringing out an old battered leather suitcase. She got out, carried the suitcase to the lamp post, then went back to help Adele from the car.

Adele struggled, attempting to knock Lillian with her head, and kicking her. But Lillian finally got her to the lamp post, ripped the tape off Adele's hands, undid the handcuffs, then re-handcuffed Adele's hands behind the post.

From the suitcase Lillian took a long skirt, which she pinned to Adele's waist. It was striped, and had three lines of braid parallelling its hem.

'This is your costume, seashell,' Lillian said rather breathlessly, cramming a black straw hat with a veil on to Adele's head. 'You're supposed to look like a suffragette, in case you didn't know. Now for the chain – they chained themselves to railings in the cause of women's freedom, did you know that?' She brought a long chain from the suitcase and draped it around Adele's body. She stood back to view the effect. 'Not the best, but it's an impromptu performance, after all,' she said consolingly. 'And for *your* audience – because you'll undoubtedly have one, don't worry – here's a label for you. Have you noticed how lots of people absolutely adore labels? We can't disappoint the folks now, can we, seasnake?' She dipped into the case once more and brought out a crudely lettered card, which had a scarlet ribbon looping from one end. Lillian slipped it over Adele's head. Over in the far corner of the parking lot, two children on bicycles stopped to stare.

I AM A VICTIM OF THE SALEM WITCH HUNTS, said the card.

'People are going to ask you what this means,' Lillian chuckled, 'I wonder what you'll say.' Her voice was sober. 'Maybe you could think about it. Because you'll know, if you do. Women have been burned as witches because they had almost too much knowledge – they really knew what it meant to be a woman. Do you, Adele Viner?' Adele stood stoically, eyes on the two children across the parking lot.

Lillian stopped speaking and stood back from Adele, looking at her with compassion now. She thought for a long moment, then unzipped her jeans and put her fingers into her vagina, brought them out, redolent with her own scent, and held them under Adele's nose. Adele jerked her head away, but Lillian stroked her fingers under Adele's nose, along her cheeks. 'That's a woman, Adele Viner, the smell of a woman. You're one of us, with a cunt that smells like the centre of the sea. You betrayed a woman, do you realise that, do you? And what that means?' Lillian paused, zipping up her jeans, then stepped close to Adele and said in a whisper 'It means you betrayed yourself, Adele.'

She started back to the car, then turned and bowed. 'End of Act One!' she said gaily. 'Exit, Lillian!'

She got into the car and drove away, passing the children on bikes who turned to stare after her, then began to pedal slowly up to Adele.

When Lillian got home, she didn't mention her afternoon with Adele. Darlene was full of her visit to Alice, and Min was an encouraging audience.

'I think I dragged her away from her painting,' said Darlene ruefully, 'but Min, you're such a good listener!'

'What are you painting at the moment, Minnewanka?' Lillian asked, 'I haven't been up in that rainbow tinted tower of yours for ages.'

'Come and see,' said Min, jumping up. 'If you really want to,' she added, uncertainly.

'Nah,' said Lillian getting up and holding Darlene's hand as they went up the three flights of stairs, 'your painting is so boring Minnewanka, I mean it's only lines and colours on a bit of tatty canvas. I mean, have you ever thought how many boat sails are hanging inside on the stuffy walls of art galleries. I wonder if they ever pine for the scent of salt, lust for a whiff of ozone . . .'

'No, didn't you hear,' Darlene put in, 'the Sails of the World united to protest about the newfangled dandy nylon, for all the – oh!'

They had arrived in Min's studio. They came in through the south wall; the other three walls were practically all window. To their left, the setting sun was painting a sultan's skysscape, streaking lavish areas of purple and gold and flame. The display stretched into the northern sky, which was tinted Maxfield Parrish blue, deepening to indigo in the east. The studio was flooded with heavy golden light. They stood bathed in it, blinking like moles. Min stepped over to her easel, surveyed the canvas on it. The other two blinked rapidly, breaking the spell of the light, and followed her.

The painting was big, the canvas about four feet square. At first glance, it looked like a fine old table with a superb bowl of fruit in front of a vase of flowers. But there was something odd, that drew your eyes deeper into the painting. And then your vision switched and you could see the naked woman who was bent nearly double with the weight of the table she was carrying. She had a child on her hip, and its little arm was going upwards to support the table too. There was sweat and pain in the woman's face, but determination and dignity too. The fruit and flowers on the table dissolved into two sturdy boys of about eight and ten, with stiff rough hair and slightly plump bodies dressed in brightly coloured shirts. They were fighting, pulling each other's hair, the foot of one poised to kick the other's groin. At their feet was the cause of the fight, a marble or two and some scattered coins.

'I call it Still Life,' said Min with a grin.

'It's superb,' said Lillian, after they'd gazed at it for a while. 'Minnewanka Bell, it's just – superb. What can I say that won't sound fatuous?'

'Nothing,' drawled Darlene, 'but we're used to that.' Lillian pinched her.

'I haven't quite finished it,' said Min, 'I want to deepen this bit here, and I'm not happy with this bit.' She put her fingers to the children's coins.

'I can't have a painter's eye then,' said Darlene, ''cause it looks just great to me.'

'Does it,' mused Min absently, 'that's nice . . .'

Lillian laughed and grabbed Min about the waist, twirling her around and squeezing her tightly. 'Stop, stop, stop, Ms Bell, it's playtime. You can't be a painter right now . . .'

Min shrieked until Lillina put her down and the three talked in the deepening light, until they heard the downstairs door bang, saying that Shirley was home.

'I've had quite a fruitful day,' said Shirley. The others looked at her expectantly, Min with food poised on her fork.

'Tell, tell,' urged Lillian, reaching for the last radish at the same time as Darlene. She slapped Darlene's hand lightly, grinned at her, took the radish and cut it in half with elaborate care. Then she gave Darlene the smaller portion. Darlene protested. Shirley waited until they were once again listening to her.

'Well, the Society for Research on Women had sent out to the twelve firms on the list, as we'd hoped they'd do, and today they got back answers from seven of them. Three of the firms enclosed statistics they'd had, three more promised answers within a short time as they were just beginning to look at that area themselves. And one said they used the Society's statistics when they needed them, but said that a sociologist who was using their computer time was in the middle of doing what seemed a very in-depth research study. They suggested we might like to get in touch with her, and invited me to call them. So I did. Her name is Suzanne Hatherly. They gave me her name, but they didn't know where to reach her, because she usually comes in at least every other day. They said they'd be happy to pass on a message from me. So I left a note for her, which they've promised to deliver.'

'A woman,' groaned Lillian. 'What a bummer.' Shirley nodded, mouth full of the perfect baby potatoes she'd just popped into it.

'That's interesting,' said Darlene slowly, 'because I heard about a woman called Suzanne today, too.' She related what Alice had discovered when going to the address of the man who'd taken the photographs on the march. She told them how Alice had scratched her calf with a nail, and they all cheered. Then she described Suzanne, and the fact that the man she lived with, John Meredith, worked for American Vehicle. Min noticed how animated Darlene looked and silently blessed this diversion from her own problems.

'Well,' said Shirley, 'and well again. I think Mr Meredith and Ms Hatherley's work deserves further investigation, don't you?'

'What do you mean,' asked Min, 'investigate it how?'

'I'll make a computer to computer request. In my position, that won't be too hard. All the computers are cross-linked anyway, which of course the public doesn't generally knowl It's like telephones, in a way, making an international call. It's really a matter of being "reputable" when you make the request. I can do that, no trouble.'

'I know an easier way,' said Darlene, grinning impishly at her sister. 'Mind you, it's not very scientific, or anything like that, but it works, I betcha.'

'What?' asked Shirley.

'No, I don't think I'll tell you.' Darlene's eyes were dancing. 'I'll let your fantastic scientific brain figure it out for itself!'

'I know!' said Lillian triumphantly. Darlene quickly put her hand over Lillie's mouth.

'Don't say,' she begged.

'What about me,' wailed Min. 'I'll never figure it out. Tell me.'

'Nope,' Darlene shook her head, 'maybe I'll draw you a picture, Min, but for now, I'll just let my dear Toby-jug figure it out for herself.'

Shirley sucked speculatively on the chicken bone she'd eaten. 'I'll

101

get it eventually,' she said finally. 'Probably – if it's that mundane – while I'm doing the dishes.' She threw the chicken bone down on her plate, licked her fingers then wiped them on her jeans and began to stack the dishes. Lillian pulled Darlene into the next room.

'What's your way,' she demanded in a whisper.

'You tell first,' Darlene whispered back.

'Well, I thought of a little sort of Perry Mason routine,' said Lillian.

'You've got it,' Darlene grinned.

'Let's do it!' hissed Lillian. 'I've got no rehearsals tomorrow because we open tomorrow night. Let's get up early, go to that apartment house Alice discovered and follow either him or her – or both!'

'There probably won't be anything in the apartment, though.'

'All the more reason to find out if they have an office.'

'But we don't know what they look like . . .'

'We know their apartment, Alice told you the number, didn't she?'

'Ye-es . . . er – 1210. And she described Suzanne, too.'

'Well then! Oh, let's do it, darling dolphin, please!'

Min came through the kitchen door. 'What are you two giggling about?' She smiled, questioningly, but they both just shook their heads and danced back into the livingroo.

Darlene was dreaming that she was eighteen again and she and Shirley had just told their parents that they were lesbians. But this time, instead of their father dismissing their words with a grunt and a 'you just need to meet the right man, that's all,' and their mother bursting into tears, haranguing them, saying she was disgusted and repelled one minute, and imploring them to tell her how she could help them the next, they were being kissed softly, and murmurs of pleasure were surrounding them. She had her arm around Shirley's waist and the two of them were chuckling with delight. She swam closer to the edge of consciousness and became aware that the nuzzling and the kissing were real and that she did have her arm around a waist, belonging to Lillian, not Shirley. Her room was not quite dark, pre-dawn grey pushing at the night.

She turned to Lillian, returning the kisses with fervour. After they had made love Lillian slipped stealthily downstairs, returning with bread and butter and fruit and two large mugs of tea. They ate quickly, pulled on their clothes and were out of the house before the sun was high.

They walked Darlene's bike some way from the house before exploding it into life, then left it parked a hundred yards away from the apartment block on Grove Poplar Drive. They worked out a strategy: Lillian would go into the apartment block, plant the invitation to the Ceramics exhibition she'd got through the theatre, and wait until Meredith picked it up. Then she'd come back to Darlene and they'd follow him downtown. They agreed that, if they got separated that day, each would wait with the motorbike for an hour, before leaving. The other would find her own way home.

Darlene watched Lillian go to the double doors, saw her enter the first set and become a shadow moving murkily beyond.

Inside the building, Lillian was scanning the door buzzers, just as one of the tenants came out. She smiled at him radiantly and grabbed the door before it shut.

The foyer was squarish, two elevator doors directly ahead of her. On the right wall were the mail boxes and, immediately past them, the wall dipped into a small alcove where a magnificent rubber tree stretched. On the left wall were three very bad paintings; that wall ended in another small alcove which proved to be the entrance to the caretaker's apartment, with three narrow steps leading down to a miniscule porch area. Lillian listened at the caretaker's door, but heard nothing. She went to the mail boxes and half stuck the envelope into the slit of 1210. Then she retreated to the steps of the caretaker's apartment and did her making-yourself-invisible exercise, drawing all her energies and vibrations into herself, being not there. One by one and in twos, the apartment people came out; but no one saw her, and no one claimed the note. After a while Lillian heard noises from inside the caretaker's apartment. The lock on the door started to click. Lillian sprang up and went to the elevators, pressing the UP button.

Out of the caretaker's apartment came a woman with curlers in her hair, carrying a milk bottle. She glanced at Lillian. The elevator bell pinged and the door opened, two people getting out as Lillian slid in, pressed the door for the first floor and rode the elevator down again. As the doors opened on the foyer, she could see the caretaker returning. She stayed in the elevator, which was summoned to the third floor where several people were waiting. Lillian stood well back as they crowded in. Back on the ground floor, she saw the caretaker chatting with a couple of the tenants. Swiftly, she decided that valour was the better part of discretion and made her way across to the mailboxes behind the backs of the moving group, grabbed the envelope and headed back for the elevator. The doors of the second elevator opened, disgorging another group of people. She got in, standing out of the line of vision of the caretaker, and pressed the button for 12. On that floor, the door of one apartment was open; a man was kissing a woman goodbye. Lillian turned and walked the other way, checking the door numbers as she went. They went down to 1201, which meant 1210 had to be the second from the far end of the corridor. The kissing man got into the elevator, the doors shutting on his final wave. The corridor was now empty. Lillian walked up to 1210 and rang the bell.

A man of medium height with a tanned, pleasant face and light grey eyes opened the door. His hair was tousled from sleep. He wore a short terry dressing gown and his feet were bare. He looked at her enquiringly.

'Good morning,' said Lillian brightly. 'I've got a pleasant surprise for you on this sunny morning – we're giving these to all the folk in this block,' and she thrust the envelope in his hand, 'just because we'd like to have an excellent turnout, and because we think our work is very good!'

'What work?' inquired the man, taking the envelope.

'Read it and see,' encouraged Lillian. 'Have a nice day,' she said cheerily, flashed him a smile and turned away to another apartment. The man shut the door. Lillian raced for the stairs, running down to the tenth floor before she caught the elevator to the ground.

The caretaker was now giving the rubber plant a drink. She looked hard at Lillian who walked quickly out of the building and down the street.

10: Time-stream Two

It was very dark, the only light in the room coming from Bonita's scarlet hair which was coated with the new phosphair colouring, and from the brooch Marla was wearing which picked out its design in pale green phosphorescent paint. Bonita's skullstars gleamed in the light of her own hair, making an effect I was sure her spacetrash colleagues would approve of. Through the glass doors, a dim glow lifted the blackness a little.

After the lights went off, we waited for the attack, but none came. Berenice decided to slip out and see what she could discover. While she was gone, Marla stood guard. Bonita, Moochie and I tried to raise something from the board, but it was as lifeless as a time-emptied body. Berenice returned. Comnet was definitely under siege, she reported. There were two people by each lifter, and by the stairway. The people were in a sort of uniform, she said, each carrying lazylights and stunners. We bolted the doors again and triggered the deadfall, wishing there was some way we could opaque the vast stretches of glass.

We felt sure that whoever was besieging us would eventually make their way here, for if it wasn't for the facilities here in this room, what reason would they have to mount an attack on us? We reviewed our position: we had water, but no food. We were all healthy – in fact, Berenice and Moochie said they would stay by the doors so that they had a chance of overpowering whoever came in, since their weight and the element of surprise would give them at least a reasonable chance of succeeding, especially if Bonita, Marla and I could be seen at the board. For the first time, I was angry that none of us at Comnet wore percoms. But we had no need of them in the building since we were surrounded by a vast computer network that was tuned in to us at all times. No matter where you were in the building, you could talk to anyone and, from the veeyouers, see whatever you wished to see. And at home, we valued the privacy we had, relying wholly on our veeyouers there to keep us in touch.

The minutes dragged by. We speculated uselessly about what was happening and what action we could take. Bonita felt particularly strained to me, so I began to talk to to her, trying to turn her thoughts away from nowtime. She'd been in the far south of Region Ten, in New Zealand, which was a highly productive part of the Food Sector. New Zealand was known as one of the most harmonious of the world's places. Its distance from everywhere else seemed to give it a special essence, for few people who chose it ever transferred from there.

She told me of some of the places she knew. A perfectly symmetrical dormant volcano set in a blue, blue sea. Another exquisitely symmetrical mountain, this one inland and crested with snow. A scatter of smoothly rounded islands in a calm and acqua gulf. The mountain city of New Auckland, built in the tree-studded Waitakeres after the decimation of Old Auckland by the horrendous ripping earthquake along the Kermadec trench.

I asked her about Borda, and as she talked, I picked up an image of a slender, almost too thin woman in her middle twenties, brown skinned with roughly cut wavy hair and tense shoulders. Eyes warily earnest. Borda had been her first love-lover. She was older, more assured, strong. She introduced Bonita to the dark green magic of forest and hills; they made love under giant ferns and by rushing skeins of water. Borda had pleaded and implored Bonita to switch to Agmin, but that spark of Bonita that wasn't wholly affected by Borda kept her shaking her head, held to the idea of the computer board she'd been bewitched by at twelve. After that, Borda changed, becoming more curt, having less time for her. A bewildered Bonita was shattered, confronted for the first time by the painfilled face of love. They had kept up a distant interaction until about six months ago when, for no reason that she could fathom, Borda had put a block against Bonita's callsign.

'Perhaps if I'd become a Twopee,' Bonita said wistfully, 'we could have had at least that in common.'

'So Borda was a Twopee,' I reflected, my voice low and lazy to keep her memories from becoming too vivid. Well, little one, I thought, you've had quite a good escape. For the vivacity Bonita displayed in her hair, dress and speech, the Borda she'd told me about was quite wrong. Nervous and domineering with religious needs. Not quite the right match for exuberant, laughing, adventurous Bonita. And of all the religions available, the First Church of the Profound Principle was probably the most severe, its rigidity arising from mathematical discipline.

'If she'd heard me call her a Twopee . . .' half giggled Bonita. To laugh at past lovers is to heal yourself, I thought.

'Smog no!' she explained. '"I am a Founder"' she mimicked, '"and I know you'll do me the courtesy of not following whatever slang is used by the Basics".' Bonita giggled again, half choked bubbles of laughter snorting through her nose. 'In our last fight, I told her I thought her head was as swelled as their Domes, and that in fact the only thing I liked about their religion was the Domes.'

'The Dome is so beautiful,' Bonita continued. 'I think I fell in love with this building the first time I saw its dome. I was coming here for the first time, and my flick was probably two miles away and I saw this warm orange glowing ball way in the distance – it was the winter sun catching and filling it, but that first time, I thought it was all the love in the world held in one source point. Silly, hey?' she finished, inviting me to share her own pleasure in her youthful romantics.

I laughed a little with her, then a silence fell between us in the dark. I could hear Berenice and Marla murmuring together and a tiny snagging sound that said Moochie was dozing.

Into my mind slid a picture of Vemare going into a Dome. I jumped inside my skin. I recalled the scene again and it was fast with the surety of truth. There was Vemare, black trousers and severely tailored jacket with its slashes of silver across the shoulders and down the centre back, disappearing into a Dome with several other people dressed in similar uniforms, but of different colours. From what I knew of the Twopees, initiates attained ranks according to numbers, each colour-coded. Then I remembered the Settlement Infosheet, which had Vemare talking on a Twopee tenet.

'What number was Borda?' I asked Bonita. 'In the Twopees, I mean.'

'Oh, not high, about a thirty, I think. But she hoped to be a twenty-five before the end of my training.'

'What colour was her uniform?'

'Pale blue with dark blue stripes on the shoulders and back. Quite nice, actually, though not a good colour on her. Still, she didn't care about that.'

'Berenice?'

'Yes?'

'What did the uniforms on the people by the lifter look like?'

'Just sort of tailored trousers and jackets, different colours, why?'

'Were they Twopee uniforms?'

A long pause. Then, 'Tiamat's tongue, Lydya, you're right, they were.'

I tried to remember what I knew about the First Church of the Profound Principle. It had been started by a group of mathematicians and scientists, none of whom believed in personal aggrandisement, so the founding group had not acclaimed a leader or prophet. But the group's beginning was popularly attributed to Rela and Arjilixtra Black, who trained together and were devoted to the science of mathematics. They believed that only numbers had the purity of real truth and that the principle 'The whole is the sum of its parts' was further extended by the example of a single molecule of holographic image, which contained in it the three-dimensional image of the entire image. The importance of that knowledge had, they felt, lain dormant for decades, but it was that knowledge which caused them to add the clause 'and the part is the sum of the whole' to that first principle. This was their so-called Universal Inversion Truth, which Vemare had spoken on. I also had a vague memory of their day of celebration being Einstein's deathday, or birthday, I wasn't sure which.

None of that really bothered me, or anyone else that I knew – after all, its logic was undeniable. The aspect of their religion that I found so distasteful was introduced after Rela and Arjilixtra died, when was added a belief in the power of uniformity, a subservience of the individual to the group. Their membership was graded in a manner so like the now defunct hierarchies that I felt physically sick when I first heard of it. It was too much like the old armies. Members moved up to higher ranks by demonstrating their ability to put aside individual – and very human – desires. Twopees were very seldom found in the Discovery Sector, the few who were there soon transferring to Food or Work. They were excellent workers, but their dislike of individuality was one I'd felt personally. Vemare found me very hard to acknowledge. I realised now that her look of triumph on the day she'd told me of my dismissal was part of that. Why couldn't they see that subservience simply meant more power to those at the head of the hierarchy? And did any of their number question the accountability of their Number One? Still, religion was a private affair, and the twopees were too small to worry about globally.

'But the Twopees wouldn't do this,' whispered Marla loudly. 'It doesn't make sense. What would they want with Comnet stations? Even supposing their idea was to grab them and bombard the collective ears of the world with their message, where would it get them?'

'And where would they get the money?' added Berenice. 'It's not as if they're a major religion, or even a small and wealthy one.'

'I don't suppose that stops them wanting to be a major religion,' yawned Moochie. 'These steps are smogging hard to sleep on. What's happened?'

'Nothing,' answered Marla. 'Lydya has collected impressions that make her think the people in the corridor are Twopees, and Berenice says she thinks they are wearing Twopee uniforms.'

'What do you suppose they're doing, whoever they are?' asked

Moochie, 'and how long do we calmly sit here in the dark? Why don't we do something?'

'What for instance,' snapped Marla, 'go and ask them to leave?'

'Why don't we try a mindtap?' suggested Moochie as if it was the easiest thing in the world.

There was a breathless hush. 'On who?' asked Berenice cautiously.

'Well, why not one of the people by the lifter. Can you visualise one?'

'I can try,' said Berenice with vigour. 'If you all agree.'

'I've never done one before.' Bonita gave a little gasp. 'Maybe you should do it without me?'

'No, five heads are better than four,' said Moochie cheerfully. 'Just trust us.'

I was a little hesitant, but I too wanted to do something. There was every chance that, if the mind we tapped was aware of our intrusion, he could follow us back. But it was worth a try. Berenice would have to lead, since she'd seen the guard, but she was also strong and experienced and the element of surprise seemed to be the only defensive strength we had.

We gathered over by the door, sitting in a circle and holding hands. I told Bonita to breathe deeply three times, long and slow, and try to focus her mind's energy wholly on Berenice. We began breathing in rhythm. Moochie's hand was large and warm and plump in my left hand, Bonita's bony and cool in my right. I concentrated. I closed my eyes, filling my mind with whiteness, and on that whiteness slowly developed Berenice's face. I centred on her eyes, sending my self-energy to her. Only distantly was I aware of a series of soft gasps.

It was impossible to tell how long we were connected, for when I came back to myself it was still dark. I still held Moochie's hand in my left, and Bonita's in my right, but now Moochie's hand was sticky with sweat and limp in my grasp. Bonita was gripping mine so tightly that I had numbing tingles running along the nerve from my little finger to my elbow. Moochie let my hand go.

'Did you get anything?' Bonita panted. 'Berenice?'

For a moment there was no reply, then Berenice grunted 'Yes. I'm just trying to sort it out. I have to be quiet a little.'

From the position of Bonita's shimmering head, I could see she was drooping. Moochie touched my arm and whispered 'Ciggie?' I aimed my Candeez in her direction. Her arm fumbled along mine, found the package, and she lit the pale green tube with her hotwire. As she dragged, the brief flares of light showed me Bonita with her head bent, elbows on knees, Marla leaning backwards on her hands, brooch a flare along her collarbone, Berenice covering her face with her hands, legs crossed, and Moochie with her legs stretched out, half reclining on one elbow as she drew on the Candeez. The smoky mint smell made me aware of other smells, body smells and the hot plastic smell of machines.

'I went in from the back. He had the automatic half shield up in front. I wanted to be quick, but I don't know – there was a pile of things to get through. The usual mess, love problems, fear, excitement flashes. But there was one thing he kept going back to – a big room packed with people, a few speaking from the centre. Four centre people, three men. Dressed like Exceeders, flamboyant colours, excellent fabrics. With those I got images of the guard I was in dressed in Leader's clothing, being rude to Servers. And another of him fucking two women at the same time, and another of him alone inside a gigantic flick, followed by this crazy image of him on a wooden horse, bumping up and down. He was staying in this holding pattern. Holding pattern.' Her voice stopped; soon she sighed and said 'No more. That's all I can hold. Very glowing about the meeting, hero-worship vibes, all that.'

'No questions?'

'No. He seemed to have taken the whole thing in quite uncritically. A bit like the religious ecstacy feeling.'

'An alliance between the Exceeders and the Twopees?' said Marla thoughtfully. 'Is it likely?'

'It explains what's happened,' answered Moochie in a low voice. 'And it turns on hundreds of blazebeams in this murky head.' It turned blazebeams on in mine, too. Couple the ways of the Exceeders with the fanatic subservience of the Twopees and you had a brew uncommonly strong – one which would, if it had its way, return the dominance of money to global sway. A return to the clawing, biting, hacking times, to the clang of the chains of slavery. And killing for profit, the apocalypse that we had seen so many times. My stomach heaved.

Bonita was still holding my hand, not as tightly now, but with the need of a child. 'I can't bear fighting,' she whisper-sobbed. 'I can't bear it.' Her voice ended in a whispered shriek which made my hair move.

'Are you going to lose control and snivel your way into a liability,' hissed Marla sharply. 'That's the last smoggy thing we need, you shorting out.'

'Mmmn, turn your energies our way, hotlocks,' Moochie softly chuckled. 'You're not here alone and you're not stupid. You shorting out could make things worse – that's no way to be a woman, is it?'

I squeezed Bonita's hand, sending calmwaves, and soon I felt her fearfuls subside and balance begin again. Through my own head, our heritage came flashing. The World Summit Meeting of Christmas 1995, with India, China, most of Africa and all of South America except Brazil aligned against the combined powers of America, Canada, South Africa, Russia, Brazil and Japan. The threat of nuclear war had finally been voiced by these combined Third World countries, a threat that had been swelling over centuries of tribalistic behaviour, often made worse by religious fervour. Huge populations, poverty and nuclear weapons provided the impetus for the challenge to the financially prosperous megapowers. From within those megapowers, groups of people who had been concerned for years about the state of the planet Earth supported the Third World countries, and, for days, the world hovered on the brink of a war no one really wanted.

So the Summit was called and the long days followed with the world erratically ticking like a weary clock. Then the hesitant carrying out of a blueprint for survival, the basic rules laid down only when unanimous approval had been won; the control of birthing, and the sharing of land and money and knowledge. The Birthrights system was begun in 2001 by the pool of money commandeered from the knowledge provided by the IMF and the major banking powers. Next was the introduction of the Global Sectors – Work, Discovery, Exceeding and Food, and the structuring of world government, a United Nations that had one representative per country, with equal vote power, and the beginning of simple agreements to pool money, food, resources while honouring each separate cultural identity. Finally, the recognition that we were one people, one world.

The agreement was won only after long and arduous days of debate that the World Feminist Network would be in total charge of communications, which also included education. Their case was won both on a stringent assessment of their principles and on a recognition that they had, since the eighteenth century for certain, been denouncing the social values and structures which had led directly to this crisis point. Feminist media, because of their autonomy and consequent freedom from restraint by big business, had been able consistently to present analyses of the very actions that had brought the planet to this point of annihilation. They had, in short, hundreds of years of understanding the problem. The Information Centre came into being, composed of a feminist representative from each culture. It had the specific duty of assessing all information before it was used by Comnet – the place from which all educational and informative communications came. The honour of the feminists was doubted at first, but after a few months and much 'accounting', the trust was earned. Hundreds of feminists were called into the project. Eventually, Comnet became the centre for a settlement of women. Once they were together, without fear, their transient telepathy deepened, firmed. Their first major New Age teaching was in telepathy.

It was agreed that political and religious ideologies must remain private convictions, for our history showed only too clearly that a dominance in these ideologies always led to war. All military forces were translated into action units and nations' boundaries became cultural only, no longer barriers to the free movement of all people. The globe was divided into ten Regions, running vertically as do the lines of longitude, each one being 36 degrees wide at the equator. Administrative groups were each linked to the central global offices, which were not huge and relied on computer efficiency for the vastness of their administration.

All citizens had to work in the Work Sector for seven years, following the completion of their education-training at seventeen. You could opt for where you'd like to work, but had to give two other choices and, even so, if those areas were full, you could end up in an entirely different workfield. But it seldom happened. After your seven years, you were free to choose from the other three sectors. Discovery was where you went if you wanted to follow your creativity and be a musician, say, or a researcher, an anthropologist or a dancer. Your Birthrights gave you your living and you could devote your time to the pursuit of your subject knowledge.

The Food Sector controlled the globe's food production and its population. The two had to be kept in balance for the survival of everyone. The Exceeders was the Sector set up in recognition of the competitive force, the drive to pit your wits against others. The Exceeders benefited the whole world, for they supplied over and over again the surplus garnered when the business game is played well. Citizens in the Exceeders Sector forfeited their Birthrights while they were there.

It worked well; but for the six years between 1995 and 2001, I knew from the old vids that the raging giants of cruelty and fear had, in all their faces, waged a terrible battle before they were subjugated.

As I'd been mindflipping, I'd had my eyes on Moochie. Her face was a little weary and the black and green robe crumpled; with a shock I realised that I could see her. I looked towards the doors. Lazer light stunned my eyes as two streams of power touched Marla and Berenice. I screamed, rolling to one side and standing against the wall, then found myself streaking for the Projection suite, Moochie's breath on my neck. I heard Bonita wail and half checked, but it was too late, the doors cracked crazily and I wide-felt people coming in.

Moochie and I pushed the huge door to the Projection Suite shut, flipping the light barrier to wide. But it would not take much to get at us. The narrow window showed us the scene beyond. Two people upheld the deadfall with antigravs, while a third scrambled along the wall looking for its switch. Bonita stood at the console, eyes huge with terror, mouth open soundlessly in protest at the first living volence she'd ever seen. The deadfall switch was touched and instantly a throng of people poured into the room. Two grabbed Bonita, who fainted at their touch, and the last I saw of her was her yellow and blue painted legs being pulled out of the doorway.

Two people approached the board. One was in black with silver slashes and the other in white with black slashes. The one in white spoke to the percom on his wrist. The one in black positioned others around the room. She'd seen us, I felt sure, because she put three by our door. Suddenly, the Transmission room lights blazed, the red light began its frenetic pulse and the warning tape flared into life. The man in white touched the panel on the board; the images died, the red light paled away. He spoke to his percom again. Within a few seconds, a new image appeared on the big screen. I felt Moochie leave my side. A click, and a voice came into the room, the voice of the man who was talking on the image, the voice of the man in white at the board.

'. . . for fear. While these actions may seem aggressive and violent to you, they are not intentioned that way. There is nothing to fear. We have taken steps which we feel necessary to keep our world safe. We have proof that many of the representatives of Nations have been in collusion. But there is now nothing to fear. We will bring evidence before you to support our claim, and we will ask all of you for your support. There is nothing to fear. The future is safe . . .' His voice was rich and warm and comforting, stroking all my nerve ends.

'Got the Enricher on,' snorted Moochie, 'smogging faker.'

'Where's it coming from?'

'Direct from our central computers, from the looks of it,' she said. 'They must have got into the basement.'

'But how?'

'Who knows?' she shrugged. 'Someone inside opened the door, possibly. They're unquestionably in.'

The rich voice went on, soothing and reassuring. The man at the board nodded with satisfaction and turned the sound off. The image was still being transmitted. The big map winked its reception in the centres around the world.

The woman in black approached the man in white. Their conference concerned us, for she gestured towards our window. Even though we were standing back from it, and there was no light in our room, I felt they knew we were there. They came towards us. Faintly, through the window I heard that rich voice; he was talking to the guards, asking them what the room was that lay behind the door. One of the guards replied, and I recognised her voice as being one of our Comnet workers. She told him the truth: that the room was quite small with no other doors or windows, full of equipment and little else. Don't worry then, he said to the woman in black. If there is someone in there, they'll perish or come out. Just keep an eye on the door. The steel in his voice made me shiver, but the cold chill in my bones came from the truth in his words.

11: Time-stream One

Shirley opened her eyes to the sunshine on the green bank that ran down past her bedroom window. The slope was a tumbled mass of small shrubs and taller trees, where occasionally the shy shade-flowers peered through the accumulated layer of leaves. On the first let's-see visit to the house, it was this room that had told her she wanted to live there. In this room, all the dark enchantments of woods and hill magic were immediately brought to the front of her mind.

There was no incongruity for her in her awareness of that pattern people called the supernatural. It was as obvious and as explicable as the science base of computers, and it obeyed the same sort of laws. She had been nine when Darlene had fallen off a toboggan, hit her head on a rock and been unconscious for three days. The first night Darlene was in the hospital, Shirley had not wanted to go to bed. Her parents had talked to her, trying to convince her that Darlene was going to be all right. With only a few protests, she had gone to the bedroom she and Darlene shared.

There was a small nightlight in the room, low on the wall and shaped like a candle flame. Shirley had lain in bed, staring at it. It glowed fixedly, the curves of dull opaqued glass forming an unmoving flame. Then, almost imperceptibly, the curves had moved and Shirley found herself looking at a tiny spot of light. She could see the whole room and herself lying in the bed, gazing at the nightlight. The thought formed slowly in her mind: I am out of my body. Her deep running curiosity and the strength gained from all her years in a nurturing home, kept her from fear. After the initial cold-water-douche of shock, she opened her senses to impressions. At once, she could feel Darlene, far away and indistinct, but steadily there. She realised her parents were right, Darlene was going to be OK. She wondered with a flash, instantly thrust away, whether other people could understand the pain of the thought of Darlene's death.

It was a long time after Darlene got home before Shirley

remembered her experience fully. It stayed at the back of her mind, but instinctively she felt it wasn't something she could share with Darlene; and she didn't know what to do with things she couldn't share with Darlene.

By the time she was seventeen, she was in the worst turmoil of her life, recognising that what she must be feeling was love and lust, for she couldn't get the hair and the lips and the curves of Melissa's body out of her mind. Everything Melissa did or said or liked or hated became the absolutely right thing. Melissa was so good to be with. It took much longer than her friendship with Melissa lasted for her to realise that she was a lesbian. Once that piece had been put in place, she relaxed. So that was why. It made sense at last. It took her longer again to realise how very hard it was for other people to accept that. She became aware of women, women's achievements. She wondered why there were so few who achieved. Was the reason that men were, on average, more intelligent, more gifted? But that certainly wasn't true of the young men at university with her, and she came quickly to the conclusion that it wasn't true at all. She was led to looking deeper for those reasons, and she saw what is there for everyone to see.

This last year had been a very satisfying one for her. She felt challenged and rewarded in most areas of her life. Coming to live in this big house had been the final satisfaction, for in it she could put space between her and Darlene without going too far away.

She woke knowing that Darlene was not in the house. Darlene's being interacted with hers in what Shirley thought of as a kind of sonar, so that when they were apart, the bounce of their vibrations backwards and forwards stretched, felt cooler. Gone for the milk, she thought, or eggs for breakfast. She threw back the covers and got out of bed, her feet touching the smooth cool of the dark wood floors with pleasure. On her way downstairs she looked in Darlene's room, and in Lillian's, seeing the mugs and the empty beds. Min was making toast and four glasses of orange juice stood on the table.

'Wake them up, would you?' said Min. 'This is nearly ready.' She gestured to the pan where scrambled eggs were thickening.

Shirley raised an eyebrow. 'They're not up there; I thought they were down here with you.'

They looked at each other blankly; suddenly the whole sequence assembled in Shirley's mind, like a computer board sliding into place and the programme completed.

'The silly idiots,' she said, instantly angry. She had no doubt they'd gone out to find John Meredith, even though the first and implacable rule of their group was to let a couple of others know, and never to expose themselves unnecessarily. They worked together, carefully, through the network, that was the agreement. Darlene knew that, and Lillian too. It was that laughing wildness which they shared. Well, she'd just have to trust them, resourceful as she knew them to be. With annoyance, and a sting of fear at the back of her mind, Shirley made light of it to Min, ate her breakfast and drove off to work.

Meredith dressed with reasonable care, thinking of Kendal. The Head of Special Projects was a large, deceptively hearty man in his late forties. Little escaped him. Meredith knew Kendal would sum up his situation within minutes. A small smile played briefly round his mouth. He wasn't afraid of Kendal. It would surprise him to see Suzanne at the airport, but Meredith had his own reasons for having Suzanne accompany him. She appeared behind Meredith in the mirror, her head held on one side questioningly. He surveyed her dark green open-throated collarless dress, the discreet gold chain at her throat, and smiled.

Kendal came off the plane in the middle of the passengers. Meredith thought how like Kendal it was to remain half hidden at all times, quite a feat when you remembered his bulk. They greeted each other with hearty handshakes, Kendal's eyes icecube cold. All the way back to the office, Meredith felt Kendal's eyes at the back of his neck. He dropped Suzanne downtown, saying, as they had agreed, that she wanted to shop; they made arrangements to meet at seven at The Snooty Fox for dinner which, laughed Suzanne, should give them plenty of time to talk lots of business so that they could have an embargo on business talk at dinner.

She slammed the door and waved goodbye as Meredith pulled away.

Kendal said 'Why?'

Meredith glanced at him. 'Cover, what else?' he replied calmly. 'Plus available tail.'

'Cover? Who do you thing you are, James Bond? There are plenty of single sociologists around.' His voice was venomous.

'Look, basically what I've got to do is find out about the actions of a group of women who don't particularly like men. I need a woman as a front. And I had to have one I could trust. I know her, she checks out. I brought her up from New York.'

'On whose cash?'

'Look, get off my back, will you? I'm not a juvenile. I know what I'm doing, and I need a cover.'

The attack strategy worked. Kendal grunted and changed the subject. On the way to the office, Meredith ran through the setting up of the apartment, the first meetings, the Women Only restrictions and his decision to bring Suzanne up.

They reached the office building. Inside, a youth in motorcycle gear, delivering a letter, waited with them for the elevator. They were silent until they were both inside the room, the door shut and a coffee made. Then Meredith ran through the meetings he'd had with Philippe Manet, the information Manet had supplied, the contact woman at the school and the trickle of information now coming from her via Manet.

As he reviewed it with Kendal, he felt pleased with himself.

'My next move is to get into this Place of theirs, plant a bug. More coffee?' He took Kendal's mug and filled it with whisky-laced coffee.

Kendal studied the sheets in front of him, saying nothing. Meredith put the cup beside Kendal and sat, relaxed, in the swivel chair. He waited, answering Kendal's terse questions. Finally Kendal shoved the papers to one side and picked up the cup.

'Cheers,' he said to Meredith, who saluted with his cup.

'What's it like elsewhere?' he asked Kendal.

Kendal hunched his shoulders. 'About the same. A central group, more or less active depending on the brains, and more or less successful, depending on the actions. This one seems to be one of the best. Or worst, I suppose. They've got their act together. When you gonna bug 'em?'

'Tomorrow; come and have a look.'

Kendal shook his head, finishing his coffee. 'Nah. Unnecessary and probably boring. You're on your own, chappie.'

Meredith drained his coffee cup, the rim hiding the gleam of jubilation in his eyes. He'd passed muster. With relief he saw it was 6.30; he got Kendal's coat and told him dirty jokes all the way to the restaurant.

Darlene and Lillian had kept watch all through the morning. They followed Meredith out to the airport, back into town. Lillian hopped off the bike to follow Suzanne. Darlene trailed the two men to the building, saw them start to park the car. She nipped the motorcycle in between two cars at the front, and went into the foyer. She kept her helmet on, hoping to look like a delivery boy. She waited until she saw them at the door, then pressed the button for the elevator. Meredith pressed the fourth floor and looked at Darlene inquiringly. She nodded and looked away. Her heart was pounding. They paid no attention to her, getting out of the elevator first and walking to Meredith's office door. Darlene walked past to the stairway, and ran down to the street. She drove to the front of Hudson's Bay, where she and Lillie had agreed to meet. She waited for an hour, then went to Grove Poplar Drive, where Lillie waited for her under the trees of the morning.

'Success?' asked Lillie, her face glimmering with a smile held in. Darlene nodded. 'Me too,' said Lillie triumphantly. 'Home James, for a session of show and tell!'

At dinner, both Lillie and Darlene were so exuberant that Shirley's annoyance dissipated. She told them tersely how bloody silly they'd been, then listened with interest to the description of Kendal, Meredith and Suzanne, and the location of Meredith's office. But the coup went to Lillie, who had followed Suzanne from downtown to the Rehab Centre, where she saw her go in and come out a short time later with a large brown envelope. She'd then gone to the centre herself and with casual questions elicited the information that Suzanne was a sociologist using free time on the Rehab Centre's computer.

The meeting they called at the Place was set for two nights later, mainly because Lillian opened in her new production the night before that, and many of them wanted to see the play.

Meredith ran through the list again. Champagne. Sleeping junk. Skeleton keys. Electronic redirection unit. Wirecutters. Hypodermic with enough sedative for a two-hour blank. Stethoscope. Balaclava. Rubber gloves. And of course the bug.

When he got home he chuckled inwardly to see the table set with candles and flowers. He knew his Suzanne. She was delighted by the champagne. Meredith crushed ice and chilled glasses while she finished preparing the meal. They ate half a dozen superb oysters each, toasting Kendal's visit with the champagne. The onion soup was excellent, the crayfish mornay splendid. Meredith insisted on stacking the dishes. Suzanne poured more champagne. They made love on the floor, laughing and spilling champagne on each other, relishing their bodies and the chemistry that ran between them.

They went to bed, taking the champagne with them. While Suzanne was showering, Meredith drained her glass and refilled it, stirring in the sleeping draught. An hour later he was on his way to the Place. It was nearly three o'clock.

When he got to the door, he heard the dog. He filled the hypodermic, found the alarm circuit and put the redirection unit to work. The door swung open as the skeleton key turned true. The dog rushed him. At the last fraction of a second, Meredith moved the upper part of his body to one side, thrusting the needle deep into the dog's neck. In a moment, the dog lay limp. He pulled the body into the room and shut the door. Planting the bug didn't take very long, and after he was satisfied with its position he began to look around.

Soon he was aware of how vast an array of information he'd stumbled across. The files contained some of the most damaging data he'd seen in public hands in a long time, cross-correlated to point out the exact areas of contact. He went through the files with increasing interest, fascinated rather than surprised at who had the dirty on whom and how much it was worth. But it was a slim red file nearly at the back of the third drawer down that turned his brain to ice. Here, in several sheets of paper, was evidence that AmVec was part of the funding of nuclear processing plants in several areas, the benefits of having fuel and fissionable weapon material not being spelt out, but obvious to anyone who thought about it. How the hell did they get this stuff, he wondered. No picture of a secretary taking an extra copy and slipping it into her bag crossed his mind.

He replaced the files as he'd found them, pulled the dog into the centre of the room and locked the door behind him. He slipped the redirection unit into his pocket and took the long way home.

Farrimond was interested and succinct. 'Get the noon plane tomorrow. You'll be met. Kendal will bunk you down overnight.' Click.

They met in the executive wing of AmVec, in one of the 'sweat rooms', small, informally arranged, designed for body ease and mental action. Farrimond was, as usual, impeccably dressed. Beside him, Michael Carr looked overly casual, jeans, open-necked gingham shirt, soft tan jacket. His eyes were half screened behind tinted glasses. Meredith was pleased he'd worn his blue suit, and next to Kendal's big rumpledness, felt at one with the group.

As the room quietened, Farrimond's eyes turned to Meredith. Meredith began with the contents of the file on the nuclear plants. The room was as quiet as deafmutes talking. Farrimond doodled on his pad, then lifted his head. 'What else?' he asked.

'There's a file on every major politician in the whole federal game up there, and one on all the provincial boys in Ontario and Quebec. Plus a cross reference system which clearly relates to stuff held elsewhere on the other province's politicians. It's quite extraordinary. There is a file for instance – well, not one, several – on who knows whom in business. It goes way back too – there's even some stuff that relates to Watergate pressures. And there's a whole set of files about the Alaskan pipelines, the Mexican gas and oil game, sitting right next to statistics on the dollar flow in and out of Canada.' He pulled out a small notebook and read out the notes he'd made. He talked for a long time.

Farrimond at last leaned forward. 'Was there anything to indicate what they're going to do with all that information?'

Meredith shook his head. 'No. But they could do anything – look at the possibilities. Give it to the press. Blackmail. Or a book. It'd made one helluva book,' he said appreciatively.

'H-h-h-how a-a-accurate is it?' stammered Carr.

'The stuff I saw was dead accurate, what I knew about, anyway.'

'Did you see any indic-c-cation of wh-wh-where they get their mu-mu-money?'

'No. Didn't stay long enough, didn't see anything like that.'

'How many are involved?' asked Farrimond.

'Near as I can make out, twenty-four or five, no more. My contact up there, a guy called Manet, has been keeping tabs on them for a long time, and that's what he reckons.'

They began to toss it backwards and forwards. Finally Farrimond brought it to an end. 'Then we're all agreed. Take as much of the stuff as you think we can use, and dispose of the rest as you see fit. A fire or something would be good – er, cleaner. And we'll do something . . . Give them something else to think about. The rent, for instance, becomes quite a problem when you haven't a job.'

Meredith nodded, thinking of the teacher who'd just lost her job.

'Yeah, I understand,' he smiled.

The mid-afternoon flight back was only three-quarters full. Meredith sat near the back, half drowsing in the hum of the jets. One of the stewardesses reminded him vaguely of Suzanne. He thought of her big, well built body with pleasure, his penis thickening. The warmth of the thought of her flowed in his mind. He slept.

Amanda looked round as the twins and Min came in. Lillian had bewailed the fact that her play had just started its run and she'd miss the meeting, but they knew nothing would keep her away from the stage.

'Terrific,' Amanda said, 'now we can start.'

The room was full. Shirley's glance told her that Lillian was the only one not there. Amanda ran over the schedule of action from the last meeting. It was despatched with speed. Actions arising were decided on and noted. Then Amanda gave Darlene and Shirley the floor. The women listened and cheered at the recital of the chase. The finale of Lillian's visit to the Rehab Centre was left for Shirley to tell, who began with her own findings and ended with Lillian's discovery of Suzanne. After several minutes of laughing interchanges, a more sober air settled over them.

'Well then,' Amanda said finally, 'What are we going to do?'

'What we need is to know what *they're* going to do,' declared Lorae.

'Why don't we kidnap the woman?' drawled Tally.

'Oh, what a good idea!' exclaimed Cora, eyes alert in her thin brown face,

'But what do we do with her afterwards?' objected Lorae.

'Hang on, let's think clearly,' said Shirley. 'Is kidnapping the woman a good idea? And if so, how, when and who?'

Most of them agreed it was likely Suzanne had something to tell them. The half-hearted suggestions of striking up a casual conversation with her, whether in a restaurant, shopping or at her apartment all met with the same objection. How do you get her to be specific without being specific yourself?

'Look, she's up here from New York,' said Alice. 'When we've finished with her, we'll take her back there. Simple.'

'I'll tell you something else,' murmured Lucy, 'maybe it's a good thing to question her, because I think someone's been in here.'

'Why do you think that, Luce?' Cora asked.

Lucy shook her head. 'All I know is the string was broken this morning, that's all. All the doors and windows were locked and the circuit was on, and Boadicea was inside. *But*, the string was broken.'

'You and your string,' laughed Cora. 'We've got five thousand dollars worth of top-rated alarms and protection devices here and you still run a string across the door! It was probably Boadicea.'

Lucy stroked the tawny coat. 'She's never done it before,' she said. 'I suppose she could have – but it could have been a person, too. Couldn't it?'

'Anything missing?' asked Darlene.

'Not that I can see,' replied Lucy. 'There's so much stuff though.'

There was a general move to check the filing cabinets, the cameras, the photographs, the indexes. No one could think of something that wasn't where it should be. Cora spread her hands out to Lucy. Lucy shrugged. They settled back to discussing the kidnapping and worked out plans to do it the following day. They discussed where to take her, vetoing the Place because it was in town. Tally suggested the sleep-out in the yard behind her home, which fitted the bill. Six women, none of whom were working the next day, were detailed to kidnap Suzanne: Cora, Tally, Darlene, Isu, Lillian and Farm. Darlene had volunteered Lillie's name, grinning at the thought of her squeal of delight.

'What about the man?' Amanda asked, 'won't he get suspicious?'

'Send him a telegram saying she's gone off for a few days to think things out,' said Lorae. 'That should work.'

'Why should it?' asked Cora. 'Perhaps they're perfectly happy.'

'Men always understand that sort of thing,' said Lucy scornfully. 'They take it totally for granted that women get emotional about little things and have to think them out. Which they mostly do,' she concluded sadly.

'What if they're doing it together?' said Isu suddenly, and there was a shout of laughter. 'No, idiots,' she returned, 'I mean, what if she's in on the whole thing. She could be.'

'Nah,' Alice shook her head. 'When I talked to the lady, she was just a stooge, I thought.'

'Suppose she's not a stooge,' said Farm, swinging her arms back and forth, 'all the better, she can tell us much more.'

'My concern was his reaction to her absence if they're partners,' said Isu seriously.

'Hey, there are some things you can't solve before they happen,' said Shirley. 'If we are agreed to take the woman, we take her and solve the problem afterwards. Have we agreed to kidnap the woman?' She sounded like a kindergarten teacher.

'Shirley!' said Cora indignantly. 'You often talk like we're retarded, that really bugs me, it's so damned insulting.'

'And patriarchal,' added someone.

'Hey, who else am I working on this one with – Tilly, Isu, Farm and. . .' interjected Darlene.

'What am I, invisible all of a sudden?' demanded Cora.

'Oh yeah,' said Darlene apologetically. 'I just forgot for a sec, sorry. Look, shouldn't we get together first thing and plan it? What about our place?'

Successfully diverted, Cora plunged into a discussion of how, where and when which left little to be accomplished early in the morning.

The kidnapping was extremely easy. The took Farm's station wagon and parked it a short distance from the apartment block. Cora, who was the smallest, lay in the back groaning artistically, a part that Lillie laughingly coached her in. When asked by Isu to come and help her sick friend, a blanket was hurriedly thrown across Suzanne's head as she peered into the back of the wagon. Strong arms dragged her inside. Darlene drove the wagon easily down the suburban streets, taking turning after turning until they reached the security of Tally's home. Isu and Lillian pulled out a protesting Suzanne and half-wrestled her into the house. Though the streets appeared empty, Darlene thought it was quite likely they'd been seen by someone. She hoped people's fear of 'getting involved' would protect them.

Suzanne was piloted to a couch, sat down and released from the blanket. She was stunned to see a smiling woman come into the room with a tray full of coffee cups steaming in her hands, followed closely by another bearing a large platter of carrot cake. She was, just for a moment, literally open-mouthed.

'How do you like your coffee, Suzanne?' said Lillie casually. 'We've got milk and cream.' She looked up from pouring and smiled warmly at Suzanne. 'If you want both, say so. I always have both, I'm a slut about coffee.' She handed over a full cup for Suzanne, who took it automatically. Lillie held the sugar bowl and spoon out to her. The others helped themselves to coffee, murmuring now and again, but their ears really tuned to Lillian and Suzanne.

Suzanne stared at Lillian for a moment, then said, 'Er, one please.'

Lillian spooned sugar into Suzanne's cup. 'I hope you agree with brown sugar,' she said, 'white's just so bad for you. Actually honey's the best of all, but we're out of honey. Cream?'

'What am I doing here? Why have you brought me here? Who are you?'

Lillian smiled and poured the cream into Suzanne's coffee and gave her a candid glance. 'You're about to have a cup of coffee. And we've brought you here because we wanted to have you over for coffee, but we didn't want your man to know that. And my name is Lillian. OK? Have some carrot cake. It's very fresh, Tally made it this morning.' Lillian smiled over at Tally, who nodded to Suzanne. The sun streamed through large dusty windows. There was a reassuring old piano in the corner, a mound of mending or ironing on the fat, seam-burst footstool and a pile of pillows thumped into a comfortable shape in the corner. Suzanne cautiously sipped at her coffee, looking at all of the women in turn. Lillian passed the cake.

The next six hours were very full. Suzanne got angry, tearful, sullen and silent by turns. The women with her remained cheerful and kind, talkative and sympathetic. She was never left alone. When she went to the toilet, a woman went with her. They asked if she'd like a shower or a bath, because she had got dusty in the back of the station wagon. She agreed, hoping to have a moment to herself, but not only did two women accompany her, one of them scrubbed her back while the other mixed the vinegar rinse for her freshly washed hair.

She still half hoped somehow she could get in touch with Meredith, and heard without surprise her captors dictating a telegram to him: FEEL THE NEED TO THINK THINGS THROUGH AM OK DON'T WORRY WILL RING WHEN RETURNING LOVE S. Anger thickened her head as she saw how well such a message would work with Meredith. The tall blonde called Lillian took it with her when she left at six.

She wondered what they would do with her and was growing restless when they did nothing. There were always four or five of them in the room with her, and they talked to one another, occasionally trying to draw her into their conversation. As they talked they gave glimpses of a lifestyle so very different from her own that Suzanne was half bewildered, half intrigued. They talked about love affairs, laws, breakdowns, job successes, of travelling. Hidda was in Sweden, Gloria in Zambia, Erryl in Spain. Marsha had just come back from Panama and Cathy had scooped the board at the Edinburgh Arts Festival. Geraldine had just left her husband and needed a place where she could have her three kids. Della had split with Mary Ann and was very down. Slowly Suzanne realised that everything they talked about was to do with women. It gradually dawned on her that her captors were feminists.

The day drifted to a close. The evening meal was made by everyone, Suzanne allotted the task of shelling peas. Later in the evening, several more women came. Suzanne recognised two from the march, one called Lucy and one called Woolly.

'I took it to remember Wolstonecraft,' she said briskly to Suzanne when they were introduced, 'but that's a bit of a mouthful so I shortened it. I couldn't hack Mary. I mean, look what the Catholics have done with that name. Well, more than them, I suppose, but –' she flopped down on the floor in front of the couch.

'They had to push Mary when they tried to convert the Irish, did you know?' asked Isu, who was sitting next to Suzanne. 'It's quite wonderful. According to the stories, the Irish had a very strong woman-goddess cult, and they didn't take to a male-lead religion at all. Anyway, the bastards finally figured that out, and started to push Mary, whom they hadn't paid any attention to really. And finally the Irish accepted it, I suppose they realised they had to give in in the end. So much blood. Sorry, am I boring you?' she said suddenly, peering into Suzanne's face.

'No, not at all,' said Suzanne, before she remembered where she was.

'That's good,' Isu said happily, lighting a cigarette and leaning back again. 'Yeah. So how about that. And in Elisabeth Gould Davis' book, *The First Sex*, the redhaired goddess of the Celts comes through loud and clear. Isn't it nice to know our heritage?' She puffed contentedly.

Suzanne didn't answer. She didn't know what to say. She'd vaguely heard of the book, but never read it. She knew about feminists, but it didn't apply in her life, she felt.

She said to Isu, 'Are you a lesbian or a feminist?'

'What?' replied Isu, looking startled. 'Oh, it's you, sorry. Well, it's possible and prolifically real to be both, you understand, but I'm not a lesbian that much. I've had a couple of male lovers, a couple of women lovers. I sort of can't make up my mind, I suppose. But I'm a total feminist. I disagree with some of the ways we do things, but I'm all in favour of the doing. What about you?'

Suzanne had never thought of having to classify herself in either of those categories.

'Neither,' she returned shortly.

'Aw, c'mon,' said Isu. 'It's OK not to be a lesbian, but surely you're a feminist. I mean you're a woman. How can you not be a feminist?'

Suzanne shook her head. 'But I'm not.'

Isu dragged at her cigarette and sighed. 'Oh well, I suppose you just haven't thought about it. Still, you'll have to now, won't you?'

'Why?'

'Well,' said Isu as if it were completely obvious, 'you can't have an experience like this and not want to know what we're on about, can you?'

This point of view hadn't occurred to Suzanne before, but as she considered it, she felt a bubble of laughter rising in her.

'No, I suppose not. I hadn't quite seen it like that.'

'Well,' said Isu, considering, 'I'm into viewing everything as a learning experience, so I was only seeing it from what I'd feel like if I were in your place. Mind you, I don't know anything about you except what's obvious, so . . .'

'What is obvious about me?' interrupted Suzanne, curious.

Isu described a vertical arc with her hand, comprehensively going from Suzanne's head to her feet.

'Hair, dress, shoes. Middle-class conformist, man-woman, I believe the current jargon is. Nothing I couldn't see on a thousand other women, is there?'

She smiled at Suzanne, her head tilted like a cheeky child. 'Like another coffee?'

'Er – yes,' said Suzanne and handed over her cup. With Isu's departure she was alone in that little corner of the room, in the corner of a couch. It was the first time she'd had a chance to look at her captors when they weren't looking at her. They were sitting round in little groups, talking. There were pools of light, fading gently into the shadows. The windows were open wide, the scent of night fresh among the smells of coffee, incense, cigarette smoke. Gleams of colour from scarf, an earring, a striped sock. She yawned and realised how tired she was. Tension had filled her for hours. Her nerves were just beginning to settle again. She wondered what on earth she was going to do, and what they were going to do with her. She wondered what would be happening if the room was filled with women all dressed like her.

The police had come to the theatre that night, and the next morning Lillian appeared in court formally charged with assault.

ACTRESS KIDNAPPED ME ALLEGES TEACHER, the weekend sensationalist paper screamed. ASSAULT CHARGES AGAINST PARELLI reported the commuters' choice. The play she was in was already a hit, and her performance had received glowing reviews.

The assault charge had her besieged with reporters, but she spoke to no one. She decided to stay in the theatre, to keep the mess away from Min and Shirley and Darlene, but Darlene packed a small bag and came to stay with her in the musty dressing room behind the stage. The theatre was jammed that night, the director half furious, half delighted.

Shirley and Min were both furious, but not for the same reasons. Min was outraged at the things the paper said, but privately thought it was very likely that Lillian had slapped Adele. Shirley thought of the group and of Darlene. On Sunday morning, disguised in a man's jacket and trousers and hat, Lillian slipped out of the back door of the theatre and got into a car; a few minutes later Darlene left by the front door and got into the van. She drove out of the city into the country for thirty miles before she turned back. Then, taking a long right-angled route, she went back to the city where Lillian was waiting at a gas station. They drove to a large hotel, booked a room for two nights and locked themselves in it.

'You know what, Lillie,' jerked out Darlene who was lying on her back, pedalling her legs, 'I keep wondering what role Adele Viner played in all this. I mean, why did she get me dismissed in the first place?'

'Money, seashell, the old salt substitute greenback,' replied Lillian, who was standing on her head in the middle of the room, something she did every day for half an hour, to feed her brain, she said.

'Yes, but that doesn't explain much really,' grunted out Darlene. 'I wonder what the story behind the money is. Like – who is she in the script?'

With a final surge of pedalling, she dropped her legs and lay flat, turning her head to meet Lillian's upside-down eyes.

'Well, you know her best,' replied Lillie. 'What do you think?'

Darlene considered. Adele had come to the school last year, immediately a loner. She was bitingly satirical in the staff room, but Darlene knew that she was a competent teacher. She was well dressed. A few times Darlene had seen her climb into a Renault, driven by a small neat city-dressed man. But that seemed only to last over the autumn. After Christmas, Darlene had seen her once with a woman who was obviously her mother, but no one else. She knew about money. Once, in a discussion of the new budget, Adele had revealed that she was part owner or shareholder in quite a large company, Darlene thought.

'Something to do with housing, or real estate, I think,' she added after telling Lillian what her musings had produced. 'Or maybe it was market gardening or landscaping. Something like that, you know?'

'Well, that's very helpful,' declared Lillian. She picked up an imaginary phone. 'Hello? Please give me the name of a housing or real estate or marketing gardening or landscaping company Adele Viner owns shares in? Thank you.' She put her hand over the mouthpiece and said smugly 'Public records – very efficient!' Darlene threw a pillow at her.

'Hang on a sec,' exclaimed Lillian as they wrestled on the floor, 'maybe it's in the stockmarket pages.'

'What a good idea!' said Darlene.

Room service delivered seven papers to them half an hour later. After scanning them closely, Darlene finally put her finger on the name Golden Westlands Ltd.

'That's it,' she said positively. 'I'm sure it is.'

Lillian craned her neck. 'Golden Westlands,' she read out. 'Nice name. And suitably vague. Could be anything from a travel agent to a rest home. Golden Westlands,' she repeated. 'Well. We can check it out tomorrow in records.'

They ordered a meal and some drinks and turned the television on low. They were waiting for Shirley to ring and report what the lawyer, and the group, had to say. It was nearly eleven before she did so. The lawyer had the case set for hearing in three weeks. The group was worried, but behind her one hundred percent, though many of them wanted to know exactly what had happened. But Lillian only laughed and wouldn't say; she hadn't told the whole story even to Darlene.

Darlene's breathing was soft against her. The noise of the traffic had thinned to a random hum. She thought of Viner and wasn't sorry; she only wished she'd foreseen this happening, intimidated her more. She felt a grudging admiration for Viner's determination. Golden Westlands. Well, if she was a property owner, she knew the score. It would be a fight. Golden Westlands. Good psychology in the name. They were part of that development in the south side of the city, she remembered drowsily; bet Viner made a packet on that.

She was almost fully asleep when the impact of her thought

snapped her awake. How did she know about the south side development? Where had she seen that? She remembered then some stories in the paper, but more clearly in her mind was a logo, a golden G intertwined by a W. She pushed her brain furiously, then it spewed out the piece of information she wanted. It was a sponsoring advertisement on one of the theatre's programmes a few months ago. She woke Darlene up.

'We've got to go back to the theatre, all the programmes are there,' she concluded.

'Aw, Lillie, I'm tired,' protested Darlene in a small voice. 'Let's wait till morning.'

'No, now,' Lillian insisted, 'while there's no one around and I can move without being hassled. C'mon, pearl of the Occident, flash your flippers.'

Grumbling a bit and insisting on coffee first, Darlene slowly talked herself awake enough to go.

At the theatre, Lillian found the programmes and the advertisements quite easily. At the bottom of the little badge-monogram that was the Golden Westlands company logo, there ran the words: A Division of Consolidated Earthworks Ltd. They looked at each other, in both their minds the same piece of knowledge, the file at the Place on Consolidated Earthworks. It wasn't a new name to them. With one accord, they left the theatre and drove a circuitous route to the Place.

Two things pissed Meredith off when he got home. One was the telegram from Suzanne. What the hell was the matter with her? And where had she gone? He thought about ringing her in New York, then shrugged. If she wanted time off, let her have time off. The second thing was to discover he hadn't activated his end of the bug. OK. So they hadn't been there – who'd know the difference?

He spent the next day getting ready. He bought a '48 Chevy in drivable condition, and four large suitcases. A contact supplied him with the tiny amount of plastic explosive he wanted. A blast caused fire, and was thoroughly destructive. He thought Farrimond would approve. He filled the hypodermic again and slid its case into one pocket. In the other, he had his little .22, a tiny gun hardly visible in his hand. Stocking guns they were called, and when he'd bought it from an antique dealer it was because he had thought it was cute, not lethal. But lethal it was at short range, and damaging enough up to fifteen or twenty feet.

He arrived at the Place about an hour and a half after midnight, parking the old car close to the door. He took the suitcases in as far as the locked door, and repeated his performance with the keys and the dog. When the dog was out, he dragged it to one side of the room. Then he started sorting through the files and selecting those he thought Farrimond would most like to have. When he finished with the files, the suitases were all full. He removed the bug from inside the fireplace. He scanned the wall, taking down names that offered self-defence courses, encounter group therapy, assertiveness training, battered wives refuges. There were three cameras on the table, one of which could have been the Nikon he'd been left with at the march. Two had film in them. He wound each one back and took out the cassette. He riffled through the papers on the table, hurriedly slipping some into the suitcase. It was a quarter to three and the dog was beginning to stir. He dismantled the small gooseneck lamp on the table, packed the base with explosive, added the fuse and put a match to it.

He had taken the first two suitcases out to the car and returned for the other two when Lillian and Darlene arrived, coming down the hall, anger and determination on their faces. He moved swiftly towards them, which surprised them momentarily. He took the gun from his pocket as he moved, shot Lillian in the kneecap, and carried his motion through to a swift uppercut to Darlene's head, catching her on the side of her jaw, and knocking her out. Like an automaton, he pocketed the gun, picked up the other suitcases and went past them without a glance. Behind him, Lillian was crying and swearing and calling Darlene's name.

She patted Darlene's cheeks, her tears dropping on Darlene's face, blood seeping from her knee to stain Darlene's jeans. Darlene opened her eyes, bewildered, but she knew where she was in a second or two. She shook her head, got up and looked at Lillian's shattered leg.

'I'll get help,' she gasped and ran to the inner room in time to receive the full lethal brunt of the blast Meredith had laid.

Lillian knew only that she mustn't give in to the red mist which throbbed and burned and sucked at her brain. She crawled to the wall and stood up, creeping towards the furnace that was raging beyond the door. The hope that Darlene was alive was shattered as terribly as Darlene's body had been. With screams bursting from her, Lillian turned away, dragging herself back along the wall to the outside door. The cold night air hit her and the quiet of the night rocked her reason. She lay against the van, gulping and hysterical. The street was deserted. She knew she had to do something, but she couldn't quite remember what it was. Slowly, she opened the van door, pulled herself into the driver's seat, her shattered leg hanging down, the open door against it. She put the van into neutral, started it, crammed it into first. Juddering, the van crept down block after block, an eternity of empty road and bleak street lights. There in the distance was the beacon, the haven, the sanctuary. With the black swirling invitingly, she stalled the van and spent long seconds summoning up her strength to get out. The telephone box waited stolidly. She dialled the three figures with shaking fingers and with the last of her consciousness told the voice what it had to know.

'Toby. Toby, wake up. *Toby*!' Shirley woke to dim room, only starlight giving lift to the dark.

'Jess,' Shirley murmured. 'C'mon then,' and held back the covers for Darlene's body to slide in beside her as it had done a thousand times before. Darlene came close, but not inside the bed.

'No, no, I can't get in, you've got to get up, dearest Toby, Lillie's hurt, she needs you.'

Shirley sat up, the urgency in Darlene's voice bringing her wide awake.

'Where is she, what's happened?'

'At the phone box on the corner of Montpelier and Duval; she's unconscious. *Hurry*.'

Shirley threw back the covers and groped for her clothes.

'Yes, baby, OK, don't panic. Turn on the light, I can't see a bloody thing.'

'I'll wake up Min,' said Darlene. Shirley snapped on the light but Darlene had gone. She pulled a heavy sweatshirt on, and struggled into jeans and sneakers. She met Min coming out of her bedroom, face troubled, blankets on her arm.

'Darlene says Lillian's unconscious –'

'Did she say what happened?'

Min shook her head. 'No, she just wanted me to hurry.'

'Where is she?'

'Gone out to the car – here.' Min thrust the blankets into Shirley's arms. 'Take those, I'll grab a thermos of hot water and honey. Start the car if you like,' she called after Shirley, 'the keys are by the door.'

Darlene was standing by the car. Shirley unlocked the doors and put the blankets in the back. Darlene climbed in after them. Shirley went to the driver's seat. As she was putting the key in the ignition, Darlene said 'Toby, I love you.'

Shirley looked round and said: 'Don't worry, Jess darling, we'll get to her.'

Min came out with the thermos and climbed in. Shirley coaxed the ancient gears to move. Min gently questioned Darlene who half-sobbed out bits and pieces of the events of the evening.

'But why is Lillian at Montpelier – why didn't you bring her home or take her to the hospital?' said Shirley, puzzled.

'I can't drive like this,' replied Darlene with despair. 'All I could do was to get to you.'

'OK, OK Jess,' said Shirley quickly, soothingly. 'It's OK, we're nearly there.'

As they turned into Duval, they saw the red and blue dance of lights that signalled the ambulance and police. Shirley ran over to the ambulance, Min close behind her. A policeman barred their way, but let them through when Shirley said Lillian was her sister.

Lillian lay unconscious. The ambulance attendant answered Min's flurry of questions with a shake of his head. Lillian had lost a lot of blood. The wound was to the kneecap, which had shattered and was known to be tricky. That was all he could say. He invited Min to ride in the ambulance with Lillian, which Min said she'd like to do if there was also room for Darlene. They looked round for Darlene. Shirley went back to the car.

Darlene was huddled on the back seat, whimpering and shivering. Shirley climbed in, slid across the seat and put her arms around her. The blanket crumpled and fell into her lap. Like the blade of a knife through her brain, she stared into the truth. Darlene was dead, She'd been putting her arms around a ghost. She twisted and jerked back from its reality, but there was no avoiding the implacable rightness of its gaze. With a soft groan, she lost consciousness.

12: Time-stream Two

Through the narrow window, we had watched the tape through twice. It wasn't complicated. The man, who introduced himself as Corlon Four, made the same general statement in about three different ways. He and his people had discovered wide-ranging corruption and bigotry amongst people in trusted positions in the Regional Administration. They had proof of these charges, and would bring it forward in due course. He introduced the woman in black, Quirelle Argent. As he said the name, I remembered her. Quirelle Argent was Number One in the First Church of the Profound Principle. I tried to remember why the name Corlon Four was familiar, but couldn't. Between the two broadcasts, the group transmitted relaxers, tapes that showed soft and tranquil images, overlaid with music that stayed wholly in the middle ranges of sound, in a gentle, measured pace. Clever.

On the interlink vidscreens each of the satellites checked into our suite, showing that Corlon Four and Quirelle Argent now controlled all the regional centres. I wondered if they had reached the Leaders, since no mention had been made of them, and whether blood had been shed. Moochie watched through the brown glass slit, muttering oaths and banging her fist softly against her thigh. Her presence was flashing with anger, streaming vividly about her as she blazed her rage and cursed low.

I felt a knocking in my mind, recoiled and automatically threw my shield higher. I turned in that direction, questing. It was a timorous tap, which reassured me. In a moment I identified Stella. I pulled at Moochie's arm, whispered 'Stella. Minding.' Moochie cut off the outside sound and became open with me. Stella retreated a little at the force of our attention, but came through quickly when she realised what was happening. Question, question, I sent and she began.

She played us the room she was in – my office. She had been sleeping there, curled up in my big chair, not wanting to go home.

She'd been awakened by noises in the corridor, and opened the door to see a dozen people in Twopee uniforms carrying lazerstuns. One caught sight of her, came in and overpowered her. Not difficult to overpower a slender child of fifteen. Two of them were now rifling my tapes while a third watched her grimly. She sent the face of that one and without much surprise, I recognised Vemare. She ended with a query.

I sent her our own position, Moochie chiming in now and then. As to her query, there was nothing I could do, and sent so. All we did was send a permanent welcome and keep my shield aware in her direction. Moochie suggested we try Berenice and Marla. We could see their still forms huddled on the step. Marla was completely silent, but there was a faint flicker from Berenice. The stun must have been deeply set. We would have to wait a few minutes more to rouse them.

In the room before us, Corlon and Quirelle sat at the board, sending instructions and information and receiving satellite reports. Uniformed people came and went with food and drinks, attending to the two at the board, then to the guards at the main door and our door. We drew back from the window, but my mouth reacted to the sight of those glasses of clear yellow sweetwater. I sat on the floor and told my body lies. Who, I thought furiously, who could help us? All of the people at Comnet were impossible, for even if they'd escaped being under guard now, they were almost certainly watched. Then I thought of Cheva. I didn't know what she could do, but at least she was someone on the outside I had mindbonds with and who, if nothing else, could tell the outside what was happening here.

Moochie touched the top of my head and beckoned me to stand. Berenice had put a hand to her face. We locked in and sent a stay still image repeatedly until she acknowledged. She asked a question, so we sent a single picture of the situation. With a final request to her to centre on Marla and send the stay still when she surfaced, we broke. I word-told Moochie about Cheva, and the distance involved; I didn't think I could go that far alone. Moochie had met Cheva only once, but she remembered her face.

Back to back we sat, my body gratefully relaxing against Moochie's broad warm back. The smell of her was armpit and Chanson Bleu, the scent she wore, mingling with smoke. I word-told her where the Settlement was; she adjusted her mind to that direction. Then I mindpainted the Settlement, leading the way to the house Cheva shared with Meriol. I flashed up Cheva's picture, followed it with Meriol's thin brown face. I signalled I was ready. Our heads fell back to touch each other and we began.

The dark countryside slid beneath us, Moochie a fraction behind me and sending so strongly. I pushed steadily ahead from every signpost, the tall black towering hills, the lights of the first Settlement, the silver smear of the river pointing in the direction I had to go. With Moochie's energy, the movement was steady and sure. I felt a rising exhilaration as I realised we could make it; our movement flickered and Moochie reproved my dip in concentration. I steadied.

I felt my Settlement, the heat of it rising, its shape. It gave me strength somehow. I passed my own home, and sent a ripple of greeting to the silver birch; almost I thought I heard one in reply. I grasped my way from point to point until slowly, there was Cheva's house, palpable as a pyramid in my mind. To its heart we went, knocking, knocking. The force of Cheva's selfshield hurt my head; I withdrew slightly, sending myself reassurance. I felt her bounding surprise and a murmur of query that was Meriol. Cheva opened. With relief, Moochie and I sent the images of our plight. We played the sequence twice, imaging Corlon Four and Quirelle. She sent understanding, then query query query. But we had no answers to give her and my energy was thinning. With a last plea for help, we broke the connection. This time, Moochie led the journey, my strength centred wholly on staying with her.

The Projection Suite was still dark, the air thickening. I was so drained.

'I have to rest,' I whispered to Moochie, and slid away from her back to lie on the floor. My body trembled and my mind wavered. I tried to hold myself together, but the pull was too great. I let go and drifted down into the whirling dark. It was full of fearsome faces, dancing up to me and back as I stood pinned into place by a force I could feel. Great bells rang from behind and ahead, their tone compelling. But I could not answer their call. Corlon and Quirelle stood mocking me, the world held in their hands. They threw it up and caught it, not once, but several times. Its radiant blue dimmed each time their hands cupped it and prepared it for the next throw. I was terrified that they would drop it. Each gasp of my fear was noted by Vemare, who laughed and laughed and urged them on. Corlon smiled meaningfully at me.

'We won't fail, my dear, you'll see to that. Don't you see, you are the one who will hold it up for us. There's only you, only you, only you . . .'

I struggled into consciousness with Moochie shaking me, whispering urgently, 'Lydya, wake up, they're coming through.'

'Who?' I whispered back, trying to shake off the sticky fluff of night.

'Berenice and Marla. Open and listen.'

I rubbed my face over with my hands as I turned to Berenice and Marla. On a low energy level, they sent the image of them overpowering Corlon and Quirelle. I sent image query of the guards, looking at Moochie. Her expression showed alarm and doubt, an echo of my own. She shook her head. Wait, we both sent, and broke.

'That's crazy,' I whispered urgently to Moochie, 'they haven't a chance. Did you tell them about Cheva?'

'Yes. But they don't see what she can do from there. We've got to stop this ourselves, they think. And I agree. While you were asleep, I opened the sound again. They are backed by the Exceeders. The Exceeders want more play room, and the Twopees too. Money and religion. Dangerous, Lydya, and terribly effective. If they get a proper hold, they'll be invincible.'

'I see that, I see it. Just let me think a minute.'

I pushed and hammered and pounded at my reason, but it swirled like new syrup. A hiss from Moochie brought me to my feet in time to see Bonita dragged back into the room. One of her feet kicked Berenice as she was pulled by. Moochie touched a switch and their outside voices jumped into the room.

Bonita's face was pale and drawn under her scarlet hair, but her eyes flashed anger and she drew away haughtily when Corlon Four touched her arm. So the little one had conquered her terror. I felt a quick stab of pride.

'Now now, Technician, I intend no harm,' Corlon said to her. 'I would just like the benefit of your help. You are the operator of this board?'

Bonita said nothing. The guard who'd brought her in shook her slightly. Corlon Four immediately told him to leave her alone, beckoned another to bring up a chair for her. She refused to sit in it. Corlon Four waved his hand and glanced at Quirelle, who came over and stood face to face with Bonita.

'I understand your feelings,' said Quirelle in a reasoning tone. Her body was rounded and full and firm. Thick black hair curled lushly around the clear amethyst band across her forehead. From her ears tiny glitterglobes, faceted from lilac to violet, swung.

'We mean you no harm. Won't you help us? We have worked long and hard to expose the fearsome knowledge of the traitoring at Leader level. We are not harmthrowers. Our every desire is threaded with peace.' She had the most beautiful voice I'd ever heard, and her control was remarkable. She held at that pitch between caress and hypnotic, a stunning combintion in a contralto. I saw Bonita relax. She flushed and looked away from Quirelle. Above my head, Quirelle laughed softly as she stepped to Bonita's side and began to stroke her breast. Bonita shuddered, but she kept her eyes shut. Corlon was sitting back in a chair, watching a performance he was clearly familiar with. Quirelle was stroking Bonita as if she were a pet cat. That wonderful voice was reciting a strange litany.

'Be at one with me, part of the wholeness. All is one, through time and space, and each is part and each is whole. Join with me in the oneness, join with me.' She kept stroking Bonita, who trembled and jerked under her hands, and keeping up an intonation of the litany.

Suddenly Bonita trembled violently, then stood quite still. She opened her eyes, gazed at Quirelle, and said quite tonelessly, 'I will join with you.'

Quirelle smiled more widely and glanced at Corlon in triumph. Her hands gave Bonita one final stroke. She said, very low into Bonita's ear, 'Union is completeness,' and stepped away from the rigid figure. As Moochie and I regained our control, I heard Corlon instructing Bonita to remove the emergency tape and prepare the board for a full channel seaming and translation exercise. Moochie's face looked weary and full of its years.

'What now,' she whispered, the stain of resignation colouring her words. Before I had any answer to give her, Vemare thrust Stella through the door.

'This one makes me uneasy,' Vemare said roughly. 'She knows something. She's too composed.'

Quirelle and Corlon appraised Stella, who stood fearlessly in the centre of the room, courage clothing her with its firm bright warmth.

'Who are you called?' asked Corlon. Stella glanced at him, then turned her eyes to Quirelle.

'I know you, Quirelle of Medtronics,' she said clearly. 'You held my sister in a mindmode, and you took my mother's mind. I declare myself against you.'

'What a pretty little unit it is,' said Quirelle calmly, 'though clearly in need of some form. Does it belong here?' At Vemare's nod, Quirelle ordered Stella to a chair. Stella didn't move. Corlon rose and took Stella's arm, pulling her over to the chair he left. He thrust her into it. She pulled herself up immediately.

'Leave me alone,' she said fiercely. 'You are only a man.' Her vehemence drew a chuckle from Moochie, but by body tingled with fear.

'What is your name, little fraction?' asked Quirelle. 'The balance is tilted when you have mine.'

'I am Stella, sister of Rilla, daughter of L'avrille.'

Quirelle waved her right hand. For the first time I saw its blazon, a ring which streamed with cold hard light of mirror interfaced to light-locked mirror, the core of the lazer, the numerically perfect colour of nought.

'A mindmode,' breathed Moochie with horror.

'Ah yes, I remember. Quite good minds, though a trifle fractured. The mother broke, I recall.'

Stella sprang at Quirelle and the ring came into her hand. She held it out in front of Quirelle, breathing fast.

'Now, Quirelle Argent!'

Quirelle laughed. 'Such energy,' she said, 'and all to no avail. Poor little fraction, did you think I'd allow the mode to work on *me*?' She stepped over to Stella, took the ring and slid it back on her finger. Then she turned to Corlon.

'This one is undoubtedly against us. Like her mother, unstable. Pity.'

Corlon motioned to the guard, who raised his lazer. I screamed and ran to the door, punching back the light barrier and wrenching it open. But the guards held me fast as I watched Stella crumple, tendrils of smoke curling up like her hair.

Corlon Four turned to where I stood, and as he pushed his neck forward between his black striped shoulders, I remembered why he was familiar. It went back to the days of my training, the 'desic domes of the Learning and Living Centres colourless echoes of the rounding green hills. He had been there too, a thin boy with slightly oversized head and a loud defiant manner. I could see why he had been one of the boys chosen for educating with us, because he had already been sent to the Lovers three times and they had charged us with the task of making him see himself more clearly. His name then had been Dovo.

'So,' he exclaimed softly, turning a smug look to Quirelle. 'Senex Brown. Just when we need you. I am Corlon Four and this is Quirelle Argent. We are your new Leaders.'

'You are nothing of the sort, Dovo,' I replied, wrenching my arms from the guard's grasp. Quirelle nodded, and he let me go. 'You just have big ideas. You always did. What have you done to this child?' I went over to Stella, my heart in my mouth, terror stroking my edges black. Beyond Stella, Berenice lifted her head slightly. Her black eyes regarded me directly.

'Dovo?' quizzed Quirelle. Corlon muttered something. Quirelle raised her voice to the guards. 'Send four more of your number, at once.'

Throwing a quick alarm to Moochie, I bent over Stella. She was dead. No flutter under her half formed breast, no pulse coursing along her fragile neck. I felt myself turn to ice, my brain stiffen and stand to attention with the cold fire of anger shocking me into strength.

'This child is dead, Dovo,' I said coldly. 'Perhaps you'd like to have her removed. And perhaps you'd like to tell me what you and this – person – are doing here?' I indicated Quirelle.

Corlon held himself theatrically erect and bent the parody of a charming smile on me.

'You were always ordering people about, I'd forgotten. What we're doing should be quite obvious, I'd have thought, especially to someone who was never noted for – relaxed learning, they call it, don't they?' Again the charade of a smile, with the china eyes blue and hard. I ignored that and glanced at the woman. She was looking at me with a sort of pleased amusement, which startled me. It was almost as if she was glad to see me.

'Yes?' I asked her, involuntarily, wondering what she wanted and feeling the strong warm aura of welcome she was sending out.

Quirelle nodded and took a step towards me. 'Lydya!' she said with deep satisfaction. 'I have been looking forward to meeting you.'

'Why?'

'Because you're a woman, of course,' she said matter of factly. 'We think alike. Men aren't nearly the challenge, are they?' She smiled at me with such warmth that I had to think to check the rising of my cheek muscles.

'I'm sure you didn't come here to talk about men,' I flicked at her. She just smiled again appreciatively, and turned to Corlon.

'Have you brought the tapes?' He nodded. 'Then I suggest you put the little unit to work sending them, while I brief Senex Brown on her new assignments. Oh and by the way, Senex Bleu is in the control room behind you and those,' she said, pointing to Berenice and Marla still lying huddled by the door, 'are Senex Redskin and Grey. Try to make them all comfortable, won't you?'

Corlon's signal of assent was knifelike. He didn't like taking orders. He motioned to the guards. Moochie was brought from the inner room, Berenice and Marla dragged to their feet. Other guards came. I opened narrowly to Moochie, but felt a block as if someone had slapped my mind.

In my ear Quirelle said, 'I don't think so, Lydya,' almost an undercurrent of glee in her voice. My body felt as cold and hard as the stellik of the dome. Since when, I wondered frantically, had she been listening. Since Stella? Cheva? And how was it that I hadn't felt her? No one had ever touched my thoughts without my being aware of it. Then I remembered her ring, its implacable direction.

The mindmode was a device initially invented to help re-order those minds twisted by hyperactive fear and suspicion. It allowed the Helper to have some idea of the strength and destructiveness of the images disturbing the mind so that the Helper could apply the most effective images to calm and allay the fear. And, of course, it had instantly found use where others wanted to have a line into your brain for less altruistic reasons. Mindmodes were in strictly limited use, their use having been cleared by several think-it-to-death boards. As far as I knew, there were only a half a dozen in the whole world.

My instant reaction was to conceal how shocked I was by her revelation. I met her gaze stonily. Her own was chuckling, warm.

'This should be fun,' she said to me, as if we were sharing the viewing of some splendid new entertainment. Corlon was over with Bonita. A guard brought forward another pile of holovid tapes. The boxes were strangely marked with numbers, but the shape was unmistakable.

'Distinctive, aren't they?' remarked Quirelle. 'Distinctive messages too. Corlon is going to get your pretty little unit to send them out. Such an exuberant one, all that scarlet hair. I like units that young. So – malleable, don't you think?' She cocked her head on one side, inviting me to laugh. 'Why don't you sit down, Lydya,' she said after a moment. 'You've had quite a day – and this could take a tiny bit of time.'

I just looked at her steadily. After a long moment, her eyebrows raised and she smiled briefly. 'They're your legs, my dear.' She turned from me to the board. I held myself still and opened just a fraction. No barrier. Cautiously, I moved out, but before I'd gone more than a few feet, there was the slap. Quirelle grinned at me over her shoulder, her headband running a clear ring of violet with the movement of her head. I realised two things. One, that at the moment I could do nothing. I could think of no action that would be succesful, or lead to success. I was very much on my own. And two, that I was tired. I would need every atom of strength I was capable of summoning some time soon, there seemed little doubt of that. Quirelle was quite right – I should sit down. I went to the chair and curled into it, giving it all my weight, letting every muscle go. As I put my head back, I caught the gleam of Quirelle's ironic look.

13: Time-stream One

The pain screamed along Lillian's body, the buzzsaws in her mind and leg seesawing into one giant ripping agony. She yelled anger at the pain, pulled her shoulders away from the nails of iron. Cool hands, the sting of a needle. She was very heavy, sinking into the old black water, but each time it swallowed her, she was plucked to the surface by the insistent beak of pain. With her whole body, she felt an urgency pushing her along. Now she couldn't burrow into oblivion's deep mud. Time flowed. She opened her eyes. Sitting close to her, studying her face with a worried frown, was a woman. She had a strong, narrow face with large cheeks and a jutting nose. Her eyes were deep-set and clear grey/black. Nice person, she thought. She studied the thick hair, the wide neck. She became aware that the woman was speaking to her.

'Lillie. Lillie darling, Lillie? Lillie, it's me, Min. Lillie, can you hear me?' The words meant nothing to her, but she recognised the strength of concern in the woman's voice. She was clearly worried about someone. Out of the corner of her eye something white moved. She turned her head slowly. At the foot of her bed, very blurry, stood another woman. Lillie blinked to clear her vision. The woman was smiling at her. She had clear, bright blue eyes that were sending her warmth. Her hair curled down on the scarlet jacket she wore. She blew a kiss to Lillie and disappeared. Lillie frowned. There was something she had to remember, something big pushing for admission at the doors of her mind.

'No,' she said loudly, denying that hugeness entry.

But light slid through in tiny slits, rivers of white running softly up to the rooms of her mind, until all was light and Lillie was herself. Anguish shook her, painting the walls black.

'Min,' she rasped and the tears poured. Min put her arms around her, holding her close and whispering into her hair. Presently she began to croon a little, rocking the woman in her arms in the mother's ancient rhythm.

It was many days before Lillian could talk coherently. Her guilt swung her in violent circles. The thought of Shirley was too much to bear. To the patterned dance of the turn of the sun, she fought for her reason. On the seventeenth day, clutching Min's hand, she asked about Shirley. Min studied her face, but what she saw there reassured her. She drew her chin into her neck, and sighed.

'Not good,' she said shortly. 'But better than she was.'

'Where is she?'

'About three rooms down from you,' Min replied, 'but I don't know whether you can see her,' she added hastily.

'Why not?' asked Lillie, fear snapping her eyes wide.

'No, no, it's nothing to do with that,' Min cried. 'She's just not conscious most of the time. They're keeping everyone out. There's a nurse there all the time.' She saw the shock and sorrow run like spiders over Lillie's face. 'She'll be all right,' Min said quickly. 'It'll just take a while, that's all.'

The nurse had come and done the final round, soothing sheets and plumping pillows for the long night. They gave her two capsules, a scarlet one and one blue and white. Lillie obediently put them on her tongue, swallowed down the water. The two tidied her bed round her, so that she felt like a paper doll in an envelope bed.

Her legs weighed a thousand kilos each, the right one full of moving shards of glass. Her mind swirled. She was dragged downwards into muffling grey. Through the mist walked Darlene, urging her on. She groaned and came up to wakefulness. The room tilted, pulling her eyes around, then steadied to an acceptable level, though the window wavered in the corner. Slowly she pushed the blankets aside and slid her legs to the floor. Her good knee buckled and the other one screamed. She clung to the bed, panting a little as she fought the drugs. She stroked the white counterpane, her nose buried in its antiseptic texture.

She pushed herself up and focussed on the silver stroke that was the door handle. Snarling at herself, she launched her body's motion towards the door. It opened with a little sigh. Down the long corridor, the floors shone under the globes of light. She lurched along the wall to her left, counting doors. The third door stood open: there was no one in the bed. She slid down the wall and sat staring, blankfaced. Presently, she shook her head and grinned at herself, then, dragging her leg in in its cast, she crawled her way back down the hall, beginning to count as she passed her own door. She pulled herself up, hanging on to the doorknob of the third door, and peered through the tiny window. She saw a shape in the bed. She opened the door intent only on her purpose, not even considering the nurse. But that woman had gone for a quick cup of coffee, it being nearly three. Lillian hobbled the centuries between herself and Shirley; she plucked and pulled at the blankets, heaving herself on to the bed beside the still figure. She pushed her arm under the dark head and arranged the covers over them both. Then, once more, she slept.

Suzanne wondered what the hell was happening. Even in the few days she'd been here, she had learned what the rhythm of the house felt like. Though Tally was a stocky no-nonsense woman with little time for fripperies, she also had a strong sense of proportion, and a passionate interest in Peru and its culture. She was enthralled by Andean flute music. She had climbed the mountain to see Macchu Picchu; had heard the flutes play up there where the air was too fine to breathe. Suzanne could imagine Tally's sturdy body hacking in the sullen fields, children around her. The feeling in Tally's house was as solid as the mountain and as precise, lilting and ordered as the piping of the mountain's flute. Since the phone call yesterday, the feel of the place had changed, and it seemed to her as if she'd suddenly been caught doing something dreadful, or had a contagious disease.

She went into the kitchen to make herself a coffee. Tally, Farm and Isu stopped talking so abruptly, stared at her so stonily, that she involuntarily cried out, 'What is it? What have I done?'

Tally broke the strain of the silence. 'It's that fine man of yours,' she said, a wealth of disgust in her voice. 'He's shot one woman, and blown another to bits.'

The words hit Suzanne in her belly. She staggered a little and sat down. Isu put her arm around Tally. Farm and Cora stared at Suzanne.

Tally began to hit her fist against the table, softly at first, then harder and harder. Words broke out of her mouth.

'Men. Fucking men. Conceited, arrogant, prick-driven beasts. They drive us into madness and marriage and whoring. They smother us, torture us, rip up our cunts and our minds. I hate them I hate them I hate them, the goddamned abnormal ignorant diseased mutants. They should die, all of them, die. And,' she said softly, head thrust close to Suzanne, 'I'm going to take personal pleasure in getting that prick of yours and cutting his balls off – one at a time, slowly – animal!' she screamed.

Farm and Cora clustered around her, rubbing her back. Tally seemed totally oblivious to them, her whole being concentrated on Suzanne, her eyes wild. Suzanne said nothing. She sat absolutely still. The turmoil inside her spilled around her brain. There were fragments of thought she didn't want to think, and images of Meredith's long white back, arms thick and smooth, strong fingers with a gun in them. She was very cold.

Farm made some coffee and slugged some brandy into it. Tally protested when Farm set a cup in front of Suzanne, but both Isu and Cora said simultaneously 'She's a woman,' and Farm added, 'Like we all are, Tal.' Tally held her head stiffly, looking into their faces. Finally she drew several long breaths and nodded.

'You're right,' she said. She looked at Suzanne. 'I'm sorry,' she said brusquely. Suzanne dipped her head, gulped her coffee.

Tentatively they began to talk about Darlene and Lillian, not including Suzanne in their conversation, but not keeping her out. Suzanne fought against believing the things they were talking of were things Meredith had done. But somewhere inside herself she recognised he had a darkness in which he could have done them. She longed to be able to talk to him, to hear his side of the story. She could see no reason why it should be Meredith. Even though the conversations she'd had with him made her know he was interested in their activities, she could see no reason why it shouldn't have been thieves or something.

'Why couldn't it have been thieves?' she said out loud. 'How do you know it was him, you didn't see him, did you?'

'No,' returned Tally grimly, 'but Lillie did. Wouldn't you remember someone who shot you and killed your lover?'

After that, Suzanne kept quiet.

But they did not keep her from the things that were happening. They told her of Lillian's condition, of Shirley's coma and the attempts Min made to find a way to organise some kind of a service for Darlene. They asked her for information about Meredith, and she gave it freely. But the only things she had to tell them were his New York address and some details of his private life. The rest they knew. She wanted to ask them what they were going to do with her. Though she was no longer guarded, she could no more walk away than fly. In some way she felt an obligation to stay. With them, she watched the television reports and listened to what the radio had to say. She learned that Lillian was an actress, saw clips of her performance. Darlene's dismissal from school was brought up, and for the first time she realised Darlene and Shirley were twins. There was no mention of Meredith: the police were seeking anyone who could help them with their inquiries. She wondered what they were going to do, and when. She didn't realise that the women were waiting out the time until Shirley and Lillian were among them again.

The hospital had finally given in to Lillian and moved her bed into Shirley's room. Each time they had taken her back to her own room, she had struggled her way out of bed, painfully lurching back to Shirley's side. It was the nurse who noticed that Shirley breathed more naturally when Lillian was with her. She convinced the matron to let Lillian stay. They put the beds together, to stop Lillian from getting into Shirley's bed.

For the days that followed, whether asleep or awake, Lillian touched Shirley somewhere, holding Shirley's hand, or an arm across her shoulders. The nurses came and went, changing Shirley's drip and bathing her unresponsive body. She had lost weight and her skin had the waxy translucence of old polished bone. At times her body jerked and shuddered, and groans so jagged they seemed capable of tearing her throat burst from her. Lillian would stroke her face at these times, watching intently, kissing Shirley's cheek and keeping up a steady murmur of sound until Shirley was quiet once more.

Nearly three weeks later, one quiet dawn, Lillian woke to Shirley's sobbing. She put her hand on Shirley's and Shirley turned to meet her eyes. Tears sprang at the sight of the depth of wild lonely misery in those caves of acheing blue.

A week later, they were back at home, Min's calm strength and hot meals making a supportive cocoon for them. She shielded them from too many visitors, wouldn't let them answer the phone, and insisted they go to bed early.

One morning, Shirley leaned across the table to kiss Min's cheek. 'Thank you, dearest Minnie. I wish there were a more adequate way to say thank you.'

Min smiled and blinked rapidly as her throat tightened.

'And I know you're going to protest, but I have to see the others, start doing things again. I am all right. I can handle it. But don't you see, we must have a meeting soon.'

Min's whole body began to protest, but she realised swiftly that it was healthy for Shirley to begin to grab hold again. Shirley took one of Min's hands and looked over at Lillian, who took the other.

'We want you to – do you think you can stand to be involved?'

'In what?' asked Min.

'Vengeance,' replied Shirley, and smiled gently at Min's decisive nod. The smile left her face quickly. She looked so very different that sometimes Min didn't recognise her. The features were familiar, but the spirit that moved them had altered their expression radically. When she wasn't talking to Lillian or Min, her face was as sharp and hard as a warrior mask. Shirley recognised the changes in herself, and that gave her a small satisfaction. For the battle she wanted to fight, she wanted no softness, no gentleness, no humanity. When she thought of a man she felt a surge of nausea and hate. She knew it was irrational, but she fostered it, hung on to it, and fed it. Men were an enemy she would vanquish. She would not be beaten again.

The group gathered at Min's two evenings later, when the deep arching blue of the summer night was stitched all over with stars as fat and bright as glass buttons. They mostly arrived in small groups, but Cora came by herself, warning that Farm, Tally and Isu would be bringing Suzanne since no one wanted to stay away and she couldn't be left. Lucy arrived bearing a ring of strudel, raisins bursting through the flaky top dusted with icing sugar. For the first time, Min saw a real smile spontaneously leap to Lillian's eyes. Lucy plucked two raisins from their nestings and put them into Lillie's mouth, then sat down beside her. Min felt so full of love for Lucy she thought she would burst.

Within a few more minutes, Min's large livingroom was crowded with women. There were hugs of greeting and desultory chat. Soon, the hum died; in the little silence, each woman turned her face to Shirley.

She sat crosslegged, very slim, ivory face slightly hued by the dull red of her shirt, dark hair lustreless from her long battle. She seemed to distil the stength of stone. On her other side, Lillian leaned back against the dark chair, her leg thrust forward on to a stool, cast now scribbled all over. She too was thin, eyes rainwater grey in her colourless face. For the first time in weeks, Min felt the flash of desire to paint.

'I need you,' said Shirley without preamble. 'For one month. at the end of that, they will be broken. I promise you. Who will give me a month of their lives?'

In the silent room, a soft rustle rose as, one after another, every woman but Suzanne put up their hands.

The next day, Suzanne was taken to a small wooden cabin somewhere in the northern bush. Isu, Farm and Tally drove her there, a bag of clothes from Farm and Tally's wardrobes thrust into her hand. They had a large box of groceries and a dozen bottles of wine. At the cabin, they were greeted by three deeply tanned women, the laughlines around their eyes standing out like make-up in the dark amber skin. Suzanne was introduced to them simply by her first name, and no immediate explanation other than 'she's resting from the city,' was given to her hosts. Clo and Rima welcomed her, while Surne carried the wine into the cabin, a big grin flashing over the case's cardboard rim.

Wine was opened, glasses gathered and the seven drifted down to the lakeside, Farm carrying the inevitable smudgepot. In a small clearing by the wide blue lake, they made themselves comfortable. Clo rolled a couple of joints. The sun was high and hot, the light knifing into Suzanne's eyes. The others took off their clothes, but she only opened a couple more buttons on her shirt. After a time of lazy chatter, Farm began to talk. Her voice was lazy and full of sorrow. She told of the past weeks without bitterness or malice; when she stopped speaking, no one interrupted the persistent note of a complaining crow.

Minutes later, Farm resumed her monologue. 'This brings us to

Suzanne. Suzanne is the sister who has been with the man Meredith. Without knowing what she was doing, we think, she has been helping him to destroy us. We need her to be in a safe place while we now proceed with what we have to do. She shows no sign yet of being ready to hear us, but neither does she seem to want to harm us. So we have brought her to you.'

The cabin women nodded thoughtfully, inspecting Suzanne with newly searching eyes. They asked many questions about Shirley and Lillian and Darlene. As the rest talked, Suzanne sat, confused. Who was she? She squinted at the flickering water. Depression covered her. She decided to get drunk and reached for the nearest bottle of wine. By the time the sun was painting the west, she was much too drunk to notice the pitying concern on the faces of the others.

Shirley went into work and had an interview with her employer. She tried to resign, but he would not accept. She needed time to get over her terrible loss, he said and, whenever that was, she would have a job to come back to. She clutched the arms of her chair and looked at the wall, not wanting his sympathy and fighting the waves of nausea it caused. He waited for her to regain control, shifting the papers on his desk, then lighting a cigarette with much deliberation, emptying the ashtray, fiddling until she broke the silence.

She thought carefully. She needed at least one week of the two weeks notice she'd given to retrieve the data she had stored. That was vital.

'Thank you.' She spoke brusquely. 'If you could put up with me working sporadically, it would help. But I might be here for hours, then not back for days. Could you put up with that?'

'Why not just rest, Miss Coral? Your services here are invaluable, but like mine, not indispensable.' His voice was gentle, underlined with humour.

She shook her head. 'Sometimes I need to – lose myself,' she managed. 'I need – something big to think about. But I get – tired.' He met her eyes and she saw with satisfaction that his were full of concern. He hesitated.

'Please,' she said simply.

'OK, Miss Coral,' he said. 'Work whatever hours you please. We'll pay your wages just as usual for the next six weeks. Then we'll have another talk, if that's all right with you.'

'Yes.' She sighed. 'That's all right.'

She took her savings out in cash, leaving only five dollars in the account. The teller asked her if she was going to buy a diamond ring. No, Shirley replied, something much better – a victory. The teller's smile was uncertain, but she wished Shirley good luck anyway. She had fifty-one hundred dollars. With the money given by the other women, the total was just under twenty-five thousand. It was not enough, but it would have to do. After the planning meeting at Min's, she returned to work.

Lillian, Lucy and Woolly drove out towards the airport and rented a motel room, Woolly doing all the negotiations while Lillian and Lucy stayed in the car. She asked the switchboard for an open line because they had so many long distance calls to make. The woman at reception was aloof at first, but Woolly's explanation that they were setting up the next stage of their Christian crusade reassured her, especially when Woolly said she'd be happy to leave a healthy pre-payment for the calls, and gave her a list of the places they were to ring, which covered cities all over North America and Europe.

In each place, they contacted a woman from the list before them. What they had to ask in many cases brought silence and cautious questioning, in some cases instant understanding and assent, and in one or two cases the type of reluctance that needed the most persuasive skills of Lillie to overcome. In the end, all of the women contacted agreed to help, to do what Shirley needed them to do .

At one point, the receptionist came to the door to tell them that their phone bill was now over fifteen hundred dollars. Lucy thanked her softly for her concern, rummaged about in the satchel by the telephone stand for a moment, then thrust a handful of notes out to her.

'I think there's enough there to reassure your employers. Thanks for keeping an eye on it for us. Don't worry – you've heard people say that the Lord will provide – well, it's true, sister!'

The receptionist took the money, protesting that no one had thought they couldn't pay, that the owners just wondered if . . . Lucy smiled and tossed her hair. She gave the receptionist a swift hug and gently thrust her out the door, still protesting, but clutching the money with both hands. Four days later, the list completed, they paid their bills in cash and slowly drove the slogan-bedecked car home.

Alice, Margo and Amanda compiled a list of things that would be needed and spent days hiring equipment. They paid a cash advance on each item, from the scaling rig and its crampons to the light meter and extra lenses for the Bolex.

Farm and Tally drove across the border at Windsor and slid into Detroit as heavy globes of late summer rain began to fall through the grey afternoon. They dawdled down Woodward Avenue to Grand Boulevard, past the General Motors building, the Henry Ford Hospital and into the southwest suburbs. There they got a motel for the night. The next day, after much cruising of the area, they spotted an old warehouse that had seen little activity for years. They told the leasing agent they were artists and he happily accepted three months' rent in advance for the loft, shaking his head at the idea that anyone could find anything arty in the neighbourhood. The electricity was on, but many of the bulbs were burned out. They bought new ones, and a second-hand stove and fridge. They bought cheap slabs of foam rubber from the factory and threw blankets and sheets over them. Tally, with a mischievous glance at Farm, bought an applemint plant and two vases, which she filled with flowers. Straightfaced, Farm paid over the dollar fifty the junkshop proprietor demanded for the yellow plastic doily and, with elaborate wrapping, brought it back and presented it to Tally. The giggles hung in the corners of the loft, echoes of home. Later that night, they drove out to American Vehicle for the first time, and took note of the huge spread of lawn.

Cora, Lorae and Isu worked from Min's home, collecting and collating. They went to newspaper files, library files and public records. Cora spent a day visiting the big psychiatric hospital on the city's west side, talking to Berri who worked in the records department. Shirley worked at retrieving data each day until she was exhausted, arriving home to Min's concerned care. Min, who had never massaged herself let alone anyone else, nightly made Shirley strip and be massaged. Most times, Shirley fell asleep as Min's hands kneaded quiescence into the clenched muscles of her neck and back.

At the end of two weeks they were ready. On Friday, Min organised the needs of the trip, particularly Lillie's comfort, for Lillie still wore the heavy cast. They would go to Detroit on Sunday. Tomorrow, they had to fetch Suzanne.

Suzanne had spent two of the most startling weeks of her life. Never before had she been challenged again and again about what she really thought, really felt. Through the sunny days and nights with the kiss of coolness, she and her guardians talked. From the first they had treated her like a friend, and even their guardianship was relaxed. By the end of the fourth day, no one accompanied her either to the ancient wooden toilet, or down to the lakeside.

'Honey, you wanna go walking, you go,' remarked Surne, 'an' when you get tired of reaching nowhere, you just hurry on home again.'

Suzanne had wandered in the bush around the cabin, but she had no idea where she was, or what direction the city was. And she felt less and less like leaving. She had begun to wonder about a lot of things, and her wonderings brought about the first tentative questions. Their answers led only to more wonderings. Her real problem was the nights, when desire crawled up, shivering through her labia and making her womb ache. One night, restless in her bunk, listening to the sounds from the other room, she half sobbed out loud. Through the thick dark, she heard Surne's whisper, 'Ain't you ever heard of the five wise fingers?' It took her a moment to work it out.

Shirley decided the trip to the cabin should be in the van, because Lillie needed the drive in the fresh air. Min went with them ostensibly for 'the ride', but really because she now could hardly bear them to be out of her sight. Shirley was still quiet and scarcely ate. Lillie too was changed, no trace of her former exuberance and warmth. Min wondered how long it would take before the harm to their minds stopped taking its toll on their bodies. She hadn't been able to paint for weeks. At first, each time she entered her studio, the room seemed to cry out to her, so that she felt unable to cope with the demands the mute canvas and paints seemed to be making. Her mind was full of red flashes hastily veiled by soft black, or the hard white of an end-of-film light. Finally, recognising that she could drive herself frantic, she put everything away and shut the tower door. She hadn't been back there since but, today, organising the trip had only taken until three. There was nothing left to do. Lillie, Cora, and Isu had just had a huge tray of cookies and tea taken into the workroom by Lorae. Instead of joining them, as Min knew they expected her to do, she was drawn upstairs by a sudden impulse as strong as an electric current.

The tower room was full of afternoon light. Min closed the door and felt the room welcome her, its warmth lapping around her, soothing her as the greeting hug from an old friend would. She sat on the small stool just to the left of the door, her head back against the wall. On three sides, the sky and trees danced to the breeze's trifling, tossing glimpses of houstop, the flash of a car, colours as 'rich as a jewel in an Ethiop's ear'. The faint susuration of the breeze was the only sound. Slowly, her body relaxed, calm soothing her spirit. After a time, sorrow rose palpable as pain, stabbing. Then, clearly as if she were there with her, Min heard Darlene whisper 'It's all right, Min, it's all right.' For the next few minutes, she cleared her heart of tears.

She dried her cheeks and stood up, feeling light and buoyant. At her workbench, she pulled out her sketchpad, rummaged for pencils. In a short time, she had a full-length figure of Darlene, dressed in Sherwood green, arms triangled on hips, legs apart, one hand clutching a soft green hat; the face looked out with laughing friendship. She smiled as she looked at the figure – the eyes were so warm and friendly. She leaned the pad against the window, seeing then that the sun had moved a long way across the sky. With an involuntary sound of surprise, she hurried out of the studio, Darlene's eyes laughing at her retreating back.

On the way to the cabin, the light of the day gathered thickly under swelling clouds. A storm. The air was moist and cottony, the deep green of the pines sinking to black near the ground. The wind of the van's passage stirred brittle roadside grasses, shaking off dust which then hung in pale wisps over the stalks. As they reached the cabin, the van's temperature needle was nudging the danger zone and the first thing Shirley did was to lift the lid, let the radiator cap pressure off slowly, then pour cool lake water into the steaming hole.

Suzanne saw their arrival with dismay. She felt not the slightest desire to get re-involved in the mess of the city. She knew intuitively the women in the van had come for her and her whole being shied away in revulsion from a situation that smelt of death and despair. She went down to the lake, pulled off her shorts and shirt and plunged into the water, swimming away from the land as if she could leave it all behind and find refuge in the waters of the north.

At the cabin, beer was poured, crackers, cheese, salami and tomatoes put out and little mushroom-and-potato tarts that Min had made the day before. When Shirley looked around for Suzanne, Clo assured her that she'd be back. Where could she go?

'What's she been like?'

'No trouble at all,' replied Surne. 'Helped out round here, did her share with no hassles. I like her.'

'Did she open up to any of you at all?'

'Sure,' said Clo, 'what do you want to know about her? She's from New York, folks are Irish. She's one of six, left home at fifteen to get a job, find her own place. Family's not too well off, but not on the breadline. Started out as a file clerk for a propane company and was with them until she came here. Sort of ran the filing department and also put out a recipe-type newsletter and home hints, which got given to people who bought appliances, stuff like that. She met Meredith about a year or so ago, when her company supplied the stoves and water heaters on contract for some company houses of American Vehicle. She was sent out to have a look – he was the liaison officer. Bingo.'

There was a little pause. Shirley's cheeks bunched. She looked into the trees and took another drink of beer.

'You taking her back?'

'Yeah. I need her. A little like a hostage, I suppose.' She pushed her hair. 'Fuck, it's hot, I wish it would rain.'

As if the sky had been waiting for her to voice this wish, huge drops of water began to plummet down. The tiny breeze picked up strength, scudding through the clothes, papers and food lying in the clearing outside the cabin. The women hastily thrust their debris through the cabin door, then for several minutes let their heat-stifled bodies be sluiced by the gathering force of the rain.

'Where's Suzanne?' shouted Clo to Surne, who shook her head and pointed in the direction of the lake.

'Will she be OK?'

Surne shrugged. 'She's a big girl,' she shouted back. Clo kept looking at her, then the two of them started down the trail to the water's edge.

The wind was slapping the water along, curling it high into rows and rows of dervish lace. Suzanne was nowhere to be seen. The two women went along the length of the little beach, darting in and out of the shaking trees. Back at the beginning of the path, they again scanned the wide, rocking waters. Surne spotted the dark ball of Suzanne's head first. She and Clo watched intently. Time and again, the waves battered her under. Finally, Surne swore, turned to Clo.

'You go and bring towels and something warm. I'll do it.'

She stripped off her jeans and lunged out in Suzanne's direction, brown arms chopping away at the continuous swells. Clo watched for a moment longer, then ran back along the path.

Surne ploughed through the water steadily. She didn't know if Suzanne had seen her. She dived under the waves, going down below the surface agitation, her body thrusting more easily through the current. Repeating the dive several times, she made steady progress, though in the soiled depths she couldn't see more than a few inches ahead. She came up, looked about her, and for a frantic minute thought she'd lost Suzanne, then saw her quite plainly only a short way away, anger and fear obvious in her face. When Surne reached her, the sight of her eased the fear in Suzanne's eyes.

'Tired,' she mouthed to Surne.

Surne shook her head. 'You can make it. You're OK!' she shouted over the noise of the water and wind. 'C'mon!'

Suzanne looked grim and concentrated on the shore. Her arms moved slowly. The waves continually hit her face. She blinked, choked and ploughed on. After some minutes, she looked at Surne despairingly and slid beneath the waves. Surne dived and grabbed her, fingers pulling hard at the thick hair.

'Don't be a fool,' shouted Surne with all her force. 'I'll do it, but help me. *Help* me.' Together, slowly but steadily, they beat their way through the long yards to the shore.

Suzanne half crawled out of the water and was hardly free of it when she began to vomit, choking up water and bile until there was no more, lying panting and shaking in the mud. Clo threw a blanket over her and when the vomiting stopped, helped her to her feet. Suzanne looked down at her naked body thickly plastered with mud. She smiled weakly at Clo and walked back to the water's edge to wash it away.

At the cabin, Suzanne was helped to her bunk, given huge cups of hot sweet milky tea. For an hour her body shook, but eventually the tea and warmth had their effect and she fell into a heavy sleep. She rose out of it to hear voices. Slowly the afternoon came back to her.

'. . . are already there. We go tomorrow. We'll make the film next week. There's a lab and editor waiting, and we've cued up dubbing it on to tape. And we've got women everywhere alerted to receive it.'

Shirley's voice, thought Suzanne, the twin of the woman who had been killed. She thought of her own three sisters and recoiled at the picture of one of them dying in such a way. She shook under the thick sleeping bags piled on her, and tried to shut out the voices. But the rooms were too close together and her ears too interested in what was being said.

'Will it work?' That was Rima, lovely Rima who had been so kind to her, laughing her out of her blues, explaining the lore of the woods.

'Oh, it'll work all right.' Shirley was positive. 'Which of us doesn't know how the media like a good story? And this is a goodie!'

'And then what?' asked Clo. Scrappy little Clo, like a terrier with her tousled hair and cracked voice, finding the space to be herself in the woods, where neither leaf nor flower nor fern cared that half of her face was stained deep purple with the marks of her birth.

'A big stink, we hope, at the very least. Prosecution at the best.'

'You'll get the stink, for sure,' said Clo, 'strong as a skunk's convention. You prepared for some of that to stick to you?'

'What d'you mean?'

'Honey, they won't take what you do lying down,' drawled Surne, and the listener in the other room felt a flood of warmth. 'They'll find a way to make some of that stink yours.'

'I don't care,' said Shirley fiercely. 'I don't give a double fucking damn what they try. One way or another we're going to tell the truth, out loud and so that some of the world can hear.'

Before they left, Suzanne asked Surne if she wouldn't come too. Surne looked at her speculatively before shaking her head.

'No, babe, I don't go into the city much. And this ain't my part of the fight. But you're welcome back here when you wanna come back. I'll keep an eye out.'

She reached for Suzanne, the two of them of a height. As Surne hugged her, Suzanne felt the pump of her heart, smelt the smoky musk of her hair and body. She hugged the other woman fiercely, trying to thank her wordlessly for her life. And she knew she would come back.

The rain stopped an hour before they left. For a while, Lillie, Min and Shirley talked a little, but fell silent as the crescent moon nicked at the night. The last hour of the journey, no one spoke at all.

As the van groaned up the hill to the house, each woman drew long breaths as though preparing to face a new encounter. There was a forced casualness to their getting Lillie out of the van and settled in the lounge, bringing the cartons of clothes and food in. Suzanne offered to make coffee, and Min, seeing the plea in her eyes, checked her refusal and motioned to the cups and the kettle. When they all gathered in the lounge, each one recognised the time for talking had come.

'I want to say something,' said Suzanne quietly. The others looked at her and Shirley gestured with her cup.

'You've got the floor,' she said.

'Let me go,' Suzanne said quickly. 'I'm truly sorry for what happened, but I didn't have anything to do with it – I didn't know what was happening. I don't want to harm anyone. I just want to be left alone. Please.'

Shirley and Lillie looked at each other and Min's gaze went to the floor. Shirley shook her head.

'You don't understand,' she said quietly. 'We need you. I apologise for making you stay with us, but at the moment nothing is more important than what we've got to do. and as far as I'm concerned, you owe us.'

'But I can't see what you want me to do.' Suzanne cried. 'You seem to know as much if not more about Meredith than I do. It's him, not me that you want.'

'It's not just Meredith we want,' replied Shirley. The utter implacability of her voice sent a clutching through Suzanne's gut.

'But what can I do?' Suzanne almost shouted. 'For godsakes tell me.'

'Oh, nothing difficult,' said Shirley. 'Just make a couple of phone calls, that's all.'

Suzanne sucked in her breath. The Judas goat, that was what she was going to be, of course.

'Are you going to kill him?' she whispered.

'No,' said Shriley with scorn, 'we're not murderers. We're simply going to tell the truth about him and his company. That should be enough.'

'Who will you tell?'

'As much of the world as will listen,' replied Shirley. 'do you really want to know?'

Suzanne's thoughts raced. She saw Meredith laughing at her, and he turned into Lillian crying, turned into Surne coming for her through the water, turned into her mother hugging her goodbye, turned into Min gesturing her to carry the tray into the big warm room. Her stomach rolled, nausea rising so that she clutched her arms over her belly and rocked herself. She felt all alone on a wide flat blackness, only space and solid air around her. All she could think of was Meredith. Even if she walked out of here tonight, she didn't think she could go to him, be with him. She felt dizzy, spots blinking on and off in front of her. A point of blue held her, steadied her. She found herself looking hard into Shirley's eyes. There blazed only strength and, far at the back, a question. To that question she finally shuddered out the demanded words: 'Yes. I want to know.'

Tally and Farm watched the white van slide to stop below, and rushed down to greet them all. They carried Lillie upstairs on crossed arms, plonking her in the middle of the thick sheets of foam. They were quite proud of the loft, pointing out its features to Lucy and Min. Shirley gave a small sigh of satisfaction when, an hour later, Alice arrived in her mini-van, its interior crammed with gear. Their group was now complete: Tally, Farm, Lillie, Min, Lucy, Alice. And Suzanne, whom Shirley saw not as one of them, but as necessary as the cameras Alice had hired, or the coveralls Tally and Farm were modelling for an amused Lillie. She could feel nothing for the woman who continually reminded her of Darlene's killer.

She hoped that now she was so close to their goal, she would be able to calm her brain to sleep deeply, if only for a short time. It was so hard to sleep. Darlene walked through her days and talked with her at night. They had discussed all the details of the plan. Shirley had no doubt that Darlene was really there, just as she had no doubt that Lillian was really there when she heard her talking in the next room. That's all it was, Darlene being in a different room. But her arms ached to hold her sister's flesh, to hear her giggle down the hall. Even during the times of wild jealousy, of tearing anger, nothing could break their trust. Deep down, sure as the core of the earth, true as the flight of a swallow. Unutterably certain, imprinted on their chromosomes. They were one and the same: no job, no lover, no friend, no happening could even nick the umbilical cord that twinned them. And when she remembered Darlene in the car that night, she realised even death couldn't do that. This knowledge had steadied her through those first piranha-edged days.

She went over in her mind the tasks to be achieved in the next few days. The film to be made, the soundtrack to be done. The editing and finally the transfer to tape. She glanced at the pile of red and white courier bags. It would work. It had been planned with military precision, which was apt, because this was war. It would work.

Suzanne had agreed to call Meredith when Shirley asked her. She didn't like the idea of being the Judas goat, but she saw that she had to. Though he'd been away for a month from the apartment, the

Toronto women knew when he came back.

As soon as she heard Meredith's voice, she began to cry, great gulping sobs that came rising up in hr throat, shattering her words. She could say very little; Meredith kept asking her where she was then, becoming impatient, roared at her until she gasped out the name of the Detroit motel she was in. He said he would be with her by that evening.

The big car spun easily through the rush hour streets, its radio giving traffic details, smatterings of gossip, and drive-easy music. Meredith was quite pleased that Suzanne had turned up again, but what she was doing here in Detroit, he couldn't work out. He'd not missed her much, but hadn't felt much desire to take up with anyone else, and the stuff she had in his apartment he'd left lying around. He wondered what she'd been up to over these three months, and what the storm in her head was. Actually, it had worked out quite well, because Farrimond had sent him down to Acapulco for a bit while they smoothed things over. He'd been pleased at the speed with which Meredith had despatched his orders to cleanup the business; a little oil was often necessary.

The last couple of months in Toronto had been quite interesting, seeing a lot more of Manet. AmVec felt he should remain there for a while just to keep an eye on things. There seemed little possibility of discovery, and it didn't hurt his sociologist-sabbatical cover at all.

It was a bit odd to be here in Detroit and not on company business, he reflected, as he turned the corner into the motel's street, but he had told Farrimond he was going there to pick up Suzanne. AmVec had been a bit irritated by her disappearance. Meredith promised to ring in that night.

Number Sixteen was at the end of a long line of units. The door was shut and the blinds drawn. At his knock, Suzanne opened the door. Her eyes were red and swollen. He smiled at her mockingly.

'Madam rang?' he asked.

She looked at him for a long moment. It seemed as if she were seeing his face very very clearly for the first time. It was a face she knew each line of, exactly how the thick hairs lay on his eye socket to form his eyebrows, the tiny circular pucker where a boil had been dug out below his ear. But his eyes. So cold, so wary. Now she could see the man who killed in the man she loved. All the words she had gathered at the back of her throat vanished. She swallowed, nodded and stepped back, gesturing him to come in. He sauntered through the doorway, looking at her quizzically.

'What's the matter, did you . . .' He broke off as the door shut behind him and Tally and Farm stood with their backs to it. Lillian sat propped on the bed, Shirley standing beside her at its head. Min guarded the window and from an inside doorway that led to the bathroom, Lucy held a large black gun in her small hand. The little white hand looked as if it knew what it was doing; the muzzle of the gun pointed directly at his stomach. Meredith's body shivered into instant alert and centred on the power in the room. Warily he looked at the woman on the bed and the woman who stood behind her, who spoke to him.

'Ah, Mr Meredith,' she said coolly. 'I am very pleased to see you. We haven't met before, in case you're wondering. Let me introduce myself. I'm Shirley Coral, sister of the woman you killed.'

He recognised her from the photograph in the paper in the clinic story. He recognised Lillian in the same brief flash. He stood perfectly still, feeling the room with his body, eyes flicking to Shirley, to Lillian, to Lucy. Behind him, he could feel the women on the outer wall.

'Bring that chair over for Mr Meredith, Suzanne,' instructed Shirley. Suzanne lifted the curved arms of a lounge chair, placing it directly behind him.

'Sit down, Mr Meredith, I'm sure you're a little weary after your long journey from New York.' When he did not sit down immediately, she spat the word at him through solid teeth. Slowly and deliberately he sat down.

'Tally,' said Shirley, and Tally came with the cord, knotting Meredith's arms and legs to the chair. She made sure each knot was double-tied. Meredith heard the rattle of the safety chain being put across the door, then a rattle of metal he couldn't identify. He had been staring at Lillian, and suddenly remembered that she was also the woman who had given him the invitation in his apartment. His eyes shifted to Lucy and he remembered her soft voice asking him to help her with the camera. He craned his neck and looked at Suzanne.

'Like that, is it?' he said lightly. 'Have you earned your dyke button yet?' Suzanne gasped as if he'd hit her.

'You – you killed someone,' she jerked out. 'Doesn't that mean anything to you?'

He shrugged. 'I didn't intend to. It was an accident.'

'And shooting Lillian – was that an accident too?'

'Do you think I meant to kill her?' he said contemptuously. 'D'you think I'm such a poor shot that I could miss my aim at ten feet?'

'But why shoot her at all?' she shouted back at him. 'Who do you think you are?'

Meredith made no answer. He looked at Suzanne for a long minute, then deliberately turned his head away from her.

He addressed Shirley. 'What do you want from me?' he asked calmly.

'Not much,' she replied. 'A chance some men yearn for, Mr Meredith. To star in your very own film.'

Meredith laughed. Shirley gestured to someone behind him.

'Action,' she said wryly. The rattle of metal he'd not been able to identify turned out to be spotlights. A short-haired woman the others called Alice set them up, while the stocky woman by the window came and took light readings. Lucy handed the gun to Lillian and was now murmuring over a three-turretted camera.

Shirley flicked over a wad of pages with Lillian. Alice adjusted the lights one final time, watching Farm handling the microphone attached to the Nagra. Farm nodded to Shirley and glanced over at Lucy, who said, 'Rolling.' Shirley touched Lillian's shoulder.

'My name is Lillian Parelli.' Lillie began, 'and I'm an actress. I'm also a feminist and a lesbian. The man that I'm pointing this gun at is John Meredith, who is employed by American Vehicle in their Special Projects Division.'

Lucy panned over to Meredith, then back to a wide two-shot as Lillian continued.

'I'm pointing the gun at him because he doesn't particularly want to be here, although he's a major character in the story I've got to tell.' Lillian smiled dazzlingly at the camera as Lucy sneaked into a close-up of her, then shot across her shoulder to focus on Suzanne.

'And this is Suzanne Hatherly,' Lillian continued, 'who is also not too happy to be here, but has been vital to the getting together of this film. She was persuaded to join Meredith in Canada, when American Vehicle sent him on a special trip up there . . .'

Succinctly, Lillie told the story, while Lucy took shots of Meredith, looking defiantly into the camera, and Suzanne's hands restlessly pushing her hair, tracing the pattern on the bedspread, as she answered Lillian's questions and substantiated her story.

Lillian invited Meredith to talk about the job AmVec wanted to do. He laughed harshly at her and told her to go fuck herself. Lillian smiled at the camera and said 'You see?' The camera stopped whirring. Lucy waved to Farm, who switched the Nagra off.

'Reload,' said Lucy briefly.

'I have to piss,' Meredith said to Shirley.

'Tough shit,' she shot back at him. 'Hold it or wet yourself. None of us is touching you till we're finished.'

On the second reel, Shirley talked about Darlene, held up the papers. Lillian described the last night of Darlene's life. Then they turned off the lights, packed away the Nagra and the camera. Meredith stayed tied to the chair while Lillie was helped out of the motel room by Min and Shirley, Lucy running out to open the doors.

Farm helped Alice pack the gear in her mini-van, and motioned Suzanne to go with her. Tally sat on the bed and watched Meredith. The gun looked much smaller in her hand. Presently, Shirley and Farm returned. Meredith heard the sound of cars going. Shirley caught his look to the window.

'Don't worry, Mr Meredith,' she said, 'they'll be back. You haven't seen the last of us just yet.'

14: Time-stream Two

I didn't actually sleep in that big chair, but I relaxed as fully as I could while still staying this side of sleep. Bonita became immersed in the work, her fear disappearing as she was given tasks to do that she understood. At first, my thoughts ran round like jitterbeans, but I used the litany that calms and so sank into a monotone daze. I stayed there for a long time, then brought myself up to an awareness of the room. I focussed on the three at the board, their faces dappled with the wink of the working lights. There were about thirty tape boxes at their feet. Corlon kept consulting a list and shuffling the boxes about in accordance with some pre-destined pattern. Quirelle and Bonita ran the board, Bonita running tapes through to Quirelle's instructions, backwards and forwards. I could see that they were well done amateurish jobs, by someone who was unaccustomed to interfacing but definitely had flair.

There was a small differential between their tapes and our machines, which Bonita was attempting to minimise while she was seaming. She had totally escaped into work, the technician won over by the need for her machines, the content of those tapes entirely overlooked as she spun and patched and smoothed. She was adept with the board, but only able to single facet, which was why the job was taking so long, and why Corlon had to keep track of the boxes.

Every seven minutes, the master machine sent out the calmtape, two minutes of soothe, soothe, soothe. On the smaller machines, screens flickered with images that Bonita spun, making connections in my mind. Whoever had assembled the images knew the motivating forces that people react to. I caught sublim work too, on my innerscreen, children blanking, fire sheeting, lazers melting flesh. Same old stuff, but none the less effective for that.

There were very ordinary people, tiny amid the looming shafts of the city, there were dark alleys fearful with paintings, with grunts of death plunged into protesting bodies. There were huge-bellied women, beaten swaggering men, unconcerned flicks rushing overhead. I wondered how long it had taken to get all the images, certainly there were such places, on the fringes of the Exceeders' Wondercities, where people gathered who had taken the gamble and lost it, who had allowed pride to stop their return to Birthrights, who grubbed and stole and fought for their meagre needs rather than admit defeat and return home.

In the end, what more could you do for people who were fully in control of their own lives and would not take those steps necessary to allow themselves to live in peace? But their cases were in the minority. This tape made it look as if they covered the world.

The next tape Bonita seamed through was logical, showing the quarters of the androids, by inference saying we preferred machines to people. But it wasn't so, it wasn't so! Now here were introduced the Twopees, and the tape ran through their beginnings, their growth and their inspection by the Council, the granting of the status of religion. Here were the burgeoning of their domes through every sector. And here were the martyrs, people wearing their uniforms being turned away from work doors, seemingly denied the Settlement areas they wanted, denied Breeding permission. My anger rose at their false inferences. Those few images were powerfully combined with images of the Twopees at worship. The insides of their domes were full of shifting mists of colour. People stood in squares, each uniform of one value being part of that square, each square abutting the correct one in its sequence.

High overhead, suspended from the centre of the dome, a cube hung. Its crystal beauty was etched with the strange tracery of mathematical symbols. Each by each, the cube filled with a colour matching the squares below, sending the clear glow of its light to align itself with that square of people, no matter how many or few stood on it. At the touch of light, the people in the square moaned joyously and the litany of Oneness was repeated until the glow faded and the crystal ran clear. It was hypnotic viewing.

I wondered where the crystal was being controlled from. There must be a viewer to get that spread of light matching so evenly, to keep that liturgy going exactly the right length of time. After all the squares had been 'touched', there was a pause. Then Quirelle appeared inside the square, filling it with a perfectly sized holovid image. No matter where you were in the dome, you would see Quirelle, the creamy lushness of her skin and hair radiant, the clear purple of her shining glass headband a contrast to the whiteness of her forehead. She smiled lovingly and recited: 'All is one, through time and space. Join with me in the Oneness.' Below her, the people chanted in response: 'We join with you, One to Oneness.'

Bonita spun and faceted and seamed. The next image was crude but devastatingly effective. The 'desic domes of Twopee worship being set ablaze, people screaming and writhing. After the scenes of worship, this apparent slaughter was sickening. I didn't believe it for one minute. Had there been such persecution, I would have known of it, even if only by gossip or oblique reference. Anyway no one cared about religion these days, not enough to try to stop anyone else's credo, or stop the formation of yet another group's desire to promulgate their own credo. By making it seem as if their group was under some kind of persecution, the Twopees gave themselves a credibility that they – and all other religions – lacked on a global basis. I could see the effect that the images would have on viewers.

I wondered what the punchline would be. I glanced at the floor: there were no more unspun tape boxes there. Bonita was spinning the reels back. Corlon and Quirelle talked, nodded and turned towards my chair. I let them approach, eyes shut now. As Quirelle bent over me, I smelt the thick scent of her body and hair, a perfume tangy and spicy and very like my own. I would not open my eyes. She chuckled once, deep in her throat, then I felt two soft full lips on mine. I recoiled and she chuckled again.

'The nicest way to wake up, don't you think?' she said lightly. 'A method old as time and still good! Feel refreshed? I do hope so, for now it's your turn to work.' She stepped back from my chair and looked around for one she could sit in. She raised an eyebrow to Corlon, who looked mutinous, but went to get one. As she sat down, I swung my feet down and sat erect, pulling my garments straight. Corlon dragged another chair over and sat.

'What did you think of our tapes, Lydya?' Quirelle asked, and I thought again how lovely her voice was.

'Amateurish,' I yawned, stretching my arms above my head. 'And unimaginative.'

'What a pity,' she replied, 'they were based on your own techniques.'

'So?' I returned, pulling my sleeves back into place.

'So nothing, you're right of course, lovely Lydya! I'm sure in that case you'll positively jump at the chance to make them better!'

'No,' I said, indifferently, 'I have no interest in your tapes, either in watching them or talking about them.'

'But you already have watched them,' she purred, 'and gave such an instant judgement too! And I'm pleased you did,' she said softly, leaning forward slightly, 'it'll help you make the finale stunning!'

I shook my head. 'No. I shan't make a tape for you,' I told her.

'But I think you forget your position,' interjected Corlon, 'and that of your friends, Senex Brown.'

'I will not make a tape for you. Nothing can make be do that.'

'Nothing, Senex Brown? Not even a series of neat lazer holes up and down the legs of your friends?'

'Corlon, don't be crude,' interrupted Quirelle and as I turned to look at her, she thrust the mindmode into my line of sight. The awful truth of centuries of ice held my eyes, light suffusing my skull. I felt lust stir along my legs, desire twitch my labia. My heart started to pound. I licked my lips, feeling the ache for another's. My hand slid furtively between my legs. Suddenly the desire was snatched away and I cried and held up my hands for it like a child imploring Mother Quirelle to give me back my toy. She smiled at me lovingly, told me I must obey her and I could have whatever joy I wanted. I nodded to show her I understood and stretched my arms to her again.

'See Lydya, my dear, how easy it is,' she crooned to me, the blaze now a glimmer, but still I was held by it. 'Now you will remember how Quirelle loves you, and you will remember how Quirelle gave you what you wanted. You will want to please Quirelle, won't you, dear lovely Lydya. Remember that: please Quirelle.'

The light paled to mirror flash, to snow glow, to merest smoke, and was gone. I stared about me, totally dazed. In the far back of my brain, a slow bell rang. I turned around, but everywhere I looked were strangers. The woman in black stepped to my side and took my hand. She led me, unresisting, out of the big room and down a corridor to a smaller room where the smell of something pleasant filled the air. She sat me on the floating green lounger. She put her arms around me, pushed my hair away from my face, stroked my cheeks and neck, kissed me lightly.

'This is not the way of a woman,' she half sang to me, 'oh no, sweet Lydya, there's no joy this way. Now, see, lovely one, it can be done, but let's not do it so. I want your mind in mine, my dear one, with all its power, not to lead you like a little child!'

She rocked me gently, then stood up and made me lie down on the swaying green. She stared into my eyes, the purpleglass band a cool mountain stream curving between the darks of her hair. The sombre bell rang deep in my brain. I rolled to one side and off the lounger. Quirelle laughed at me from the other side.

'I knew it! Little witchery wonder!' She crowed softly. 'Thank you for not letting me down! Now, beloved, I shall lock your body in here for one moment, but only a very little moment. We have work to do, and I must fetch the tools!' Blowing me a moue of a kiss, eyes glinting with good humour, she slipped out of the room, palming the seal as she went.

I looked round the room. Like the other rest rooms, it held the minimum: a floater, body cleansing and relieving facilities, a selection of calmers by the wallplayer next to the roomcom. I wondered where Berenice and the others had been put. The Solarium most likely, an absolutely invulnerable room. I put the seatcube on top of the floater, then scrambled warily on top of it, standing carefully. The floater was unused to such activity, but it accommodated my actions with a dignified sway of balance. I was very close to the ceiling now. I reached up and pressed my palms against its blue. Then I shut my eyes and tried to visualise where in the building I was. When that clicked through, and I could place myself in relation to the Solarium's layout, I sent a quick narrow but intense burst knocking through. I locked into images of Berenie, Moochie and Marla, hoping they were together. I sent wellness and danger and queries. At the end of my send, I felt the rising replies from Berenice, but before we could lock together, the chiding feel of Quirelle came through and I was muffled under a coat of laughter.

I got down from the floater and removed the seatcube, my anger and my frustration making my brain race. I triplewalled my mind, now afraid that she might monitor me constantly, even though I knew she couldn't do that without the mindmode. I found myself staring at the wallplayer. The dull glint of the indented buttons was ringed with a dim pink circle, as were those on the roomcom's panel. I had wondered if the roomcom was operable, a thought answered by these glowing circles of pink. Clicking the on-alert button to OFF, I touched the Solarium button. The tiny screen before me immediately gave me the first camera's view, a glimpse of the huge room partially blocked by a rigid back. Camera two gave me an empty dome, camera three two guards gesturing to one another. I punched the buttons rapidly, hoping that the ACTIVE light would not be on long enough to attract their attention.

On camera seven I found them. They were sprawled on the huge cushions where I had found Moochie so wretchedly sobbing. I pressed the OFF button and went back to the floater, thinking hard.

Knowing that they were together and apparently unharmed filled me with strength. I wondered whether I'd be able to get a look outside, perhaps even get hold of Cheva. I started for the roomcom, then stopped, realising that Quirelle would undoubtedly hear me, and I risked being on the mindmode. If I was on that, there was no hope at all of my controlling events. I would just be a puppet on her string. My reflections were cut off by Quirelle's return. She held the door open, and guards walked in, one carrying a huge covered tray that my nose instantly told me held food, one carrying sweetwater, one carrying a large pile of cushions. The guards deposited things at Quirelle's direction, then left, Quirelle setting the open-alarm circuit after them. I realised that the last time I had eaten was the food Stella had brought to Moochie and me many hours ago.

'Bring the floater down to floor level, would you precious? And we'll just throw this pretty over it and have a snack!'

In the face of her good naturedness, I could do little else. I was also hungry, and unafraid. The fact of the others' safety had filled me with a degree of elation. Whatever Quirelle might offer, I was ready for. When I had the floater adjusted to a couple of handspans from the floor, I flung the 'pretty' over it – an exquisite example of the irridescent lacework from the new spinneries at Bannerlarmi. Quirelle began to put the food she had brought on to our improvised table. There were two crystal glasses to hold the icy sweetwater. Quirelle flung me a couple of cushions, then tucked a couple under her reclining body. She watched me pile my plate, chuckling at each new morsel I put on it.

I stopped and looked at her. 'Aren't you eating? Why? Is it altered in some way?'

She laughed outright. 'My dear! What a crass thought! One couldn't distort pleasant food like this!' She began to fill her plate. 'Everything to your liking?'

'Reasonably so, considering the company,' I replied.

'Ooh! A tiny talon. But I knew you were fully recovered when I felt you going out of your head. I do admire your spirit, sweet Lydya Brown!'

'I find your manner quite offensive,' I threw back at her, dropping food into my mouth then speaking through it, something I ordinarily chose not to do. 'And your constant stream of endearments is artifical and insulting.'

She paused, looked at me. 'So it's to be like that, is it?' she queried softly. 'I suppose I was expecting too much to have it any other way. All right, Senex Brown. Any way you wish. I advise you to eat until you're full then, for it may be a very long time until you eat again.' The rich voice was now as heavy and implacable as a gold ingot.

I would have eaten well in any case, for each of the foods was one I particularly liked, because the kitchen had stocked itself for Moochie's and my midnight work. But I took a third helping because of what she had said and because, now she was silent, I had a chance to assess her, both overtly and covertly.

Her black garment fitted well across the shoulders and fell in dark spills to clutch around each ankle. Its cut was cunning, for Quirelle was not a slender woman, but the effect given was of a satutesque magnificence not of a large woman gone to fat. A semi-cape swooped from shoulder to shoulder and fell to just above her waist. The silver slashes of her rank had been thought of in the design of the garment, for they turned the eye along flattering lines. her very thick, very white skin looked even whiter because of the night-dark hair, and the purpleglass band across her forehead gave her an air of authority in an indefinable way. The lilac glitterglobes in her ears were often obscured by her hair, through which they sent pale gleams. Her mouth was very full and she used no colour on it. But the ancient kohl was skilfully used around her eyes; the combination of that black and the very pale blue was expressive to say the least. Her hands were plump, with attractive fingers, and from the central one on her left hand the mindmode winked in its sleep.

She finished eating, drank a glass of sweetwater, then touched the percom on her wrist. Instantly, the door opened. She gestured to the debris; guards cleared it away, leaving only the jug of sweetwater. The guards left. As I rinsed out my mouth and sluiced my face and hands, I was aware of her gaze the whole time. I knew that I couldn't achieve much by myself, but I knew also Quirelle would be suspicious if I appeared to give in too easily to her. I had to appear to give in to her, be beaten by her, and be forced into doing the tape. That meant going very close to the edge. Without looking at her, I went back to the floater, dialled it back to its original position, flipped up its headrest and settled myself against it.

'Well?' I challenged her.

She gazed at me speculatively, a tiny smile in the corners of her mouth. Then she drew the mindmode off her finger, stood up, placed it on the seatcube.

'Equals,' she said, coming to sit on the floater, flicking up a backrest as she did so.

'Equals,' I agreed, with just a touch of sarcasm. She looked directly into my eyes and I into hers. I could feel her knocking, but I held my shield firm.

'All right,' she said at last, 'you come to me.'

I waited a second or two, then opened very narrowly, and cautiously walked into her head. She opened widely, but I kept myself together and stayed at the threshold, feeling my way. At once, I felt sensations of welcome mingled with mockery. I waited. Soon the images began to slide through. Quirelle, wise and compassionate, solving the problems that beset us, earning the love and respect of the people around her. To that I interfaced an inversion, Quirelle, autocratic, narrow-minded, seeing only what she wanted to see, power-hungry and blind to reality. Now came Quirelle, a magnificent martyr behind sightless lazer bars, misunderstood but taking her suffering with dignity. I interfaced an ordinary offender's life, the dulling routine, the trivial chatter of fools. Then she imaged a complex woman, full of confidence and doubts, believing she had seen not only a problem, but also a solution. To that one, I opened a littler wider and interfaced a world full of such women. She replied with an assent, and for a moment, we rested.

Now began a litany of shape, of space and balance and harmony, weaving the image/sound with me merely as spectator, not keeping me out, rather making a deliberate showing for me, building layer by layer a beautiful and reasonable pattern that owed its symmetry to numbers, to sheer simplicity and austere perfection of their intangible solidity. On such a base, the universe is crafted, she concluded. In reply, I used her pattern as my base, but only in the finest lines of dullest black. Around that pattern, I spun a web of music. When the shape was whole, I held it, then silvered it down with light, light from the source of feeling larger than love, a feeling without word, an essential substance that was the universe. This is what your pattern lacked.

She smashed through it with enormous power, an explosion of elemental force, at once wiping out the delicacy of my form and obliterating the shiver of its light with an annihilating shout. In its place now stood a stone black being, old as age, invulnerable as space, with the presence of mountains. The smell of old canyons blew through, the scent of innumerable bones slowly rushing to powder, solidifying into new forms of indomitable strength.

My river ran round and battered on the black, to no avail. I threw seeds into cracks, but they were ground with the teeth of the rock, fragmenting its dinner of bone. My purest beam of light was swallowed without a trace in the all-embracing mouth of blackness. I stepped back one step and the dissonant laughter of old cracked bells started and held me to my retreat.

'Checkmate,' she said, breathing quickly, eyes snapping. I refocussed into my eyes and slowly lowered them from hers, the bend of my neck a silent assent. We stayed there on the floater for a time. Quirelle was the first to recover. She poured a glass of sweetwater and handed it to me, then poured one for herself.

'And now we make a tape together,' she said, when her glass was empty. 'Agreed?'

I nodded, my eyes still lowered.

'Good,' she said briskly. 'Let's get started.'

I was unresponsive as she got off the floater, snapped its back down and adjusted her clothing, eyes all the time on her face. But eventually I followed her motions and got off the floater myself, raising my eyes to hers as I did so. She laughed a triumphant little trill and whirled to the door, rapping on it once; the guard opened it instantly.

'Yaleen,' whispered Jacinthe, 'now is the link real, fleshhold its power.' And I felt in my hand the solidity of her gift. I slipped Quirelle's mindmode into the silent mouth of my pocket.

Quirelle took me to the Transmission room. I looked around with a strange feeling that aeons of time had passed. But there were the tape boxes just as they'd been left an hour ago, and there was Bonita, now huddled into the chair I had been in, deeply unconscious with sleep. Corlon was nowhere to be seen. Quirelle went to the board, where her tapes were still reeled.

'Where do you normally work?' she asked.

I gestured to the small projection suite and we went to its open door. Suddenly I thought of my own tape, wondering if it was still in the machine. But from the doorway I could see the empty splaynes. Moochie was clearly more farsighted than I.

'Let me tell you what I want,' said Quirelle when we were in the smaller room, 'then you can call for the source tapes and we can begin to compile. Yes?'

'But –' I protested, then stopped. 'Yes. All right.'

'But what?' she said sharply. 'Is that not the way you work?'

I glanced at her for the first time, dislike and sullenness in my eyes and voice. 'It will do.' My voice was grim.

She laughed softly. 'Oh no, Senex Brown, what I require is not an "it-will-do". I want the best of your skill.' She threw me a flicking mindlash which caught me totally off guard; instinctively I cringed. She took a deep breath, expelled it slowly.

'Now my dear? How do you work?'

'With Senex Bleu,' I replied sullenly. 'We are complementary.'

'I see.' Quirelle was thoughtful. Then, making her decision, she tapped the percom on her wrist and spoke into it.

'Corlon. Bring Senex Bleu to the Transmission Room. We are ready to begin.'

We had been working for many hours, for although what Quirelle wanted was not long in duration, the complexity of it was demanding. She would not let Moochie go to the archives of sound, so each tape had to be remembered, noted down and laboriously sought for by Corlon, who was impatient with the requests. Quirelle was edgy, querying our every move. Only the solidity of the token in my pocket kept me from losing my way again and again. In spite of ourselves, the spark between Moochie and I kept leaping through to ignite the work. And in spite of her fear, Quirelle could see the patterns growing and was pleased.

We had come to the final pattern, the image that would hold the power to stay in the minds of the viewers and swing them definitively over to amiable obeisance to the power of the Church of the Profound Principle. For this, simplicity of image and the swelling graduations of song were united to promise release from pain and experience of quiet joy. It was an iceberg that would lodge deeply in the mind, being crafted almost wholly on the subliminal plane. Michou looked at me and though our minds were closed to one another, I knew well what words they were that her eyes spoke. It had to be now; we were finished. What we had done, under Quirelle's command, was to create a pathway on which she could walk to a position of power within our world. Backed by the money of the Exceeders, and using a vile distortion of mother-love, she had, through us, positioned herself as a loving caring Leader, whose courage had seen evil and conquered it. Her stone-black being would have full sway, no hint of compassion to stop its rampage of destruction.

'What is it, Senex Bleu?' asked Quirelle. 'Is it not working? Do you require another sound?'

Michou just held my eyes with hers, ignoring Quirelle. Michou stretched out her hand to me, still holding my gaze. I took the steps towards her, put one hand in my pocket on the token, then put the other into Michou's waiting palm.

15: Time-stream Two

The white van now sported a discreet sign on either door: Greenfingers Ltd, it said, and, underneath, Commercial Gardeners, all in a pleasant shade of green. The lettering had been dried under hot lamps, to deepen and age the paint a little. Tally had taken great delight in rubbing dust along its cracks. The gardeners at AmVec were both easy to get talking to, and delighted that these two Canadian girls seemed so friendly. Nice looking too, they congratulated themselves. It wasn't difficult for Lucy to get them to agree to come up to the loft, Alice adding her enthusiasm at just the right time. The sleeping tablets in the wine had exactly the effect the prescription said they would.

Tally and Farm went unchallenged the next day as they drove through the gates, explaining that they'd been called in because both gardeners were off work. Their sturdy bodies in the well-used overalls excited no comment, and they enjoyed the day's activities on the motor mowers. At the end of the day, they put the mowers back in their shed, made sure Shirley and Lucy were comfortable in there, and drove out of the gates, calling quips to the gatekeeper as he waved them on their way. The shed was roomy and smelt pleasantly of earth and old grass, petrol and oil. Through a cloudy window, Shirley watched the building empty and the security guard make his round. In the last of the light she saw the guard going down the curving drive to the bright clattering lights of the assembly plant a stretch away across the lawn. Then she and Lucy slipped out of the shed and round to the side door of the executive wing. The skeleton key clicked home. Seconds later, they both stood in the near-dark corridor that smelt of men.

'His office will be the largest,' whispered Shirley, once they were sure the building had no one in it. They went back down the hall to the foyer. There was the reception desk, with two office doors beyond. On the long wall to their right, three more office doors presented blank faces to their inspection. At their back, another door, this one slightly ajar. Behind it glimpsed a corner office. Shirley touched Lucy's shoulder and led the way into it. Lucy closed the door behind them. Shirley was already at the desk, pulling out drawers and scanning their contents with her pencil beam.

'This is the accountant's office,' she whispered. 'Let's have a quick look.'

The drawers she wanted to open were locked, but yielded easily to her little set of keys. Her beam flickered over the files. With tiny hiss of breath, she pulled one out. Lucy was at her side in an instant. The file tab read: Meredith: Project Eleven. In it were carefully noted amounts of money, with their dates. A sheaf of receipts was pinned to the other side of the form. The items were all innocuous – purchase of three filing cabinets, installation of phone fee – but they were all signed by Meredith, and all receipts were from stores in their own sprawling Canadian city.

'Should we take them?' asked Lucy.

'Sure,' nodded Shirley, 'it puts him on the scene.'

She folded the sheets of paper and pocketed them, put the file back into the drawer and let its locks snap through. With a last glance around, she motioned Lucy to the door. Lucy eased it open. Only deepening gloom greeted them. Shirley pointed at the office door in the opposite corner. Lucy nodded her understanding and, leaving the door precisely as they'd found it, the two made their way round the wall to the opposite door.

This door was locked, and for the third time Shirley had to use her little set of keys. Inside, she gave a grunt of satisfaction.

'This has got to be it,' she hissed at Lucy.

The room was surprisingly light, the illumination due to the two huge windows which formed nearly half of the outside wall on either side and through which the lights of the assembly plant shone, outlining the assembly factory in its ceaseless rote of creation. In the room were banks of filing cabinets, a telex machine and a small computer. Shirley looked at Lucy, who nodded vigorously and soundlessly clapped her hands with glee.

'Go on! You just can't keep your hands off them, I know!' whispered Lucy. 'You're just a technofreak, Shirley Coral!'

Shirley grinned a little and went over to the machine. Lucy sighed, pushed back her hair and started on the cabinet labelled Lex-Moli. They had been working for quite a long time, getting quietly elated at the breadth of their finds, when Shirley felt a strong sense of Darlene. She threw up her head; her sister tugged insistently and Shirley felt an overwhelming urge to get out.

'Lucy! We must go. Quickly.'

'What about these?' said Lucy, gesturing to the piles of paper around her.

'Take what you can,' said Shirley urgently, 'but hurry.' She switched off the VDU and thrust her notebook into her own haversack, then bent to help Lucy. She thrust the last of the papers under her arm and ran for the door. As she reached for the handle, the door opened. In walked Farrimond, one hand flooding the room with light, a small blue-steel menace absurdly real in the other. Behind him were two men, one the pugnaciously frightened security guard.

Farrimond stared at the two women, his eyes flicking from their faces to the haversack Lucy carried, to the papers under Shirley's arm. He turned and motioned one of the men into the room, dismissing the guard, saying lightly, 'I think we can handle this, Signew, you keep an eye outside the building for more.'

Shirley pulled Lucy back so that they were standing by the huge desk, while the thin-faced man with the hooked nose watched them and Farrimond shut the door. He turned to the thin man.

'Michael, have our – er – unexpected guests sit down, won't you, while I look at which of our paperwork excites their interest.' He waved the gun thoughtfully.

The thin man started towards Shirley, who linked her arm in Lucy's and moved back behind the desk. Farrimond sighed.

'Are you armed?' he asked Shirley. She didn't reply. 'Then I really do think she should sit down. As you see, I am armed, and I wouldn't hesitate to use force against you. The fact that you're women doesn't matter a damn to me.' He motioned to the thin man who went round the desk, grasped each of them by an arm and piloted them towards the huddle of fat armchairs. Lucy hiccupped and fell forward in a faint.

'Wh-wh-what?' stuttered the thin man, startled, while Shirley shot a glance at Farrimond, who caught her look and smiled thinly.

'It was a try,' he said. 'Now ask your colleague to get up please.'

'She really has fainted,' said Shirley, bending down to Lucy. 'I was just looking to see how trigger happy you are.' Her voice was scornful and unafraid. 'Lucy. Lucy. C'mon now.'

'Well, at least we know one name,' said Farrimond behind her. 'I imagine you already know that I am Martin Farrimond; my colleague is Michael Carr. Who are you?'

Shirley ignored him, kneeling on the bundle of papers that she'd had under her arm, and chafing Lucy's wrists between her hands. Lucy was half lying on the haversack, her breathing rapid and shallow.

'Water, Michael,' ordered Farrimond, his eyes hard and the gun in his hand rocksteady. Carr fetched a glass of water, but as he started to hand it to Shirley, Farrimond told him to throw it into Lucy's face, which he did immediately. Lucy gasped and cried out. Shirley scowled at Farrimond, drawing tissues from her pocket and mopping the face of her friend. Lucy opened her eyes.

'Be quiet and lie still,' Shirley whispered insistently. 'Don't speak.'

'On the contrary,' said Farrimond. 'Michael, help the young woman to a chair.'

Carr came over to Lucy and as she struggled with him, Shirley, her back to Farrimond, half shuffled round until she was closer to him, then she moved swiftly, her leg describing two quick jagged arcs as she kicked Farrimond in the testicles, then on the wrist, so that the little gun dropped from his suddenly nerveless fingers. She swooped it up and from a half crouch, pointed it at Carr.

'Please move,' she urged him, 'I would love to have a chance to shoot you with a clear conscience.'

Carr shook his head. 'I'm no he-he-hero,' he said simply. 'Do what you like, I won't stop you.'

From the floor, Farrimond's fist banged as he struggled for breath. Carr looked at him, then at Shirley.

'Can I get him some water?' he asked, 'A kick in the balls hu-hu-hurts like hell.' Shirley nodded, holding the gun on Carr while he went over to the panelled cabinet and once more pushed the sliding door to reveal a miniature fridge. He filled a glass with iced water. As he was doing that, Lucy pulled two chairs together to the centre of the room, and Shirley dragged Farrimond by his collar to one, gun trained down on him. She motioned him into the chair. Sweating and pale, Farrimond clutched at the chair and fell into it. Carr turned with the water. Shirley's gun motioned him to the chair. When both men were seated, Lucy took the gun from Shirley and trained it on the two men. Shirley went behind him and delivered a short sharp chop to each man's cranial nerve. They half hunched and slumped.

'Whew!' said Lucy.

'Let's go,' said Shirley.

They hurried out of the room, clicking the lock behind them. Lucy headed for the side door, but Shirley touched her arm. They went back into the accountant's office; Shirley quietly shut the door, then opened a window. The ground was only three feet from the window ledge and the two stepped out into the shrubbery. Lucy ruffled the earth to hide their footprints. They scrambled through the ornamental bushes and headed away from the building as fast as they could run.

At the high perimeter fence, with its strands of barbed wire frowning down at them, Shirley rummaged in the haversack for the wirecutters. She climbed up the diamonds to the barbed wire and, holding her body close to the fence, with her head down, she clipped the top strand. It curled backwards with a vicious hiss. She lowered herself a couple of feet and did the second strand and repeated the performance with the third. Then she and Lucy climbed over and down. Twenty minutes later they had reached a bus stop. Ninety minutes from the time she had knocked the two men out, Shirley was consulting with the others back at the loft.

They'd been busy too. Min had helped Alice put the gardeners, still unconscious, into the van. Alice had then driven them to the other side of town and a little way out into the countryside, where she had eventually rolled them out into a hayfield, watched by two old bulls and a flock of sparrows. Min also helped Suzanne bathe and feed Meredith, who was hand and foot cuffed, the handcuffs around one of the support posts in the centre of the long room. Meredith had said nothing after his stream of curses had been stopped by Min who, roused to the first uncontrolled anger of her life, had hit him with the full force of her open hand.

'I'm sorry,' she had said to Suzanne, panting and blinking as she tried to get her anger under control, 'but I can't bear to hear him speak to you like that.'

Suzanne hunched one shoulder in reply, tears spilling down as she went to the far corner and huddled against the wall.

'Well done,' said Lillie to Min quietly. 'I'd have done just the same.' Min shook her head and sat down on the piled sheets of foam that formed Lillie's daybed.

'I don't know,' she said wearily, 'I just don't know.'

'Don't give in now, Minnewanka,' said Lillian gravely, 'not when we're so close to the end.'

'No, no,' replied Min. 'I just –' and she told her perplexity with expressive hands. 'I mean, when I think of my life a few months ago, and my studio with the sun and the treetops . . .' and she choked a little, holding back tears.

'Hey,' said Lillie, shifting her body down to get to Min, holding the older woman in a consoling hug. 'Hey lady. I love you.'

'Soppy cunts,' jeered Meredith, but Lillie and Min ignored him. In the far corner, Suzanne lifted her head and stared at Meredith. She wiped her eyes on the back of her hand, stood up and went to the suitcases lined up along the wall. She rummaged through one for a minute, pulling out a long orange scarf. Then she went to Meredith and gagged him.

'I can't stand any more of you,' she said tersely. Min and Lillie both applauded her, but she stood stony-faced, shook her head, and went to plug in the kettle.

In another few days the film was finished, the speed of its compilation making it raw. But it was compulsive viewing. From the moment of the opening, with Lillie lying on the bed holding a gun and declaring herself, to the moment of its close, it skewered the viewer's attention. Shirley's explanation of the actions of American Vehicle were supported by the indisputable evidence from the files. The evidence that they'd picked up along the way of corporate collusion, tax fiddles, payola and big money political graft was backed up and proven time after time. The film was damning. It ended with a group shot of Shirley, Lillie, Tally, Farm, and Alice. Min ran the camera and Suzanne set the lights and sound. Over those six pairs of unwavering eyes ran the sound: 'The way to get things done is to begin to do them. And as one condemned sister in Salem said to another – you may as well trust me, sister, they're the ones doing the burning.'

They ran it through one last time, having made their booking at Vidscene to transfer the film to tape and take the dubs. Min tried to disassociate herself from the women on the film, in an attempt to see it objectively. But she was only partly successful. She saw Lillie as herself and her talking of Darlene's death brought the silent tears. Dear stringent Shirley could never be anything other than herself; but in that final shot, with them all together and their eyes strong and cold and determined, Min saw them as warriors, as modern-day Amazons perhaps, or a small determined army. She felt a surge of warmth flooding her, a rising pride in herself and in these friends, these committed women. The projector ran free, the light from the white screen blinding.

'Rough,' said Shirley, 'but it'll do.'

They began to collect their bags. Only Shirley, Min, Lucy and Alice were left. Tally, Farm and Suzanne had gone back to Canada taking Lillie with them. They had drugged Meredith and laid him in the back of the van. Suzanne wanted to return to the cabin in the woods. She volunteered to let Meredith out somewhere isolated along the way. Tally and Farm would stay with Lillie, one of them going with Suzanne to bring the van home.

The only time they had been able to book at Vidscene was nine in the evening. But working at night was now commonplace to them. Shirley smacked the lid down on the film can and put it in her haversack.

The drive to Vidscene in Alice's mini-van was very quiet. Min had the list of names and places the tapes were to be sent to. Alice had spoken to the courier service, which was primed to take the scarlet and white bags to the airport, unaware of their dangerous contents. Alice had hired the Vidscene facilities and requested that they be able to use them without a Vidscene operator. She had had to convince them that Shirley knew how to handle the quad machines – and succeeded only by paying in advance.

There were only a couple of people in evidence at Vidscene. One of them, a young man with the still-red scars of his pimpled youth apparent, fussed around them, being protective about 'his' machine until Shirley engaged him in a brief but bewildering conversation so full of technical jargon that she finally convinced him she knew what he was doing. As they bent to their work, his shadow could be seen crossing and recrossing the double glass porthole between the main suite and the sound studio.

Shirley laid the film on to the two-inch tape. They began the dubbing, a dreary business. After the tenth tape was completed and had been taken away by the carrier van, Min went upstairs to the kitchen to get them all a reviving cup of coffee before starting on the next ten.

In the kitchen, three men sat around the small table, one of them the pimpled youth. At her entrance, they all looked at her. She nodded to the youth. She could feel their eyes on her back as she put the cups on a tray, waiting for the water to scream its readiness. She picked up the tray and headed for the door. Behind her, a man's voice said, 'I'll take that.'

She half turned to protest, and saw the man holding a gun of her. Her heart thumped, extraordinarily hard, just once, closing her throat and quickening her breath.

'You don't look like Meredith's woman,' said the man calmly, 'so you must be a friend of Miss Coral's. She has been persistently interested in our affairs. Even my nephew here has noticed her interest,' he nodded at the pimply youth, who blushed scarlet, 'and called me to see if I knew her, which of course I do, in a manner of speaking. Timely, wouldn't you say? I don't suppose you've seen Mr Meredith?'

Min didn't answer. The second man took the tray from her shaking hands.

'Lead the way, Tony,' said the man with the gun to the youngster.

'Yes uncle,' said the youth, throwing a look of adolescent contempt at Min.

'You go after him, Carr, and you next,' Farrimond said to Min, waggling the gun at her.

They made their way down the dimly lit staircase, Min shaking and confused. The youth pointed to the door of the suite. Farrimond nodded and motioned him to leave. Carr thrust the tray back into Min's hands.

'Naturally, and with no words,' Farrimond said to her in a cold low tone, and sent her forward; Min took two paces forward, her mind was suddenly icily clear, her body strong. She couldn't be the Judas goat, that she knew.

'No!' she shouted at the top of her lungs, whirling around and throwing the tray of coffee at the man behind her. She heard a soft explosion, felt a slam on her shoulder, followed by an immensely hot pain. She gasped once and fell to her knees, her stomach involuntarily heaving. Farrimond stood back from her, making no attempt to help the scalded Carr. The studio door sighed and Alice's head looked out.

Farrimond levelled the gun at her.

'Thank you,' he said, 'I want to come in.'

Alice pushed the door shut as Farrimond's bullet slammed into the jamb where her head had been. Then he was running forward to grab the huge handle and push. Carr kicked Min out of the way and added his strength to Farrimond's to slowly open the door. It yielded infinitesmally, opening inwards. Carr held it while Farrimond slid in to the left, along the inner wall of the studio.

'Pull the door to,' rasped Farrimond to Carr, whose action revealed three women behind the door: Alice and Lucy trying to pull Shirley down to them.

Farrimond promptly shot Shirley.

Darlene screamed as the bullet burned through bone and heart and lung.

Time swung.

16: Aftertime

From the cauldron of smoke around me, I, Cassie, breathed great gouts of heat and whimpered. Slow on the turning of time came down the long healing touch, the voice of knowing, the sense of self reborn. Now once again torn apart, I, Darlene, took the violence into my body, each cell shrieking with the burden it could not bear, and the smell of burning is my own flesh and bone. The slow hands soothed and the voice beckoned on. I, Lydya, have invaders in my head, trampling the carefully tended flowers, hate spraying its insecticide on colour and shape and form, until they melt and run a stench of powerful decay. I jerk under the mindlash and the touch comes through, slowly dissipating the stench with the breath of the mothers.

I am one and a million women through the ripple of time, the tick of life fracturing the carapace of death, showing the source below. I am the vessel and its water, the source of life, the bearer of the flame, the guardian of the flesh through which the spirit wells. In the white anemone and the steelgrey shark, moving at separate speeds, being seen by the Lookers who dwell on where we've been, before carrying on.

Cassie slumped against the ropes and stepped out of herself. At her side, she became aware of many women, some standing watching her burn, others weeping quietly, being shrieked at by the wildhaired ones. As she glanced along, she saw the mad ones too, faraway eyes and dancing bodies, gone where it is supportable to be. The woman next to her spoke. 'Not a good sight,' she said.

'No,' I replied slowly, looking back at the cracking flames. I watched as that thinned and paled and faded and vanished.

'Come, Yaleen,' said Jacinthe imperiously, 'you know we've got to hurry.'

I heeded her voice, passing quickly the sight of a Moebius strip of energy, both female, being shredded and torn apart, the scream of their separation too big for any other room but the universe.

Jacinthe turned, topaz hair swirling, eyes blazing with intent. I swung to match her movement. Together we found the Centre and together selected the chamber and together twinned out skilled energy to turn the Key. The Great Seal parted and we were there. I stood beside my Lydya-self, thrusting my hand into my pocket, putting the mindmode on my finger, sliding its beam home. Quirelle jerked and spun around, eyes at full stretch with the surprise of it. Across her face sped first the fear of a child, then the arrogance of youth, then the full force of elemental desire. Through the long dark stream, dusted with black glints, the beam ran and the voice said the words of the Great Mother:

. . . whenever ye have need of anything, once in the month, and better it be when the moon is full, then shall ye assemble in some secret place . . . to these I will teach things that are yet unknown. AND YE SHALL BE FREE FROM ALL SLAVERY *. . . Keep pure your highest ideal; strive ever toward it.* LET NAUGHT STOP YOU OR TURN YOU ASIDE *. . . Mine is the cup of the wine of life and the cauldron of Cerridwen . . . I am the Mother of all living, and my love is poured out upon the Earth . . . I am the beauty of the Green Earth, and the White Moon among the stars and the mystery of the Waters,* AND THE DESIRE IN THE HEART OF WOMAN *. . . Before my face let thine innermost divine self be enfolded in the raptures of the Infinite . . . Know the mystery, that if that which thous seekest thous findest not within thee, thou wilt never find it without thee . . . For Behold,* I HAVE BEEN WITH THEE FROM THE BEGINNING. *And I await you now.*

EPILOGUE

One more showing, thought Min with a small glow of pleasure. Alice was an absolute genius, those ten tapes had been shown to more people than she would ever have dreamed possible, considering it had to be in secret.

And it was working! By the Great Mother, it was working!